The Going Down of the Sun

By Jo Bannister

THE GOING DOWN OF THE SUN
GILGAMESH
THE MASON CODEX
MOSAIC
STRIVING WITH GODS
A CACTUS GARDEN
THE WINTER PLAIN
MATRIX

The Going Down of the Sun

of the Sun

JO BANNISTER

A Crime Club Book
Doubleday

NEW YORK   LONDON   TORONTO   SYDNEY   AUCKLAND

A Crime Club Book
Published by Doubleday, a division of
Bantam Doubleday Dell Publishing Group, Inc.
666 Fifth Avenue, New York, New York 10103

Doubleday and the portrayal of a man
with a gun are trademarks of
Doubleday, a division of Bantam Doubleday Dell
Publishing Group, Inc.

Library of Congress Cataloging-in-Publication Data

Bannister, Jo.
The going down of the sun/Jo Bannister.
p.   cm.
"A Crime Club book."
I. Title.
PR6052.A497G6   1989
823'.914—dc19   89-31312

ISBN 0-385-26451-8
Printed in the United States of America
October 1989
First Edition
OG

I

Saturday

After the hole in his chest had healed and the strength was returning to his right shoulder, his doctor recommended that Harry take a holiday. Since Harry's doctor had known my husband longer, and hardly less intimately, than I, I presume he made this suggestion from the safety of a locked room adjoining the surgery, through the keyhole.

Our first matrimonial bust-up had arisen when I asked where we were going on holiday. When I wouldn't take "Nowhere" for an answer Harry lost his temper, thumped the table and went to sulk in the garage. We'd been playing chess. It was three days before I found the last pawn nestling among the fronds of a Mother-in-Law's Tongue. For my holiday that year I went sailing off the west coast of Scotland. For his, Harry stripped down the engine of his Riley.

The police surgeon had taken the precaution of tidying any potential missiles out of sight, and since Harry wanted his approval to return to work he couldn't storm off and sulk somewhere either. He had to grit his teeth and bear it. "Holiday?"

A nice brisk holiday, said the doctor, with plenty of fresh air and exercise, would get his damaged lung working, free the kinks left by the bullet, build up his strength and stamina, and generally restore him to the peak of physical fitness required of a Detective Superintendent in the modern police service. Nobody outside the firm appreciates the toll that paperwork exacts; and tragically enough, it was his form-filling arm that was affected. There was a time when we seriously wondered whether he'd ever complete a 53b Drawing Pin Requisition again.

He had his back against the wall, but he gave it his best shot. "Car maintenance is a surprisingly energetic occupation—"

"No doubt, no doubt," said the doctor briskly. "But what I had in mind was more a week's sailing off the west coast of Scotland."

We picked up the boat in Ardfern, a neat little sloop of about twenty-four feet. *Rubh'an Leim* was identical in every way—including the fact that no Sassenach could pronounce her name—to the *Rubh'an Leanachais* I'd sailed here the previous year, except in one strange particular. The cabins that had accommodated four of us quite comfortably last summer had unaccountably shrunk so that Harry banged his head, or his knee, or his healing shoulder on one projection or another every time he turned round. Getting him in and out of the heads was a shoehorn job.

He couldn't get used to the idea that you can't always stand upright and move in straight lines on a boat. He was like a drill sergeant from one of the taller Regiments of Guards trying to remain a fine figure of a man under a ceiling about five feet off the floor. I was beginning to doubt the wisdom of the enterprise before the man from the boat yard had finished his doom and gloom lecture about how easy it is to blow up a boat with its own gas and gone ashore.

For two pins I'd have followed him. If Harry had said, "I can get cold, wet and cramped in my own bath" just once more I would have followed him, and cast off the warps and shoved the *Rubber Lion* in the general direction of the Corryvreckan whirl-pool before my nearest and dearest could thread his way past the chart-table.

The essence of the problem was not that he was something over six feet and built to match, nor that his shoulder still made bending and twisting awkward, nor even that he had the same natural aptitude for life afloat as a brick. The essence of the problem was that he wanted to be miserable. He was here under protest and he wasn't going to let me forget it. The police surgeon might have the power to send him on holiday, even if it did smack of cruel and unusual punishment, but by God *nobody* could make him enjoy it!

As soon as I'd familiarised myself with the gear again we got under way. I let Harry take us out on the engine while I got the sails rigged. I wasn't planning on doing much motoring this week—if you get in the way of starting the engine when it's handier than sailing you soon give up sailing altogether—but the throaty rumble and the vibration under his feet and the stink of diesel might help shift that martyred look off his face. I reminded him that you push a tiller left to steer a boat right, in time to avoid a rock if only just, then left him to play with the controls while I got on with the serious business of setting sail.

We had a choice of head-sails. With a breeze that was sturdy rather than stiff, I opted for the working jib. Later in the week, when I had the feel of the boat, I'd be using the genoa in stronger winds than this, but for now the jib was sufficient. The storm-jib was thoughtfully stowed in a red bag and I hoped not to need it at all.

I bent the head-sail onto the forestay, attached halyard and sheets, and sat back on the fore-hatch to admire the result. Then I took it all off again and put it back the right way up. I doubt if Harry would have noticed, but I'd have been the toast of Ardfern if I'd sailed out hauling my jib upside down.

The mainsail was rolled onto its boom, lacking only its battens and brute strength to set it. I unrolled it into the cockpit—Harry claimed I was trying to smother him—and fought bitterly with the battens until I realised that, while two of them were the same length, one was wider than the other and would never go into the top pocket however much I swore at it.

I moved up to the foot of the mast, bracing myself against the movement under me that always seems so pronounced on the first day and, barring hurricanes, is hardly noticeable after that. The burgee went up first and grafted itself firmly to the masthead, giving me a small thrill of success. It's harder to get a clean hoist with a burgee than almost anything in the sail-locker.

The little scrap of nylon fluttered busily a little starboard of the stern. The wind was in the south, which meant we could set sail without altering course. The main went up, the jib went up, I scuttled back and sheeted them both in; then I took the tiller from Harry and turned the key in the ignition. "Finished with engines."

He looked severely at me. "You've cut your finger."

Of course I'd cut my finger. You're constantly cutting your fingers aboard boats; also barking your shins, skinning your elbows and excavating holes in your backside by sitting on cleats. It's all part of the fun.

"Why are you grinning?" demanded Harry.

But little by little, some of the magic of the day entered his soul. The sparkle of the sun on the jewel-blue water, the whisper of the foam creaming along the bow, the small creaking and snapping sounds of the sails and the rigging; and the way the mouth of Loch Craignish widened as we stood towards it, and a little fleecy cloud that hung over the violet Paps of Jura twenty miles down the Sound, all conspired to lighten the heart and raise the spirit. Although to be honest he'd still sooner have been up to his elbows in a nice grisly murder back home in Skipley, he was finally beginning to see that sailing had its charms too.

We beat down to Craignish Point and rounded the little headland through the gap marked on the chart as the Dorus Mór. With the wind behind us now we ran up past the northern tip of Jura, past infamous Corryvreckan—even in the moderate conditions of the day we could hear the thunder of the disturbed seas and see white water flung mast-high as the tide raced through the narrow channel—and past Scarba into the pretty region around Loch Melfort, where the hills of the mainland and the hummocks of the islands folded together in a concert of pastel greys as the day's wind died towards evening.

We dropped the hook in a little bay on Shuna's north shore, and I went below to get dinner on the stove. In the cockpit I could hear Harry softly whistling to himself as he tinkered with the engine. I smiled. I didn't care what he did to the engine, as long as he got it back together again before we had to return the boat.

After a time, with the stove humming under its breath and good smells beginning to rise from the saucepans, I heard the music from above break abruptly, then the unmistakable two-tone of a wolf-whistle. I was up the companionway before you could say "Rob Roy."

"Now that," said Harry, admiration thick in his voice, "is what I call a boat."

Myself, I couldn't see it. I could see plenty of money, plenty of power. I suppose there was a certain grace in the flare of the high bows, the strong sweep of the hull. Certainly she was making enough noise as she ran down through the long afternoon towards Craignish Point, but then so would a motor-home.

On the subject of sail versus power I'm a bigot. I reckon if you're going to drive places you might as well stick to the roads: it's quicker, it's cheaper and you're less likely to hit a rock. I accept, reluctantly, the place of power in maritime commerce, but a pleasure boat without sails is a contradiction in terms.

Harry, on the other hand, considers the internal combustion engine conclusive proof of God, so this high-stepping, highly polished little gin palace riding its bow-wave down the Sound regardless of wind and tide filled him with delight.

It was only as she drew level with our anchorage that we saw the woman at the helm, blonde hair flying in the slipstream. She saw us and waved. We waved back, but the glance Harry cast me was embar-

rassed. Middle-aged detective superintendents should not be caught
wolf-whistling at blondes in power-boats. I chuckled. She'd been too far
away to hear him over the roar of her engines, and I knew full well the
bodywork he'd been admiring.

When she was gone, leaving only the taint of diesel on the air and a
last glimpse of the name on her departing stern, I went back to the
goulash bubbling spicily on the stove.

The name on the stern was *Skara Sun*.

The next day the wind had veered round into the north-west. I had
thought of pushing up past Luing, but we'd have the wind in our teeth
all the way and this was supposed to be a holiday, not an endurance
test. We headed back down the Sound, making for Loch Sween.

Corryvreckan was more tumultuous than before. It made you understand the early chart-makers who wrote "Here be dragons" in the
places they dared not approach.

"Is there actually a way through there?" asked Harry.

"Oh yes, there's a channel. But not too many people use it. It's
always treacherous. At slack tide, with a steady breeze and no sea, it's
just about passable. Most of the time it's a death-trap."

"Have you ever been through?" He was watching it, fascinated, like
a man watching a snake.

"No. I've sailed hereabouts most every summer for eighteen years,
and I've gone up close a few times to see what it looked like, but I've
never found the combination of conditions and courage to try it. I've
seen it done a couple of times, and I've known people come to grief
there. I'd love to have done it, but I'm shit-scared of doing it."

"Funny," mused Harry. "I felt that way about marriage."

I spent the day teaching him the rudiments of sailing. Through the
morning we had the wind comfortably on the beam, and I could see
the confidence growing to smugness in Harry's face. He'd thought this
was going to be difficult, and now he thought it was easy. There are
many hazards awaiting the sailing man, from sudden squalls and breaking seas to rocks gnawing at his keel and pillocks driving power-boats
with one arm round a blonde and a magnum of champagne within easy
reach. But far and away the greatest danger facing a sailor is his own
complacency.

You have to know what you can do, and more importantly what you
can't. After forty-four years of considering wind propulsion as wildly

impractical and wholly pointless, one morning with the sun on the sea
and a steady breeze on the beam had been enough to persuade him
that he had this sailing thing licked. In his own interests, it was time to
disabuse him.

We turned the corner round Danna Island, a low dark nail at the tip
of the finger of land stretching down from Crinan, and began beating
our way up Loch Sween. Immediately everything was different. The
seas in the narrow waterway were restricted, but we were sailing into
the choppy face of them. The wind in the sails heeled the little boat
onto her shoulder, and made her tug at the tiller like a dog fretting on a
leash. The sails thrummed, the rigging sang. Salt spray came at us over
the gunwales. And every few minutes one rocky shore or the other bore
down on us and we had to tack away.

Like many policemen, Harry is a cautious man. He likes to be in
control of a situation—hence the love affair with engines, I suppose;
they do what they're meant to according to strict rules, and if they stop
there's a definitive mechanical reason for that too.

But sailing isn't an exact science, sailing to windward least of all:
you're constantly seeking a point of balance between conflicting and
inconstant forces. You don't steer through the wind, you ride it—
watching your burgee and the leading edge of the sails for the tell-tale
lift that warns of stalling, you skim the eddies and billows of the wind
as if it were something you could see and touch, using its sudden
strengths to bring you up to windward, paying off before its unexpected
hollows kill your thrust. The wind is like an animal that you have to
manage, not so much conquer as reach an accommodation with. There
is an equilibrium there to be used, but it's a dynamic one, eternally
changing. Sailing is a task for the instinct rather than the intellect.

Harry doesn't much like trusting to instinct, except that instinct told
him to give me the helm. I shook my head. "No, you sail her—I'll tell
you what to do."

So he learned how to balance the boat on the edge of the driving
wind and convert its fluctuations into a useful course even if it was not
always a straight one, and I trimmed the sails and warned him of
impending shores, and before the Fairy Isles hove in view he was sing-
ing "Lee-O" and shoving the tiller away from him as if he'd been doing
it half his life. An unbiased observer might even have thought he was
enjoying himself.

There are many magic places on earth, and I've been privileged to visit a few of them, both in company I cherished and alone. But perhaps God laid his hand most lightly of all on this little ring of rocky islets, their granite bones clothed in rowan and conifers, enclosing a tiny anchorage where the seals play and the otters visit, and the sea pales first to a milky brightness and then to the silken gleam of a steel mirror, as the stillness of the long evening comes on.

Luke brought me here first, when I was a brand new doctor with ambitions to change the world and needed dragging on holiday as now I dragged Harry. I'd been back almost every year since. I'd seen it in sunshine and rain; once I came in April and it snowed, decking the Christmas trees with tinsel and rimming the rocks, swallowing the view across the loch in a ballet of dancing, swirling white. Still the magic of it touched me every time, a purely Celtic magic woven of green and silver.

And it touched Harry too, which was a bonus I had not looked for. Because of the narrowness of the entrance and the confines of the anchorage itself, I took the *Rubber Lion* in under power. But as soon as the anchor was down and holding and the chain paid out, without any prompting from me Harry turned off the engine and we just sat, hand in hand on the cabin roof, listening to the twilight.

At length Harry said, a shade quietly, as if he found it difficult, "Was this one of the places you came with Luke? You know, special places."

I didn't know what he wanted to hear so I told him the truth. "Yes."

His eyes slipped out of focus above the Knapdale Forest. He said softly, "I could find it in me to be jealous about that."

I squeezed his hand. "You know that would be silly."

"I know. He was dead before I knew you."

"That too. But mostly because being jealous of Luke would be like being jealous of my sister. If he was alive today I'd feel about him the way I always did. But I wouldn't love you any the less because of it."

For a little while he said nothing more. I could feel him still troubled by the friendship he had never understood, the deep platonic friendship between me and Luke Shaw, over whose dead body—literally—we had come together. Finally he said, "I'm glad you brought me too."

I pressed into the curve of his body. I thought then that there was nothing in my life, nothing I had or was, that I would not want to share with him.

We had been lucky in that the lagoon was empty when we arrived, and we had it to ourselves for half an hour longer. But it was a popular anchorage, even at the beginning of the season, and another boat arrived with the last of the light, a big power-boat with a flared bow to her long white hull, and though they had throttled the twin engines right back to ease into the lagoon, still the rumble of them echoed off all the rocks and filled the anchorage.

They found a spot astern of us and dropped their hook, and after a moment longer the big engines died. In the sudden silence we could hear the murmur of voices from the cabin. The name on the bows was smaller than that on the stern, but it was the *Skara Sun* again.

I shrugged, freed my hand from Harry's and went down to the galley. "If there's one thing that lowers the tone of these places," I said, "it's noisy neighbours."

But I hadn't anticipated just how much noise we were going to be subjected to. It wasn't so much their voices that disturbed us—there seemed to be only the two of them, the woman and a man, and I wouldn't say they were any rowdier than Harry and I were. It wasn't the radio, which was playing dance music and the occasional snatch of Verdi at a pitch suitable for late evening in a secluded anchorage; or even the big engines, which in the event we never heard again.

It was the fact that, at ten-fifteen the following morning, while the seals were catching their breakfast and I was cooking ours, the *Skara Sun* blew up.

[2]

Sky-high. It was as if someone had dropped a match into the Woolwich Arsenal. One moment I was chivvying eggs and sausages in a pan, and Harry was trying to shave with too little hot water in too little space, and the next a percussion that was sound and force inextricably combined hit the *Rubber Lion* from astern, the pressure wave throwing her up the anchor-chain like an elderly and unfit racehorse startled to find itself back in the starting stalls.

With the boards lurching under me I lost my footing and hurtled towards the mast-step. The breakfast followed, the hot pan missing me by inches and one hot sausage not at all. Harry, better braced in the open doorway of the heads, bounded off one bulkhead after another but at least kept his feet. As the boat resumed an approximately even keel, he was up the steps of the companionway ahead of me, foam and whiskers on one half of his face, bellowing, "What the *hell*—?" as he went.

On the top step he stopped abruptly, blocking my view. I pushed him and he stepped aside.

A column of dense black smoke reached a hundred feet into the scrubbed morning sky. At the top it broadened into a boiling anvil-headed cloud. There was some flame, but not much—there was almost nothing left to burn. Debris in small shards was pattering back into the water almost gently, some of it hitting the *Rubber Lion* and some of it further away. Angry little waves were bouncing off the shore and the islets. Birds had exploded upwards from all the surrounding trees. The seals had stopped their fishing, too stunned even to dive.

Of the *Skara Sun* there remained only a shapeless knot of rubbish that sank even as we watched it, and the upturned hull of a dinghy, and a child's toy—a clear plastic globe filled with coloured fancies that danced within it as it spun and swirled on the afrighted sea. The scurrying ripples brought it bobbing gently against the hull of the *Rubber Lion* and, with nothing else to do, I leaned over to pick it up.

Harry touched my arm. "There."

It was a body, spread-eagled in the water by the capsised dinghy. It was face down and unmoving except for the movement of the stained water. It was the man whose voice we had heard. At least, it wasn't the woman we had seen; the floating hair was short and dark, not long and fair. Of her body there was no sign at all.

Harry was kicking his shoes off. I stopped him. "I'll need you to pull him on board." I took the horse-shoe lifebelt from its cradle in the stern and cast it, trailing its line, in the direction of the floating corpse. Then I followed it.

The water flowed like cold silk along my body. As I got closer it grew thick with particles of floating refuse. I tried quite hard not to think what some of them might be.

Before I reached him I was getting that sense of urgency, like a tiny alarm bell sounding deep in my brain, that said he wasn't yet dead—that some fragment of life lingered in his floating, broken body. I can't explain that, but I've known it too often—in myself and others—even to consider it a phenomenon.

There might be half a dozen of you clustered round a coronary case, and the sister can't get a blood pressure reading and the ECG has gone flat, and you keep plugging away at the massage and the stimulants and the defibrillator because that's what the book says you do; but you know, from sources other than the evidence of your clever equipment, whether this is one you're going to save or lose, and mostly you all feel the same way, and it's not often you're wrong. It's as if a viable body, one which has the physical and mental capacity to take up a restored life, has some way of signalling the fact to others close enough to help it—a kind of telepathic distress call: "Don't leave me, get me out of here!"

That's what I got from him then. Oh, not the words, nothing articulate and inarguable, but a tiny powerful sense of panic that I wouldn't have got from a floating log or a dead man, that made me lengthen my stroke to the limit of my strength although common sense dictated that a man who had been on that boat, in that explosion, and was now floating face down in the lagoon, should be beyond any help I could give him.

When I reached him, using the lifebelt for support I rolled him onto his back and got his face out of the water. He wasn't breathing but my instinct had been right: there was a faint thready pulse at his wrist. I cleared his mouth and breathed air into him.

If he wasn't dead yet, he was deeply unconscious. His face was slack, unknowing; his eyes were rolled back, a thin white line showing between the wet lashes of his slightly parted lids. There was the mark of a heavy blow to his temple. I breathed into him again, still without response.

"Harry, pull us in!"

Weak shoulder notwithstanding, Harry hauled the two of us in on that line faster than I could have swum alone. I had the lifebelt round the casualty now and let myself be towed along beside him, still breathing oxygen into his drowned lungs. I didn't know yet if I could save him, but that urgent instinct said he could be saved.

Harry helped me out of the water and together we pulled the boy out. A boy was all he was: he might have been twenty-three, not more, and the way he looked now he'd never make twenty-four. He still wasn't breathing. I stretched him out on the boards and pumped all the water I could out of him, and kept breathing fresh air in, but nothing was happening. He wasn't breathing, his pulse wasn't picking up—only this tiny, terrified voice in my head pleaded, "Don't give up—*please* don't give up on me, don't let me die."

Between breaths I gasped, "Harry, we have to get him ashore. I can't help—if I leave him he'll die. Get the engine started. Never mind about weighing anchor, we haven't time—let the chain go, I'll buy them a new one. Take her out through the gap we came in by—slowly, you haven't much room."

While he was doing this I was breathing, for myself and for the boy. His pulse was improving marginally. I was sorry to ditch the anchor, it's the sort of blot no sailor likes on her escutcheon, but lifting it would have taken minutes and this boy was already on borrowed time.

As he turned the *Rubber Lion* towards the channel, Harry looked back over his shoulder once more and said, "What about the woman?" His voice was low with shock.

I said, "What woman?" and he nodded and took us out into the loch.

We were making for Tayvallich a couple of miles down the coast. It wasn't, God knows, the sort of place you'd find an emergency unit— from what I could remember there was a pub and a shop or two—but there was a harbour and a road, and we could have travelled a lot further than two miles to find either.

It probably took us half an hour, and that with the engine at full revs. I might have sailed it faster, but Harry couldn't have managed alone under sail and if I'd sailed the boat my patient would have died. So Harry motored us down to Tayvallich and went ashore to summon help, and I stayed on my knees on the boards, bent like a succubus over the body of my victim.

And I stayed there, with my legs numb and my back breaking, breathing now for him and now for me, until a man in a helmet with an oxygen bottle took him from me, which was the first I knew that the sudden loud wind that had blown up was a helicopter landing.

As a doctor, I went with my patient. As a policeman, Harry stayed at the scene of the incident.

A wonderful thing is the helicopter. They took us to Glasgow, sixty miles away as the crow flies, and it took us half an hour. An ambulance with a good driver who knew the road might have got us halfway to Oban by then.

Actually, he'd have survived the drive to Oban. The oxygen finally flushed his lungs in a way my second-hand breath had not, and by the time we were in the air he was breathing for himself. The damage to his skull might or might not be serious, but the odds were that if he hadn't died of it by now he wasn't going to. He had superficial burns to the right side of his face and neck, his right forearm was broken, and he had acquired an interesting collection of cuts and bruises either in the explosion or in being hauled aboard the *Rubber Lion* by whatever parts of his anatomy came to hand. Once he was breathing, none of it threatened his life.

Now I had a little time to think about it, that was the most amazing part of the whole thing. He had no business floating away from the cinders that remained of the *Skara Sun* with no more to show for the disaster than a bump on the head and a broken arm. After an explosion like that you'd hardly expect to find a body, let alone a comparatively undamaged body still with some life left in it. There was only one explanation: that he hadn't been on board when it happened.

We'd found him floating beside the upturned dinghy, which was knocked about like himself but also in better condition than you could reasonably expect. It might have been lying well astern on its painter and thus escaped the worst of the blast. But it seemed likely that the boy had been in the dinghy, rowing away from the big cruiser when the explosion occurred. Perhaps he meant to emulate the seals and catch breakfast for his lady. It was the best decision he'd ever make.

Thinking about them like that, as a couple enjoying their holiday, making a late start to the day just as Harry and I were doing a hundred yards ahead of them, and then him setting off in the dinghy to land some breakfast while she lit the stove, brought home the sheer human tragedy of it. By the arbitrary good fortune that they'd anchored in company last night instead of alone, and anchored moreover behind a qualified if somewhat out-of-practice doctor, the boy on the stretcher with the oxygen mask over his face seemed likely to escape with his life. But a moment's carelessness in connecting a gas cylinder or something equally basic had cost him the woman he loved and the boat he'd worked for.

Then I remembered the sparkling globe dancing on the shock-waves in the lagoon and my belly turned over. Dear God, he'd lost his baby as well.

He started coming round in Casualty, not enough to make sense but it was a hopeful sign as far as the head injury was concerned. When they took him to Radiography I phoned the pub at Tayvallich and, sure enough, Harry wasn't a million miles away.

I told him where I was, and that the boy had made it this far and the indications were hopeful, and asked what he'd found out at his end. "Who is he? Where had they come from? How many were on board?"

"Well," Harry began slowly, and even down sixty-odd miles of Highland telegraph wire I could tell he was hedging, "the *Skara Sun* left Oban on Saturday afternoon, about three. It belongs—belonged—to Frazer McAllister, a Glasgow industrialist, and his wife. Mrs. Alison McAllister took the boat out on her own—she told the boat yard she was picking her husband up in Crinan." A thirty-mile run: the *Sun* would have got her there in time for dinner.

"Did she often go out alone?"

"Quite often. The boat was hers, really, the husband wasn't that interested though he'd go along to keep her company. What's supercargo?"

I tried not to smile. Harry can hear me smiling across a major land mass. "It's a passenger. Someone who's less use than ornament on board a boat. Where did you hear that?"

"The yard in Oban. They reckoned Mrs. McAllister was the sailor, her husband was supercargo."

For a moment I said nothing. Now the good sailor was with all the other good sailors on Fiddler's Green, and the supercargo was slowly waking up to the realisation of what he'd lost.

And just how much had he lost? "Did they say if she had a child with her?"

"A child?" His voice sharpened. "Was there a child too?"

"I don't know. There was a child's toy—a baby's, really—in the water. I was going to pick it up when you spotted the boy. The yard didn't mention a child, then?"

"No. She was alone when she left Oban."

"Perhaps McAllister brought it aboard with him at Crinan."

There was a fractional, significant pause on the line before Harry said, "I don't think so. I don't think McAllister was ever aboard—not this trip."

I didn't understand, though perhaps I should have done: this may be the age of the Yuppie but the boy on the table down in Radiography just wasn't old enough to be an industrialist. "What do you mean?"

"I mean, the boat yard in Oban gave me a description of Frazer McAllister. I don't know who we pulled out of the water this morning, but it wasn't a fifty-year-old Glaswegian with half his face missing and an artificial leg."

There was no arguing on that score. Happy with the results of the X-ray, they put him to bed in an observation ward and I watched while he slowly recovered his senses.

He was damn nearly thirty years too young to be Mrs. McAllister's husband, and when he finally got his wits marshalled all parts of him would be present and correct. Other than the minor burn on one cheek, his face was unmarked—curiously unmarked—until today neither time nor tragedy had laid their hands on him.

Long and slender in the big bed, he looked like a tall child. The dark hair had dried in a slightly tousled fringe over his high forehead, and the lashes beginning to flutter on his cheekbones were as long as a girl's. His broken arm was sandbagged at his side. An awareness of that, and the pain in his head, was getting through to him now. His face twisted anxiously and his head moved in little fretful arcs on the pillow. His good hand twitched and plucked without co-ordination at the sheet over him. He mumbled to himself. Once I thought he said a name, but it wasn't Alison. It might have been Peter.

A little time passed. The nurse brought me some coffee. While I was drinking it I became aware that the pattern of his breathing had altered, that the little febrile movements of his head and hand had stilled. I looked up quickly and met his eyes.

His eyes were brown, the deep peaty brown of trout pools, but that little silvery movement within them was not fish but fear. If he didn't yet know what had happened, he knew something had—something vast and terrible enough to reach down to him through the layers of unconsciousness to where he had hovered perilously close to oblivion.

His lips formed words, but his mouth was too dry to get them out. It didn't matter; I could read their shape on his lips, their meaning in his scared eyes. He said, "Who are you? Where's Alison?"

I answered the easy one first. "I'm Clio Marsh. My husband and I were anchored near you at the Fairy Isles. We pulled you out of the water."

He knew what had happened; maybe not in the forefront of his mind, where his returning consciousness was struggling against acceptance, but in the heart and depths of him he knew. Still his lips framed the word: "Water?"

"There was an explosion. Your boat—the boat you were on. The *Skara Sun*. She blew up."

"Where's Alison?"

It wasn't my job to tell him. I'd broken enough bad news in my time. His doctor could tell him—I'd ceased being responsible for him as soon as we'd landed here—or the police could, or he could wait until someone else whose job it was came along.

Wait while his returning strength fed the anxiety which would rip him up like claws. Wait while the memory came back by degrees, piecemeal, fragments of a horrid jigsaw falling slowly into place and presenting its picture at last with dreadful inevitability. Wait while memory and instinct and intuition and dread together built up a cohesive account of his loss that he could begin to grieve over if only someone would tell him it was true. Until then he was in a limbo-land full of monstrous shadows but no reality.

I couldn't make it easier for him, but I could avoid making it harder. "If she was on board the boat, she's dead. I'm sorry. You were the only survivor."

I watched it fall into his eyes, and float there for a moment and then begin to sink. I was right—he had known, had only been waiting for confirmation. Tears welled and ran from the corners of his eyes into his hair. He raised his good arm with effort and laid it across his face, crying behind it. The rhythm of his sobbing vibrated through the bed. He was too weak for great paroxysms of grief, but I thought his heart was breaking.

[3]

A touch on my shoulder startled me. It was the casualty officer who had met the helicopter. "I see you've told him."

I shrugged. "He asked. So I told him."

He nodded. He was about six-foot-four in his trainers and hadn't shaved this morning. Of course, to a hospital casualty officer morning can be the end of a very long night. He wasn't criticising; I think he was relieved. "He might as well know—start his mourning while he's still close enough to what happened to value his own survival. It'll be worse when he forgets how close he came to dying too."

I was surprised. Philosophy you don't expect from a hospital casualty doctor in the middle of a Monday morning. I asked his name.

"Neil Burns." The accent was pure Glasgow; not Gorbals, but Glasgow. He looked at me with frank curiosity. "Are you really a doctor?"

I really am, but I don't really look it. I didn't really look it when I was practising, the whole medical ethos is basically antipathetic to doctors who can wear a gym-slip and travel half-fare on buses, but since I foresook medicine to make my living out of murder I have lost even that slight air of professional authority I once had.

This particular morning I was wearing damp shorts, with my forty-two-year-old knees turning blue beneath them, a dry sweater that Harry had pulled over my head after he pulled me out of the water and which I had not until that moment realised was back to front, and canvas shoes drying to a salty whiteness over no socks. I couldn't find it in me to resent that note of incredulity in his voice.

I smiled wearily. "Yes, really. Though I don't advertise the fact any more—I don't know how he knew whose boat to get himself blown up beside."

Neil Burns's big angular face with its rugby player's nose turned disapproving. He didn't mind my knees, or the subtle pervasive aroma of wet deck-shoes, but he didn't like me wasting my degree. He scowled at my ring finger. "I suppose you gave it up when you got married."

I bristled. "I gave it up years before I got married. I gave it up when I found I could make a living without being propositioned by drunks every Friday night, without having to wash other people's vomit out of my clothes; without being accused of incompetence, or worse, every time that all the skill and care and sheer hard work I put in didn't pay off; without spending my rare days off seeing my own doctor about the ulcers that wouldn't heal and the fact that the only nights I didn't cry myself to sleep were the ones when I was just too God-damned tired. I did your job for ten years, sonny, and I was bloody good at it, but I wouldn't do it again if the only alternative was sending my mother to the glue factory."

I was entitled to answer his implied criticism, but my vehemence seemed out of all proportion, even to me. It sounded defensive, as if he had touched a raw nerve. I hadn't realised I felt guilty about it.

But the disapproval in Dr. Burns's face had faded into understanding, even respect. "Aye, ten years is a long time. So what do you do now?"

I could have told him. I could have told him that all the nightmares I had worked through, all the disasters human beings wreak on one another and then bring to doctors to cure, now peopled the pages of eight books on the shelves of his public library; that I spent my days writing about murder and mayhem, and by night slept soundly between pleasant dreams. I don't know why I didn't: owning up to being a novelist isn't like admitting you're the chucker-out at a brothel, it's a perfectly respectable occupation. But instead I said, "Now I just make the occasional boat-call. Don't you think we should find out who he is?"

Burns looked surprised. "I didn't know we didn't know."

I shook my head. "We know who the boat belonged to. We know who the woman was. All we know about him is that he wasn't her husband."

"There was no ID in his clothes?"

"You saw what he was wearing." Approximately the same as me, and I was carrying nothing that would identify me either. All his property that wasn't directly about his person had gone up in flames.

"Well, he's pretty much awake now. Ask him."

He hadn't cried himself out yet, but while we'd been talking quietly at the other end of his bed the violence of his grieving had abated. Now he lay still behind the shelter of his arm, too weak to do anything else. Neil Burns was right: grief takes most out of those who have most to spare for it. This boy would cry again when he was stronger, but for now he had reached a kind of peace.

I took his hand, and his elbow in my other hand, and lifted his arm high enough to peep underneath. "Feeling better?"

His eyes were red. His hair, which had dried from the sea, was wet again at both temples. But crying had at least given him a voice. "I'm all right." It was a lie, of course. He wasn't all right; he wasn't even feeling better.

I said, "We don't know your name."

He paused a little longer than made sense. There was no question of amnesia. He remembered what had happened, remembered Alison McAllister clearly enough to break up over her—the chances of his having forgotten his own name were negligible. But something was going through his mind, and only after he had it resolved did he consent to answer. "Alex Curragh."

It was his name all right, it's such a personal thing that it's quite difficult to give a false name convincingly, but I was sure he had thought about telling us another lie and I wondered why.

But the answer was obvious enough. He had been on a boat with another man's wife when fate stepped in and promoted their discreet dirty weekend to front-page news. Her husband was going to know; his wife, if he had one, was going to know. He might have got away with giving a false name to the hospital, but plainly the police were going to be involved as well. So he told us who he was.

"Where do you live, Alex?"

"Crinan. I work on the boats." So that was how they'd met, the rich man's sailor wife and the boat hand.

"Had you known her long—Alison, Mrs. McAllister?"

Again that brief pause while he thought, a gathering of cloud in his dark eyes, and this time he lied. "A few weeks. She needed some help with her boat. I helped her out." He avoided looking at me.

I didn't believe him—a young man doesn't cry like that for the death of a casual employer—but I didn't force the issue. The police would do that. "You were crewing for her?"

"Yes." But the yard in Oban had been unconcerned to see her leave alone for the thirty-mile passage to Crinan; if she didn't need a crew to get that far, she didn't need a crew. They were lovers, all right. He was thinking of the dead woman's reputation.

"Do you know what caused the explosion?"

His eyes filled up again but the tears didn't spill.

"She was so *careful*." The accent was Highland, soft and musical. "She never turned the gas on unless she had a match lit. She wouldn't have smoking on board. She wouldn't have so much as the radio on when she was fuelling. She said she saw a boat burn up once, and she didn't want to go that way." His face twisted and the tears spilt.

I held his hand, for comfort but also to stop him hiding. His hands were brown with weather, hardened by salt and work, but surprisingly slender in design. He was not a big man. If he had been he would likely have died in the lagoon before we could haul him aboard. I said, "She couldn't have known anything about it, Alex. We were right in front of you, and by the time we got on deck the *Skara Sun* was gone. She had no time to be hurt, or afraid."

He couldn't speak. He nodded, his eyes grateful. His hand was tight in mine.

I said, "Where were you when it happened?"

His eyes flared as if I'd threatened him. "I—I'm not sure. Didn't you see?"

"We were below. We didn't see anything until afterwards."

"I was in the cabin, I think. Alison was making breakfast."

It wasn't credible and I knew it too, but I wouldn't have said anything. If there's one thing policemen can't abide it's well-meaning busybodies polishing the stories of people who are going to help them with their enquiries.

But Neil Burns wasn't married to a policeman and so didn't know the taboos. "You can't have been. You'd have gone the same way she did. But you're practically undamaged. Apart from nearly drowning, I mean."

I winced but it didn't stop me listening for the answer. It took time coming. I saw him look at the broken arm wedged at his side, think about his battered head and other injuries. I saw him consider the plausibility of what he was going to say.

"I must have been on deck. That's right, I went to check the anchor-chain. I had the forward hatch open, so I could get in and out of my cabin without disturbing Mrs. McAllister. Then she said she was making breakfast, and I leaned over to check the fairlead before going aft. She must have lit the gas then. I don't remember anything more."

Well, he wouldn't. When that boat went up she went like a bomb; he would have had no warning of whatever it was that hit him and threw him senseless into the sea. He could have been up in the bows: that would have put him, and the dinghy on its painter trailing from the stern, about equally as far from the gas stove, which would explain why they escaped the otherwise comprehensive destruction.

That left the third improbable survivor. "Alex, there wasn't a child on board?"

His eyes rounded at me with a peculiar horror. "A child? God almighty, no."

"I saw a plastic toy floating in the water. Did Mrs. McAllister have a child?"

"Aye, a baby, four months old. But he was never on the boat. She left him at home, with her husband." He swallowed. "Has he been told yet?"

Burns shrugged. "I've no idea."

Back home Harry would have been trying to contact the next-of-kin within minutes of the victim's identity being discovered. I presumed it would be the same here. "Yes, probably. Unless he's neither at home nor his office, in which case the police will be making every effort to find him before it goes out on the news. Yes, I think he'll know by now."

"There was nothing I could have done," said Alex Curragh. I wasn't sure if he was telling me or asking me. "Even if I'd been right beside her, there was nothing I could have done to save her?"

The reassurance he craved was also the truth. "Nothing. If it was a gas leak, it was always going to kill everyone in the cabin when the first match was struck. It's a miracle it didn't kill everyone on board."

For the traditional minute none of us said anything. Then Neil Burns cleared his throat. Interested as he was in the domestic tragedy of Alison McAllister's death, he had work of his own to do. I left them to get on with it. I made my way down to Reception and asked if Harry had phoned, but he hadn't.

What I wanted most of all was some dry clothes, and after a minute chatting with the receptionist I confessed as much. I could have lived with the sweater, once I got round to turning the *V* to the front, but underneath it I had a wet shirt, wet shorts, wet pants and wet shoes. I'd have been uncomfortable in my own living-room. Knocking round the public areas of a large hospital, watched curiously by staff who knew I had been one of them and thought I had gone native, and with some anxiety by civilians who didn't know the background and just thought I was peculiar, I felt singularly disadvantaged. If I'd had my purse with me I could have headed for the nearest department store to regularise the situation, but nobody takes their purse swimming. I'm not even sure that wet notes are legal tender.

The receptionist listened with sympathy and some amusement, then nodded me to a handy chair and turned to her switchboard. "I know who'll sort you out."

I would have known too if I hadn't been away from hospitals so long. The chief fixer in any infirmary is always the head porter. The hospital secretary, the chief nursing officer, the senior doctor, all these are worthy people whose contribution to running the establishment cannot be overstated. But each of them is responsible for a particular area of hospital management defined by clean-etched lines, and things like the reassembly of battle-scarred Action Men from the children's ward, and caring for budgerigars brought in clutched to the breasts of little old ladies who should be worrying about their broken hips, and dressing visiting physicians who are soaked to the skin and sixty miles from their nearest funds, never quite fit into their parameters. The head porter deals with everything that anybody else can reasonably claim isn't their job. In a very real sense, the hospital buck stops with him.

So less than ten minutes after the receptionist called him, the biggest, blackest head porter you ever saw bustled through the swing-doors bearing a stack of towels, clothes, brush and comb, even cosmetics—we hadn't actually met till now, remember—before him. He saw Little Orphan Annie sitting damply in her corner and beamed. I grinned back. I was relieved to see the succour that he brought, but mostly it was a Pavlovian response to a face that cheerful. I felt warm for the first time in hours.

I retired to the Ladies and got first dry and then decent. I put together a perfectly respectable, if not exactly haut couture, outfit from a nurse's blouse and white lab coat belted round the middle to take up the length—you don't find many lab technicians my height, they'd have trouble reaching the shelves—with a pair of backless mules for shoes. The head porter, bless him, had even scrounged me some underwear. The knickers were a pair of wholly honorable white cellular passion-killers, but the bra would have taken any two people my size. I returned it, with the towels and my thanks. My own damp belongings I stuffed into the carrier-bag provided for the purpose.

Thus warmed, cheered and upholstered in a manner befitting a middle-aged woman with a professional past, I sallied forth to court the approval of my new friends for my new image. Jim Fernie the porter beamed again with proprietorial pride, as if I were his little girl who had just dressed herself for the first time.

"Half the doctors in this hospital will be asking you for a second opinion," he said. I thought it more likely that someone would press a mop into my hand and tell me to deal with the sago on the canteen floor, but I appreciated his confidence.

I went to pirouette for Ros the receptionist too, but she had a customer. I could see her talking, her face serious, and gesturing past his broad dark-suited back. When he thanked her and limped off in the direction indicated, I went to show her my spring collection.

She was suitably impressed. "What price Bruce Oldfield now?" Personally I couldn't see where a karate film star came into it.

When she had said all there was to say about my costume, she nodded towards the lifts and said, "That was your friend's da come to see him."

I frowned. "Sorry?"

"Your friend from the boat—Alex Curragh. That was his father."

"Oh—good." I was a little surprised: although the police would have contacted Curragh's next-of-kin at the same time as they were breaking the news to Frazer McAllister, there hardly seemed to have been time for him to get here from Crinan. Perhaps he didn't live in Crinan. "He's going to need his family. A thing like that will be with him a lot longer than it takes the broken bone to heal."

Ros nodded, sympathy pursing her lips. She was a tall, dark woman of about thirty and she'd seen a lot of pain and misery and despair come through those doors in her time. "Maybe his da can help him with that too. What happened to him must have taken some coming to terms with."

We seemed to be at cross purposes. At any event, I didn't understand what she was saying. "Sorry, what?"

"Didn't you see? No, of course, he had his back to you. He must have been in a fire—not recently, but it did a lot of damage. Half his face is gone."

I could feel alarm stretching my eyes, saw incomprehension cloud Ros's. But now I understood—as well I might, I'd been told enough to identify him three times over. Even the limp—he had an artificial foot, Harry said. Alison's dread of fire presumably stemmed from her husband's experience.

There was no time to explain. I set off for the lifts at a determined jog, the closest I could manage to a run in mules, shouting back at Ros as I went. "Find a policeman. Get Jim Fernie. That wasn't Alex Curragh's dad you sent up to his room—it was his mistress's husband!"

The lift was too long coming. I kicked off the borrowed mules and took to the stairs. He had a head start on me, but I had the greater sense of urgency. Also I knew where I was going. The upshot was that I skidded round the last corner of the corridor in time to see Frazer McAllister throw open the door, stride limping powerfully into the room and lift Curragh half out of the bed by one big fist twisted in his pyjama front.

In a voice that was not merely Glasgow but Gorbals through and through, he bellowed into the boy's face, "Are you the wee shite that murdered my wife?"

[4]

I got there first but Neil Burns was right behind and infinitely more effective. He elbowed past me in the doorway, grabbed McAllister by one shoulder of his expensive suit and bent low enough to shove his young rugby player's face into the older man's ruined one. "If you don't put my patient down now, I'm going to stuff your head down the autoclave."

As a threat it may have lacked subtlety, particularly in view of McAllister's face, but it had the desired effect and I don't think appeals to the man's better nature would have done. He let go of Curragh, who dropped back onto the bed with a thump, and rounded on Burns. "Wee son, you're crumpling my suit."

I doubt Neil Burns had been addressed thus since he passed the six-foot mark, somewhere around his fifteenth birthday, and certainly not by a man he could look squarely in the bald patch, but if there was anything intrinsically silly about the big young man being warned off by the shorter, older, damaged one, neither of them acknowledged it. Burns took his hand back and straightened up. "You have no business here."

Frazer McAllister broadened visibly, like a ruffled fighting-cock. He was a strong, substantial man, a big man every way but up. Wide, heavy shoulders and broad arms filled his jacket as his thick neck filled the collar of his white shirt. His big heavy head jutted forward, like an old boxer used to taking everything on the chin. I was still behind him, still couldn't see his face, but his big skull was fringed copiously by a lion's mane of greying hair which burst out like an expression of the man's energy, slightly long and slightly frizzy. He might have had one artificial toe stuck in the wall socket.

His voice rumbled up from his deep barrel of a chest. "Sonny, I'm Frazer McAllister. There's more of my money in this hospital than you're likely to see in your lifetime. There's almost no part of this city where I don't have business."

But Neil Burns in his jeans and trainers was invulnerable to the intimidation of sheer money. I saw his lip wrinkle. "Mr. McAllister, I don't doubt your taxes run three wings of Barlinnie Prison as well. That's where people who assault my patients end up."

McAllister snorted at him, but I got the strong impression that he was not displeased. He was a man who radiated emotions, all of them powerful, like a pharos sheds light. Radiating from him now, as well as and somehow distinct from the violence of his anger, was a compound of surprise and amusement and respect for someone who was prepared to stand up to him. But then, he'd have looked the same way at a dog walking on its hind legs.

The imminent prospect of a punch-up seemed to have retreated. I sidled along the wall to where I could see what was going to happen instead. McAllister's big body swivelled like an executive's revolving chair. "Who the hell are you?"

Burns gave me no time to answer. "Dr. Marsh saved Curragh's life. If it had happened differently—if Mrs. McAllister had been on deck while Curragh cooked breakfast—you'd be standing here thanking her."

McAllister growled, "Aye," low in his throat. It was true, but it was asking a lot of him to accept the purely medical view that one life has much the same value as another, that his wife's lover was as much worth saving as his wife.

Yet he was not distraught in his grief. Mostly what he felt thus far was anger—a legitimate reaction in the circumstances—and even that was something that he possessed rather than possessed him. There was no loss of control. What he had done and said was no more or other than he had intended. He hadn't been suddenly overwhelmed by an access of unbearable passion when he hauled Alex Curragh from his bed, sending the pain beating through his battered skull and leaving his arm to trail useless as a bird's broken wing. What he had said could not be dismissed as the ravings of someone temporarily out of his mind with shock. Frazer McAllister gave a powerful impression of a man totally in command of himself and his destiny.

It was an impression which his big scarred face did nothing to contradict; though to refer to his scars is misleading. Almost half his face, from his left ear to his nose and from his eyebrow over the granite bluff of his jaw and down his throat, was nothing but scar tissue, dark and pitted and granular, as if he'd been stitched together from very small pieces—which is what grafting is. Usually it works better than this, but then I didn't know how deep the damage had gone or what complications had arisen. Also, this wasn't recent. The healing was long done. This was the best he was going to look.

And then, as quickly as that, with the man still staring at me with his eyes, including the puckered one, steady and arrogant, and his mouth, including the undamaged side, twisted into a sneer of austere interest, I felt the miracle begin—that special miracle wrought by, or on, the grossly deformed. At first sight the spoiled face, the crooked limb or the hunched back seems totally to dominate the victim, or at least the way you relate to him. You're embarrassed by your inability to see past it. You might suppose that doctors, inured by familiarity, might be better at seeing the essential human being locked up in the burlesque, but in fact we're often rather worse. It's a constant battle to remember you've been consulted by a person rather than a duodenal ulcer, at the best of times.

Then the miracle begins. The divine human gift is adaptability, and once the surprise is past the horror fades, then the pity, and before much longer even the acute awareness of difference. By the time you've known this mutilated, devastated creature long enough to know his wife's name and have seen his children's photographs, he's an individual with a background, with problems and hopes that go back further and reach out beyond the ones that brought him to you, and it's a little jolt to remember at intervals just how distorted his appearance is, and then how little it affects the quintessential humanity resident in his soul. The important things, like strength and courage and kindness, and whether you like someone or not, don't so much transcend the deformity as come from somewhere else in the first place. No-one ever liked someone less because he was ugly than they would have done had he been fair.

So, almost before I had fully mapped out the extent of his disfigurement, I was aware that what had happened to make Frazer McAllister look like that mattered much less, to him and to the world on which he imposed his authority, than what had happened to make him the kind of man he was. The face was fancy wrapping-paper, no reflection of and no guide to the contents.

The other thing you learn early about pain and suffering is that, contrary to popular opinion, they have no ennobling qualities whatever. Nice people suffer dreadful accidents and diseases, but so do absolute bastards, and the man who was an absolute bastard in his glorious entirety is unlikely to be significantly nicer if fate deprives him of one or more extremities.

It was too early in our acquaintance for me to categorise McAllister as an absolute bastard. What I was sure of, from that powerful, magnetic aura surrounding the man like a force-field, from the arrogance of his eyes and the pugnacity of his broad, square, expensively upholstered shoulders, was that he had the capacity to be one.

All this took less time to happen than to describe, so that before he'd finished his sentence I had got my attention off both his face and his personality and onto what he was saying, which was: "You saw my wife's boat burn up?"

I shook my head. "It didn't burn up, it blew up. It was gone before we could get on deck. She couldn't have known a thing about it." It felt almost stranger than anything that had happened, to be making the same reassuring noises to the woman's husband as only minutes before I had been making to her lover.

"That's something to be grateful for, anyway," said McAllister gruffly.

I said, "If you've finished threatening Dr. Burns's patient, at least for the moment, I think we should go and explain to the policeman who's on his way here that his presence is no longer required."

"Policeman?" He said it the Glasgow way, the emphasis on the first syllable, and there was something like injured innocence in his ravaged face.

"You shouldn't have told the receptionist you were Curragh's father."

"I didnae. I asked her was he here. She asked was I a relative. I said I was. She didnae ask me whose." He sounded like a schoolboy who'd got away with cheeking his Latin teacher by quoting from Catullus.

We seemed to be losing sight of the reason for his presence here, the fact that his wife had just died. I touched his sleeve. "If you'll come with me, Mr. McAllister, I'll tell you what I know of what happened."

He followed me towards the door. But there he stopped and turned back, and his voice rasped like slow machine-gun fire. "Curragh, I know what you are. I know what you've done. Take it from me, you're not going to get away with it."

Then McAllister turned towards me again and for a moment, past the bulk of his shoulder, I saw Alex Curragh's face. And what I saw there I couldn't understand. Of course there was fear—he wasn't a fool, he recognised a threat when one was snarled at him, and he had better reason than I to know the stamp and nature of the man snarling it. Fear was the appropriate response of a nobody threatened by the likes of Frazer McAllister. The shock was a hangover from what had happened to him this morning, compounded by what had happened to him just now—they'd have to do that arm again, broken limbs shouldn't be treated like that.

But beside the fear and the shock stretching his eyes was the thing that I couldn't describe, even to myself, couldn't begin to understand. Momentarily it looked almost like pride—a frightened, defiant pride. Then Neil Burns leaned over to see to his arm and came between us.

I found some seats for McAllister and myself in a quiet corner of a corridor, grouped round a plastic palm, and shortly afterwards Jim Fernie and the policeman found us. Jim looked surprised, if not actually disappointed, at the lack of blood. "Is everything all right, Dr. Marsh?"

It still sounded funny to me. I'd hardly been addressed as "Doctor" since my marriage. I nodded. "I think so. At least for now."

McAllister squinted sideways at me, a bleak humour in his eyes, which were the colour of blued steel and held the same kind of edge. "For now."

I ignored him. "You'd better have a word with Dr. Burns. Curragh is his patient."

"And then come back here, Constable," said McAllister, in the tone of a man used to command, "because I may have something to tell you."

Plainly the policeman knew McAllister, or anyway knew who he was. He raised no questions, no objection. "Yes, sir." He trotted away tamely on Jim Fernie's heels.

McAllister turned back to me with a satisfied expression. How that ruined face could express feelings was part of the miracle, but in fact it did so quite clearly. Everything he did was precise, deliberate. He left no room for misunderstanding. "OK, lassie, what was it you were going to tell me?"

I have never much cared for diminutives, but you have to make allowances for the recently bereaved. I tried not to bristle visibly. "I was going to tell you how the accident happened—how your wife died."

His jaw came up like a naval gun. "I know how she died, and it wasn't an accident. He murdered her—Curragh, the wee shite."

I frowned but also I was curious. "That's a serious accusation, you know, and now you've made it twice. I know how you must be feeling, but have you any reason to blame Curragh? For what happened to the boat, I mean."

He gave me what I can only describe as a canny look. Even the anger seemed to have gone now—gone, or gone to ground. "Your tale first, lassie."

So I told him what had happened—what Harry and I had heard and seen, and what we had done. He listened without interruption, although his face clouded as I described the efforts necessary to save young Curragh's life. I couldn't altogether blame him for feeling that way. I went on without comment and finished my account.

While I was still talking, the policeman came back and stood near us, a respectful distance behind McAllister's shoulder.

When I finished I looked at McAllister, seeking some sign of grief in him. I hadn't seen one yet. Unless he had done all his crying at home, in the few minutes between receiving the news of his wife's death and coming here to confront her lover, he hadn't shed a tear for Alison. You couldn't count the anger. It was passion enough, certainly, but not for Alison. I thought he was angry about what had been done to him.

And still that blue steel eye was undimmed by any token of his bereavement. He might have been robbed of some valuable possession, in a theft that had left him seething with indignation rather than aching with loss. Two possibilities occurred to me: that he really hadn't cared for his wife very much, or that he cared so much he didn't dare let loose the grieving for fear that it would consume him. Anger is a useful tool in many ways. If you're angry enough you hardly feel hurt at all.

"So the boat was gone, and Alison was gone, and that wee shite was floating round with nothing but a few cuts and bruises to show for it?" There was a light like wine or fire in his eye. "You didn't think that was a bit odd?"

And of course I had, but not inexplicably so. "He says he was on deck, in the bows, when the explosion occurred. The shock-wave must have knocked him into the water before much else reached him."

"Did you see him?"

"I told you, we saw nothing until after the explosion."

"Aye, well," said McAllister heavily. He looked round for the policeman, beckoned him to a seat. "You see, my wife was very careful aboard that boat of hers. Very careful. You might think she took risks heading out alone, sailing in big seas and bad weather, but actually she did nothing without she had a big safety margin. She picked that boat because it was about the toughest on the market. Not the biggest, or the flashiest, or the fastest or even the most expensive—she reckoned it was the most seaworthy. She wanted diesel engines rather than petrol. She had the radio installed handy to the wheel—she always planned to sail mostly alone. I'd go with her on a nice day but I never had that much time or affection for it.

"And she put in one of those gas detectors. It was that bloody sensitive it went off if we had baked beans on toast. I don't believe there was any gas leak. She wouldn't have fitted the canister wrong, and she wouldn't have left the tap on, and most of all that damn detector would have woken half the Western Highlands long before there was enough gas to explode. You didn't hear it, I bet."

"No. Would we have done?—we were anchored a hundred yards away from the *Skara Sun.*"

"You'd have heard it half a mile a way, maybe more, if it had gone off."

"Could it have failed?"

He shrugged his big shoulders. "Anything's possible. But she'd have checked it before she left Oban. She left nothing to chance."

He paused then, waiting to be prompted. I resisted the temptation, knowing he'd go on anyway, but the constable was made of less stern stuff. "So what are you suggesting happened, sir?"

McAllister waited a moment longer. For some reason he was looking at me. There was a kind of suppressed excitement within him, as inappropriate an emotion as I could imagine. One shaggy eyebrow went up, the other down. Finally he said, "I'm suggesting that if the gas leaked it was meant to leak. I'm suggesting that if the alarm didn't sound it was fixed not to."

He looked at me, waiting for my response. Again I said nothing.

The constable, both excited and uneasy at having one of the biggest men in the city making wild allegations in his presence, said carefully, "You seem to be implying there was some foul play here, Mr. McAllister."

McAllister went off in a small explosion of his own. "I'm implying nothing, sonny. I'm saying that my wife's death was not an accident. I'm saying someone fixed the stove to blow her sky-high the moment she put a match under the bacon.

"I'm saying that he made damn sure he was on deck before breakfast, and when she moved towards the stove he got into the dinghy and rowed like hell. It was just bad luck he couldn't get out of range before the explosion. Or maybe it wasn't; maybe the fact that he needed hauling out and pumping out will be the mainstay of his defence. Granted he cut it a bit fine, but the principle was sound."

There was a stretched minute's silence. I had a sense of something irrevocable having been done, something that would alter lives in ways that could never afterwards be repaired. I knew what he was saying, of course, and all that would inevitably flow from it—well, not all, no-one could have foreseen it all. But somehow I felt that it was the imminent accusation, rather than anything that had happened aboard the *Skara Sun*, which was the fulcrum. I didn't want him to say it. I seemed to think that if he didn't actually say it, everything would somehow work out. I glued my eyes to my knees under the white overall and said nothing and tried to think nothing. Like an atomic clock making good the hour's extra second, time fractionally expanded.

Then the constable stammered, "Whose defence against what?" and McAllister took the irreversable step.

"Alex Curragh's defence against a charge of murdering my wife. For the sake of a fifteen-thousand-pound bequest in her will."

[5]

I was never afterwards sure whether what Neil Burns did then was calculated, or ingenuous, or just a doctor getting on with his job. While the Glasgow air was buzzing with urgency and phone calls, and policemen from our young lad to (for all I know) the Chief Constable of Strathclyde were blowing dust off their notebooks and stealing themselves for a good old-fashioned Celebrated Case, and Harry was desperately trying to get himself from Tayvallich to Glasgow while his car was in Ardfern, and I was mostly sitting in a corner over a cup of cold tea, Neil Burns was prepping Alex Curragh for surgery on his broken arm. Once the pre-med was circulating in his system he wouldn't be fit to be questioned for hours, probably not for the rest of the day.

Not that he was going anywhere. If McAllister was serious, and he appeared to be absolutely serious—he might be shocked and grieving and outraged as well, but he hadn't been ranting out of that, he had been quite lucid and seemed to have facts to support him—Curragh would find himself at the sharp end of a long and pointed interrogation. But not today, when he had nearly died. He'd still be here tomorrow, and tomorrow was time enough for justice. Dr. Burns was right: medicine took precedence.

You wouldn't have thought he was right. Ascending ranks of policemen came and tried to lean on him. He was as untroubled by that as by
the power-politics of McAllister's fortune. When you're six-foot-four
and in your mid-twenties, in your own hospital and anyway probably
right, the only way even a big policeman can lean on you is by standing
on a stool, a position in which it is difficult to maintain either dignity or
balance.

Finding they couldn't subject Curragh to the third degree, or brow-
beat his doctor, the police switched their attention to me. A medium-
sized policeman in a pigskin jacket and matching shoes came over with
fresh tea and an extra cup on a tin tray, and introduced himself as
Detective Chief Inspector Baker. He had a small, immaculately
trimmed moustache and spoke with the Scottish equivalent of a Win-
chester accent. He asked me what I had seen and heard, and I told
him. As I had told it to Frazer McAllister.

I won't say he leapt to the same conclusions, but clearly he was
struck by the same significances. I saw them register in his face, and he
went over them again in his questions.

"You saw the *Skara Sun* before she anchored by you in Loch Sween,
then."

"About five o'clock on Saturday. She passed us heading south from
the Seil Sound while we were anchored at Shuna."

The names that were second nature to me after years of cruising
round there meant nothing to him. But he had brought an Ordnance
Survey map of the west coast and had me point out the relevant places.
He pored over it now. "That's on a direct route from Oban to
Crinan?"

"With a motorboat, yes. She'd have no trouble getting through the
Clachan Bridge."

"How long would it have taken her from Oban?"

"Depends how fast she was going. That isn't exactly open sea—
tootling along at ten knots, say, she'd have made Shuna in two hours,
which fits with the time she left the yard."

The impeccable moustache bristled, the neat (and matching) eyebrows climbed. "Does it? How do you know?"

I despise women who can't have their say without backing it up with
their husband's authority. "John always says . . ." "Martin doesn't
believe . . ." It's pathetic. I said, "My husband told me." It was true
and unavoidable, but I still winced.

I think DCI Baker may have despised women like that too. He regarded me down his nose. "And what does your husband know about it?"

I nettled. He wasn't offensive enough to challenge, but only because he knew how not to be. "What he was told, I presume. The local police called the yard in Oban."

Baker smiled, like a fish on a slab. "Yes, well, Mr. Marsh would be better leaving the business to the professionals."

I had him, and I took a moment to enjoy it. "Detective Superintendent Marsh is a professional. Anyway, the time the *Skara Sun* left Oban won't be covered by the Official Secrets Act." Of course, you couldn't be sure of that.

Surprise jolted through him like a small amount of electricity. He'd thought it a coincidence that Curragh was fished out of the water by an erstwhile doctor. He didn't know what to make of the fact that there was a detective involved as well. Finally he remembered official police policy towards inconvenient facts—ignore them—and moved on. "And you reckon Mrs. McAllister was alone on the boat then."

"The yard in Oban"—I couldn't resist reminding him—"said she left alone. I didn't see anyone else on board, and she could certainly have managed on her own."

"When would she have reached Crinan?"

I glanced at the map to confirm my recollection. "Shuna's about halfway, but she could do the second half faster. She might have made Crinan about six-thirty."

"Where she collected Curragh."

"I don't know that, of course, but it seems likely. I do know they were both on board when the *Sun* anchored behind us at the Fairy Isles last night."

"That was the next you saw of her?"

"Yes."

Baker unfolded his map to display all the islets and inlets of the glacial west coast. "So there was a day—from Saturday evening until Sunday evening—when you saw nothing of them. How far could they have got in that time?"

I remembered the big flared bow of the *Skara Sun*, and the big twin diesels shoving her along, and tried to imagine the range of the big tanks feeding them. "She could have got to Ireland and back if she'd wanted to."

Baker worried about that for a minute before moving on again. "So the next you saw of them was at the Fairy Isles."

"We didn't actually see him. We saw the woman and heard a man's voice."

"Were you talking to them at all?"

"No." That must have seemed odd to a landsman, that you could anchor a hundred yards apart, your two crews maybe the only living souls for miles, and still make no gesture towards neighbourliness, not so much as a shouted greeting, let alone rowing across for cocktails. It is a bit odd, but it's how it's done: you need to have met someone regularly before you even exchange weather reports. Perhaps it's because more people sail to get away from other people than do so to meet them. The ideal anchorage is one with nobody else there, and if you do have to share, by a kind of unspoken agreement you ignore one another. A bit like DCI Baker and inconvenient facts. "No, but voices carry clearly over water. They'd know there were two of us on our boat too."

"Could you hear what they were saying?"

"No. There was no shouting, if that's what you're wondering. They had the radio on, not very loud. A couple of times I heard them laughing, later on they quieted down."

"Was it a warm night?"

I blinked at the change of direction but answered anyway. "It was pleasant, but you couldn't really say it was warm. It's always much colder afloat than ashore."

"They'd have wanted a hot meal then."

Now I saw what he was getting at. He was more astute than he looked. "The stove. Yes, I'd be surprised if she didn't cook supper. I did for Harry and me, and our galley was primitive compared with what they'd have."

"So whatever it was happened between supper and breakfast. Would that fit in with a gas leak?"

"Listen, I'm no expert," I said, "I've never actually blown a boat up. But it's not that rare an accident, and you listen to all the stories to avoid making the same mistakes yourself. Yes, I think it could happen. Cooking gas is heavy; if you get a slow leak it collects in the bilges and maybe you wouldn't know until you got a spark down there. Except that McAllister says his wife fitted a gas detector, and that would warn her long before there was a dangerous build-up.

"The other possibility is that she finished one cylinder cooking supper and fitted another one to cook breakfast. It shouldn't be a problem, but if you've got a bad seal you could get a sudden release of gas. But she'd have had to be very quick off the mark to light the stove before the detector smelled it."

"If it was working."

"They're pretty reliable. They tend to be too sensitive, not the other way round."

"Could it be disconnected?"

It was a leading question, but it was his job to ask it and mine to answer. "Yes, it could."

We ended up, neither antagonists nor allies except in the search for what had happened, facing one another over the monstrous shadow that was McAllister's allegation. Baker said, quietly and a little sadly, "Then the old man could be right. It might not have been an accident. Curragh could have contrived her death."

"For the money?"

He shrugged. "An awful lot of crimes are committed for it."

"Fifteen thousand pounds? He's not going to live in luxury for the rest of his life on that."

"It's still probably the biggest sum he's ever owned."

"But peanuts to her." The figure worried me. It was too much and too little: too much for a casual gift, even from a rich woman to a young man whose company she had enjoyed, but too little for the crazy, passionate gesture of a rich woman towards the young man she adored. It was a middling sum, a calculated sum. Where on earth had she got the figure from?

Also, her will was the wrong place for it. She was about thirty years old. If she'd wanted to give Curragh some money, she wouldn't have wrapped it up where he might not see it for fifty years, by which time he too would be past enjoying it.

I don't know if precisely these questions were going through Baker's mind as well, but I could see he was as troubled by the scenario as I was. Whether Mrs. McAllister was murdered or died in an accident was only the last of the mysteries gathered about her.

Something else occurred to me. "How did McAllister know about the bequest? She's only been dead six hours, he can't have had the will read already. And if it was a bequest to her lover, she's hardly likely to have told her husband. Have you talked to McAllister?"

"Not yet. I wanted to know what you'd seen first—the only unbiased account I'm likely to get in this—and actually you didn't see very much, did you?" He sighed. He consulted his notebook. He looked up at the ceiling. "When you got on deck after the explosion, Curragh was floating near the upturned dinghy?"

"Yes, just behind it."

"Does that sound right to you—that he was on the front deck and the dinghy was tied up behind, but after the *Skara Sun* was gone they ended up in much the same place?"

And of course it didn't, and I had to say so. I could believe that the combination of wind and wave and a massive explosion would have some curious effects, and he'd need a physicist or a marine engineer for an authoritative opinion, but if he cared what I believed then I believed he was right: it hadn't happened as Curragh had said.

Not as Curragh had said the second time, after Neil Burns queried his first account. His original version, that he was with Alison McAllister in the cabin when the explosion occurred, was even less credible. Shock and concussion might have confused him, but the other explanation was that he was lying in his teeth and hadn't told the truth about the episode yet.

Not sure whether Burns would want to report his patient's initial account to the police, I did so. If Curragh had deliberately blown up a boat with a woman on board, the fact that I had hauled him back from the jaws of death in no way diminished my desire to see him pay.

I realised I had underestimated DCI Neville Baker. He might be over-educated, pretentiously accented and know nothing about sailing, but he was good enough at his job. He recognised, of course, the significance of Curragh's slip, and his lips pursed irritably at Burns's intervention. But he wasn't going to build a case of murder round it, at least not yet. It could still prove to have been an honest mistake.

Yet the evidence, circumstantial as it was, was mounting, and I could have believed that—for the fifteen thousand pounds she had bequeathed him or for some reason we did not so far suspect—Alex Curragh had murdered Alison McAllister, but for one thing. It wasn't a physical obstacle to his guilt, or an alibi; it wasn't even a good disincentive. It was nothing a defence lawyer could make capital of without having a prosecutor pull it down around his ears.

But to me, who had broken the news to him and watched him weep, the sheer scale of his grieving was a difficulty I could see no way round.

It had had a depth and a range and a power that I could not believe he had fabricated. It had shaken him to his soul, ripping through the frail fibres of his being like some cosmic disturbance. It was the sort of fierce, consuming grief you could imagine someone dying of.

I'm a grown woman, I've been around a bit, and I've seen enough of crime and criminals to know that great feats can be performed by those who want something badly enough. Maybe doctors, whose province is the sick, are more gullible than policemen, whose province is essentially the wicked. But in spite of the lies, in spite of the evidence shifting away from an accidental cause, and while acknowledging the suspect's vested interest in my sympathy, I could not persuade myself that Alex Curragh's distress was anything other than genuine and profound. I had seen it in his eyes. I didn't believe he could lie there.

But if Curragh hadn't killed Alison McAllister, why had he lied— why was he lying still? If it wasn't murder, what had he to hide?

Their affair? Surely, even in his current shocked and weakened state, he couldn't believe there was still a secret to protect? When a woman and a young man who is not her husband spend nights alone together on a small boat, there's really only one conclusion to be drawn. It doesn't take a particularly prurient mind to suppose that they were enjoying a dirty weekend.

Admittedly, people who knew us well enough to know that Luke and I were not married, but not so well as to know his taste didn't lean towards women, thought the same about us and were mistaken. But neither of us ended up dead at the bottom of the Fairy Isles lagoon. I could almost regret that: it would have been a fitter resting-place for my friend than the one he eventually found.

Besides, with Alison dead, did it matter? Perhaps, if he had a wife of his own. Yet the lies he had told would not have protected him from the outrage of either Mr. McAllister or a putative Mrs. Curragh. They could only have defended him against the very accusation McAllister had made—that he had left the *Skara Sun* before the explosion that destroyed her.

I sighed. "Where do you go from here?"

Baker shrugged. "What I need is to get Curragh under the full glare of a sixty-watt bulb back at my nick, and pummel him with astute and pertinent questions until he breaks and confesses all. Thanks to Dr. Burns that's going to have to wait. There may be another way. If the local constabulary hasn't already done so, I'll organise divers. Let's see what the late Mrs. McAllister and the wreckage of her boat can tell us."

There was something else he could do, though it wasn't my place to suggest it. Fortunately he thought of it for himself. Unfortunately, when he turned his sixty-watt bulb on Frazer McAllister he mentioned that he'd talked to me first.

Which is how I came to be kidnapped in broad daylight from the public concourse of a major British hospital, en route between the magazine kiosk and the coffee machine.

[6]

It was now late afternoon, and I was expecting Harry at any time. I'd tried the pub in Tayvallich again and got the message that he'd left. Someone had brought his car down from Ardfern and was returning with the *Rubber Lion*, while Harry hit the long and winding road for Glasgow. I hoped he'd had the wit to remove our belongings, particularly my clothes, from the boat before handing her over.

It had been a short holiday but an interesting one.

So when a rather snazzy young man in a pin-striped suit strolled over and said, "Mrs. Marsh? There's a man looking for you at reception. I think he went out to the car-park," I immediately assumed it was Harry and hurried after him, leaving my polystyrene cup and my *Yachting World* together on my seat. It had been a long day and I was too tired to notice the distinct aroma of rat.

I couldn't see Harry's car from the porch so I moved down into the car-park. I was still scanning the roofs for one that looked familiar when a car that wasn't Harry's cruised up beside me, the rear door opened and a hand reached out.

"Mrs. Marsh, it was good of you to come." The gravelly voice was enough; I didn't need to see what was left of his face to recognize Frazer McAllister.

As I said, I've been around. I know better than to get into cars with strange men. But when I stepped back from the door I sort of bounced off the pin-striped suit which had come up behind me, and the helping hands that came to steady me just sort of guided me into the car as a convenient place to recover my breath. It was slickly done. You couldn't say that violence was used against me, or intimidation. All the same, I know when I've been kidnapped.

Once I was inside and the door was shut—centralised locking could have been designed by a kidnapper—and the pin-striped suit had slid in cat-like beside the chauffeur, the big dark car moved off. Not at speed, and not very far—through the tinted glass I could see that we were just cruising round the fairways of the car-park. It was reassuring, but not all that much.

I said with as much asperity as I could muster, "Stop this car immediately."

McAllister, lounging back against his plush upholstery, passed on the message. "MacLeod, you heard the lady." I was in no way deceived by the faintly satiric note of indignation, and I don't suppose MacLeod was either.

"Yes, sir," said the chauffeur, unperturbed. "I'll find somewhere now, sir." The big dark car went on cruising the parking lot at a steady fifteen miles per hour.

But the clock ticking wasn't the loudest sound in this limousine. Me getting cross took that honour, by several decibels. "Mr. McAllister, I don't know what you hope to achieve by this pantomime, but when Chief Inspector Baker hears about it he'll—" What, change his bulb for a hundred-watter? There was probably nothing he could do: McAllister wouldn't make the mistake of crossing any line he was obliged to defend. But I knew this meeting was neither accidental nor social. "And when he's finished, my husband will want a go at the pieces."

McAllister looked at me as if I'd threatened him with my mother. "Why, what's your husband—an all-in wrestler?"

So Baker hadn't passed on everything I'd told him. It was a pity, really, that he'd stopped short of that. I fired the information back like a salvo of big guns. "No, he's a detective superintendent."

McAllister looked disappointed. "What, another wee plod?" He managed to make Britain's finest sound like a family of mice behind the skirting board, a slight but tedious irritation he would tolerate only so long before going to the chemist for something to deal with them.

I have heard Harry called some things in the pursuit of his duty. I have called him some of them myself. But I had never heard an epithet at once so mild and derogatory as "another wee plod" applied to him before. There's more than six feet of Harry, and not much less from side to side, and though he actually has a most impressive intellect he makes a good job of hiding it. There are those who would consider the words described him perfectly. Mind you, most of them are in jail and still wondering why.

Thinking this, I began to chuckle. It wasn't very nice to be chuckling, in the presence of a man who had just lost his wife, and on the back seat of his own car, but McAllister had brought it on himself.

Also, if I hadn't seen the funny side of it, I might have been getting violent by now. Us short people aren't the push-overs we are commonly supposed. Hard bits of our bodies, like knees and elbows and skulls, come at unexpected and strategic levels. If I bend at the waist and run like hell, I can sort out a six-foot mugger armed with anything less than a flick-knife and protected by anything less than an interior-sprung codpiece.

"Listen, McAllister," I said. "You can tell your driver to stop looking so feverishly for somewhere to park. I don't mind if he drives us round while you tell me what it was you were so anxious to ask me that you had to hijack me off the hospital doorstep. I've nothing to hide: as far as I know there's nothing that I know that you shouldn't know too. It'll all be said at the inquest anyway, but if you want to hear it now, ask."

I think he found it disconcerting, being offered the co-operation he had been prepared to wring out of me. But even if I disapproved of his methods, I didn't begrudge him what scant information I had about his wife's last hours. Actually I doubted there was anything he hadn't already heard, but I didn't mind repeating myself if it would give him any comfort. He hadn't had much so far today, and he could go a lot longer yet.

He looked taken aback, but only for a moment. Then his natural aggression reasserted itself, his scarred jaw jutting, his eyes glittering steel-blue. "Aw' right, wee hen, tell me this. Tell me why you told thon first wee plod that I murdered Alison."

I couldn't have been more surprised if he'd accused me of blowing the boat up. My mind did that split-second back-flip that your stomach does on the first fast bend of a big dipper. For just a moment the normal parameters were gone, the accustomed dimensions of up and down and two sides tumbled over one another and there seemed to be nothing familiar and solid enough for me to grab and steady the inverting universe.

Then the moment of vertigo passed, bringing in its wake anger and a kind of understanding. I hit McAllister in the eyes with my own and

felt him recoil. He had thought he had me off-balance, had not expected me to recover quickly enough to strike back.

In a quiet barbed voice that seemed the only alternative to shouting
at him, I observed, "Mr. McAllister, you're either a fool or a liar. I
think you may be both."

If I'd been a man, he'd have struck me. He might have done so
anyway, except that it was fair comment and he knew it. He pushed
himself back into the bosom of his upholstery as if putting distance
between his hands and my throat, and said stiffly, "I do not understand
you."

"Oh yes you do." I knew he did, but I spelled it out anyway. "DCI
Baker neither said nor suggested any such thing. If you think he was
doing, you're a fool. If you don't, you're a liar. And if you're kite-flying,
you're both."

His expression was arctic, but he seemed just fractionally unsure of
himself. I think the echo of that uncertainty in his voice shocked him
more than anything I had said. "He gave me to understand—"

I raised one eyebrow in silent but overt scepticism. Even that toned-
down version wasn't accurate: I'd seen enough policemen in my time to
know how reluctantly they convey information. What they do is ask
questions. Baker had asked him a question that had put him on the
defensive, and he blamed me.

As it happened he was right. Surly, he said, "He wanted to know
about Alison's will—how I knew what was in it so soon after—"

For the first time I saw in his ruined face an emotional reaction to
what had happened. For just a moment the clouds of anger parted and
I glimpsed his grief. It was not a little thing. He had buried it so deeply,
walled it up so carefully, precisely because the size and might of it
frightened him. In the scant moment that I was aware of it, it frightened me too.

And it changed the way I felt towards him. He was a man whose
attitudes would always provoke resentment, and by and large he could
be relied upon to deal with that to his own satisfaction. But this was
different. He was no less vulnerable than Alex Curragh because he
showed his feelings less, no less weakened by his hurts because the
wounds were internal and did not show. However things had been
between them, he had just lost his wife. If his reactions were aberrant,
it was because he was—in many senses, perhaps in every sense—an
extraordinary man.

He was rich and powerful, and he had got there despite a background of privation that was still, almost defiantly, audible in his voice; and he had stayed there despite the accident that had robbed him of part of his body and must have threatened his life. All this had made him a survivor, a man who would not easily submit to public scrutiny the private places where he felt fragile, open to attack. He was a man who could see love as a weakness to be exploited, something that could be used against him. Understanding this changed fundamentally the way I saw him.

And I was a little ashamed of how I had treated him. The fact that he had asked for it did not absolve me. I said, more gently, "It struck me as a little curious, that's all. It really is none of my business, you know."

He seemed to find kindness harder to cope with than antagonism. Lack of practice, perhaps. His eyes dimmed, remembering. "She told me. Alison. She told me about the will."

I was startled. "You knew about Curragh then?"

"Oh aye," he said; wearily, not even with much bitterness. "I knew she had a wee laddie for a friend. How old is he, do you know?"

I shrugged and guessed. "About twenty-three?"

"Jesus wept." There was a kind of despair in his voice. "Twenty-three years old, sound in wind and limb, with the next half-century at his disposal, and all he can think to do with his life is murder older women for a few thousand quid. Hell, I'd have given him the money to leave her be."

The difference in ages hadn't struck me, although I suppose I knew she'd been older than Curragh. She must also have been considerably younger than her husband, to leave him with a new baby. "How old was Alison?"

"Thirty-one," he said. He looked at me then, his eyes shrewd. "Twenty years younger than me. Go on, flatter me—tell me you can't imagine why the bitch would jump over the wall."

"Maybe to escape the monotony of unfailing courtesy and inexorable good manners?"

Immediately I regretted the jibe and started to apologise, but McAllister gave an improbable grin and nodded. "Aye, I think the humility got up her nose too, eventually."

We grinned together, the atmosphere easing all the time. McAllister went on. "No, she was still a young woman, I suppose she got to wondering if there was more to life than looking after a rich cripple. She was right, there was, but he didn't leave her long to enjoy it."

"Do you know how long she knew him?" It was impertinent to be questioning him like this, but somehow it seemed to follow naturally from this unlikely conversation.

"No," he said sharply, as if he too considered it impertinent. But after another moment's thought he answered more fully. "No, not exactly. It might have been six months. It was February she told me about the will."

"Curragh said he'd only known her a few weeks."

McAllister shrugged. "The will will be dated."

And would prove that the boy had lied once again. I wondered if anything he had said had been the truth. But the violence of his grief said he loved her.

I ventured, "Why did your wife tell you about her bequest to another man?"

He stared at me. This interview was not going the way he'd expected. Then he sighed. "We were arguing. Something I said hurt her. She threw that back at me."

"Did it work—were you hurt?"

Again he shrugged. "Not hurt so much; maybe a little disappointed. I wasn't surprised that she had a lover. I thought she might have been more discreet about it."

I'd have thought so too. He might have been the most indulgent husband in the world—it seemed out of character but it was possible— but he was still a rich and powerful man. Hurling that at him in the middle of an argument suggested Alison feared neither his power nor the loss of his wealth.

I said, "Do you really believe he killed her?"

The first time he said it, storming into Alex Curragh's hospital room, full of shock and rage at the news, it could have been the fury talking. He needed someone to blame and, whatever else Curragh had done, he had put himself in line by being on Mrs. McAllister's boat.

But that fury had mostly leached out of McAllister's eyes by now. A good bit of it seemed to have gone in the few minutes we had been talking while his chauffeur drove us round the hospital car-park. There was more sorrow than anger there now, and I thought that if his outburst had been born of that anger he would tell me.

He met my eyes without any shadows. At peace, his ravaged face had a kind of dignity. "I don't believe it was an accident. Someone else might have made that mistake, she might have made another. But I don't believe Alison let a gas leak destroy her boat. Yes, I think Curragh killed her."

"For fifteen thousand pounds?"

One grizzled eyebrow climbed higher than the other. "What else?"

I shuffled uncomfortably under his steady gaze. "I don't know. It doesn't seem—" I let the sentence tail off. The feeling I had about it was real enough but difficult to express.

I paid the price for reticence when McAllister misunderstood. A frostiness appeared in his eyes. "What, enough? You have a fine disdain for the value of other people's money, wee hen. What do you reckon the going rate for a gigolo is, then?"

I coloured a little under his scorn. It wasn't even true; I've been sufficiently hard up—twice, both as a young doctor and ten years later as a novice writer—to have a keen appreciation of fiscal values, but I couldn't blame him for his reaction when I only half understood the thing myself.

I said, "Well, the police'll sort out what happened. They're diving on the wreck now. We'll have a clearer idea what went wrong and if anyone was to blame when they recover the stove and the gas cylinder, and the gas detector. If anything has been tampered with, young Curragh will have some explaining to do."

McAllister looked doubtful. "Will they be able to tell if they've been tampered with? There can't be much left but fragments."

"You'd be surprised what forensics can do with a few twisted bits of metal." It's amazing how much survives, in one form or another, the most devastating explosion. Think of a mid-air disaster, no survivors, wreckage scattered over miles. You'd think destruction that complete would be irretrievable. But the accident investigators go for long walks with their cardboard boxes, and over a period of days stretching into weeks the pieces they bring back are slotted into the reconstruction taking place in a handy shed, and eventually they can pinpoint not only the cause of the disaster—a bomb, say—but also what sort of bomb it was and even which seat it was under.

The physical destruction of matter takes immense quantities of energy. Infinitely more matter than is destroyed in an explosion is altered in it—fragmented, twisted, crystalised, charred, burned. But people conversant with those processes can track them back to the moment of cataclysm, and say within narrow tolerances where a thing was and what it was doing immediately prior to becoming a ballistic missile. When the police divers hauled up the remains of the cooker, and forensics finished analysing it, they'd know whether accident was still a plausible explanation.

McAllister's driver made another slow sweep in front of the main entrance, and we found ourselves following a grey BMW.

"There's Harry now," I said. He hadn't seen me: even a detective doesn't look for his wife in the backs of other men's limousines. "Listen, you'll have to let me off now. Tell your driver to drop me at the main door: if he's still worried about getting a ticket, tell him I'm well in with a policeman."

McAllister nodded at his driver and the car rolled to a halt, so smoothly it was hard to know exactly when it had stopped moving. I went for the door handle but the lad in pinstripes beat me to it, held it for me with every appearance of courtesy though I could feel—possibly McAllister could not—an almost electric aura of insolence reaching out to me. I can't say it bothered me, though I've never really liked pinstripes since.

I saw Harry park the car and come towards me, though he hadn't spotted me yet. Just before I went to meet him I looked back at McAllister, sunk in his expensive upholstery like the Sultan of Sauchiehall Street. I watched him sitting there watching me, and somehow it seemed he was moving away from me, growing smaller and more remote, the damaged face setting in a basilisk mask, the unwinking regard of an ill-forged bronze idol.

I leaned towards him in the open door. "Look, if you want to talk again, Baker'll know where to find me."

He almost smiled. "If I want to talk to you, I'll know where to find you."

Probably. He probably owned half the hotels in Glasgow. I nodded. "Will you be all right?"

I think he was surprised at that. Perhaps rich men aren't used to people feeling anxious about them. His jaw came up arrogantly. Then a little of the proud disdain in his eyes melted and a small warmth kindled there, enough to show the sadness again. He said, "Aye, I shall be all right. I have my son to care for."

I nodded and turned away, and the long car drove past me down the service road as I walked, waving, towards Harry.

[7]

The sensible thing would have been to go home. I had told Baker everything I knew, and a lot I could only guess. Harry had stayed at Tayvallich until a senior detective arrived on the scene to take over. Neither of us had anything more to contribute. The sensible thing was to tell Baker where we could be contacted and get away home, and write it off as just another holiday gone wrong.

So we booked into an hotel—McAllister didn't own it; I checked—changed our clothes, had a meal, got a night's sleep and awaited developments.

The first development was nothing less than an act of God. One of those late spring storms that make the prudent Scot delay his summer holidays blew in from the Atlantic, a ripping south-westerly that still smelled of shamrocks when it tore up the moorings of the police launch at Loch Sween and sent the entire task force racing for cover in the Tayvallich pub.

Judging by the weather forecast, it would be forty-eight hours before the divers would go down again—before then the bed of the loch would be so stirred up they wouldn't be able to see well enough to work. The bottom there is a deep silty mud that sticks like treacle to an anchor-chain and smells like a sewage-farm.

Harry and I had breakfast in our room and listened to the shipping forecasts on the radio. The report for Malin told us what was happening at Loch Sween; Rockall and Shannon told us what would be happening there soon. None of the news was good. The last time I was caught out by a storm like this I spent four days of a six-day holiday at anchor in some little back-of-beyond bay, watching the spume-lashed rocks circling the boat with each tide, listening to the wind shriek in the rigging, wondering if I dare risk a half-mile dash up the coast to the next little bay just for the change of scenery. If this storm had come forty-eight hours earlier it would have ended not only this holiday but any prospect of future holidays with my husband, and quite possibly our marriage as well.

We had already exchanged notes on the previous day. If the highlight of mine was that rather benign kidnapping, the most memorable feature of Harry's—at least the one he kept harking back to—was getting hemmed in behind a wagon-train of travelling tinkers on the single-track road through the Knapdale Forest. The map shows about five miles of it between Tayvallich and the B-road flanking the Crinan Canal, but to hear him tell it he drove for hours, eating the tinkers' dust and fuming, through a forest of Tolstoy proportions. The third time he told it I expected him to add in wolves for colour.

As soon as he felt he decently could—i.e. about a quarter of an hour later than he'd have been at his desk in his own nick—Harry wandered nonchalantly into DCI Baker's office to see how the investigation was progressing. Actually, nonchalance is not something Harry does well— he's no more built for it, physically or psychologically, than a bull-buffalo.

While he was strolling round a Glasgow police station like a laid-back buffalo, and trying not to tell the local men how to do their job, I was planning a similar sortie to the hospital. I may not be much better at nonchalance than Harry is, but I'm easier to overlook. I doubted Neil Burns would resent my presence, as long as I refrained from telling him how to tie sutures, and anyway I wanted to return the clothes Jim Fernie had borrowed for me, which the hotel had laundered overnight.

But if I'm less obtrusive than Harry, I'm a lot slower off the mark in the morning. I was still stumbling round the room in one shoe when the phone went and it was Harry, already well into his day's work. He sounded at once content—to be free of this holiday nonsense, at least for now—and grim. Clearly something had come up.

"Before the storm struck last night they recovered some of the wreckage from the lagoon."

"What—the stove, the cylinder?"

"No, they'll have to go back for those when the weather improves. But they found the gas detector and the bit of bulkhead it was attached to. It appears to have been switched off."

I felt my heart sink. Even after I'd accepted his sincerity, I hadn't wanted McAllister to be right. "Shit."

"Well, it's not conclusive," said Harry, but from his tone there wasn't much room for doubt. "Forensics will have to establish that the switch couldn't have been tripped in the explosion. Or they may find it corroded up, in which case it's been like that for months and has nothing to do with what happened. But . . ."

"But Mrs. McAllister was a careful sailor. She wouldn't have had it fitted and then left it switched off."

"That's what I thought," he admitted. "But I'll talk to the boat

yard, see if they know whether it was working. If it was off all winter
while the boat was rested up—"

"Laid up," I said.

"—maybe she hadn't noticed, or hadn't got round to fixing it. She
had other things on her mind when she left Oban."

But how much mental energy did it take to check she was safe?
She'd check she had enough fuel; that her radio was working, that she
had what provisions she needed and the gas to cook them. A careful
sailor would also check the seals on her cylinders and her gas detector.
It was possible that she had forgotten, and that the yard fitting out the
Skara Sun for her had also forgotten, and that following those two bits
of forgetfulness she'd been unlucky enough to get a gas leak. But there
was a simpler explanation.

"Damn," I said. "I wanted him to be wrong—an accident, just an
accident—" I sniffed and pulled myself together. "Oh well, at least
now we know. Listen, thanks for calling. I'll take this stuff back to the
hospital but I won't hang round. Meet me for lunch?"

"I'll try to get away," he promised, for all the world as if he was at
his own desk and the Mafia was moving in on Skipley.

The hospital was no great distance, so I walked, my brown paper
parcel under my arm. I greeted Ros in reception, showed her how I
looked when respectably clad in dry clothes of my own, and asked if the
head porter was about. But he was off duty, so I left my parcel with her
to be passed on along with my thanks.

I was going to leave then, but she had a message that Dr. Burns
wanted to see me when I called in. I liked that "when": my husband
and I must have built up some reputation in the few hours we'd been in
this city.

Ros directed me to a ward on the same level as Curragh's room. I
passed his door at a brisk walk—I had no intention of seeing him again.
But Burns wasn't on the ward, and as I walked back to the lift I heard
raised voices, the scuffle of feet and the shatter of glass, and I was
through that damn door before common sense had the chance to inter-
vene and find urgent business for me elsewhere.

The little room was full of people: DCI Baker and another policeman, Neil Burns, Alex Curragh and now me. There was hardly room
for the furniture, and indeed the bed had been shoved under the window, the locker into one corner and the chair turned on its side.

Alex Curragh was in the other corner, between the bed and the wash-stand, crouched defensively in the angle. He was informally dressed, in pyjama trousers but neither jacket nor slippers, and his right arm was bulky in fresh white plaster. In his left hand he held a broken glass, and he held it by the heel with the jagged points ranged outwards.

His eyes were wild, white-ringed, the irises dark and hollow. His face was white too, the skin drawn tight over prominent bones, stained blue-black under the eyes with livid spots where the burns were. The bruise on his temple had spread all round his eye. He had his back to the wall, metaphorically as well as literally, and a glass claw to fend off a frontal assault. He looked as if he was fighting for his life.

There was something so deeply atavistic about the scene, so profoundly disturbing about the palpable fear that Curragh cast out as an aura around him, that I was momentarily rooted, shocked to my soul. It was as if I had strayed into some ancient mystic ritual, a rite of passage or of blood. Then I heard myself ask thinly, "What the hell's going on here?"

Tersely, without looking at me, Baker said, "Stay out of this." He edged along the wall. Curragh's glass dagger followed him. The points reflected the light from the window, twinkling as his hand trembled.

Neil Burns spared me a glance. "It could be an IR."

"To the anaesthetic?" Idiosyncratic responses to modern anaesthetics, particularly at a dosage adequate to set a broken arm, aren't very common, but there are always a few patients who react badly or oddly to any drug. I'd seen it before, though not this long after administration.

"Or the antibiotics. I don't know. But something set him off."

"The prospect of having to answer my questions set him off," growled Baker.

I asked Neil, "What happened?"

He shrugged, worried and nonplussed. "I don't know. Baker wanted to talk to him about the explosion. He seemed all right so I brought them in here. Baker introduced himself and said what he'd come about. I don't think he said anything out of turn, anything to provoke this. But next thing I knew, Curragh was out of bed and smashing his glass in the basin."

"I know what provoked it." Baker's voice was low, his eyes fixed on the boy's face. "I said he could answer my questions either here or at the police station."

It was a routine enough remark. It shouldn't have precipitated violence in either an innocent or a guilty man. I looked at Curragh's white face and scared, haunted eyes and saw panic. His reaction had been more hysterical than violent, not rational enough to have any meaning. If it wasn't an IR it was something equally random, something he had no control over. Even the posture with the broken glass wasn't a threatening thing. He'd retreated into the furthest corner he could find, and was using what weapons he could improvise to protect himself.

Far from threatening, he was reacting as a man under threat—not the intellectual threat posed by a policeman investigating a crime but something older, deeper, closer to the level of instinct and survival. Something—the drugs, the questions, possibly delayed shock from yesterday—had triggered a primitive response in him that, for a few moments, he had no more power to control than a sneeze or a yawn.

In his eyes bewilderment was creeping in round the edges where the panic was receding. He seemed uncertain where he was, what he was doing, and how he came by the crystal weapon in his hand. It was as if he was waking from a nightmare only to find he had brought the essence of the horror out with him. There was the makings of fresh panic in that, the incomprehensible loss of sense and self and time. I sensed it bubbling up in him, like nitrogen bubbling lethally in a diver's blood. I sensed, like before, the silent cry of desperation from his soul to mine.

He was still crouched in his corner, half naked, his plastered arm braced against the wall, the jagged glass in his hand extended towards my throat. But I knew he was no danger to me, knew how desperately he needed someone to take control of the situation and end the vicious little drama in which, unaccountably, he found himself. It was thus an act of no bravery at all when I stepped quietly, steadily towards him, my hand out, palm up.

"Give me the glass, Alex, before someone gets cut."

Neil Burns behind me murmured, "Careful," and Baker hissed, "He'll carve her."

But Alex Curragh was never going to hurt me, not unless I forced him to. His dark eyes ached for help. Compassion twisted a hard knot behind my breastbone.

His voice came with difficulty and deliberation from somewhere low in his throat. The words came out slow and measured, as if that was the only alternative to screaming them. He got out, "I don't know what I'm doing . . ."

I said, "It's all right, Alex. It's just the shock. Give me the glass."

I couldn't take it by the points. My hand touched his as I closed my fingers round the unbroken heel, and he yielded the ugly thing to me not only willingly but with relief. I heard the air sigh out of his lungs. He straightened a little in his corner and his eyes half closed.

There was quick movement behind me. Neil Burns swept me into the protective compass of his long arms, and extracted the broken glass from my fingers as carefully as I had taken it from Curragh. By then Baker and his oppo had the boy pinned to the wall, not violently but with some force: I heard his back thump against it and the rest of the air rush from his lungs, and the sharp crack of plaster on plaster.

I cried, "Don't hurt him!" and Neil shouted, "Mind that arm!"

For a moment he all but disappeared behind the greater bulk of the two policemen. Then, once they had their hands on him, they relaxed a little, their broad shoulders parting, and I saw his eyes, lonely and afraid and crying out for help. He didn't make a sound.

Baker's sergeant was reaching for handcuffs. "Don't you dare," exclaimed Neil Burns, the tremor of his anger racing through his body into mine. After a moment's thought the sergeant put them back in his pocket.

"Well," said Baker heavily, "that was some performance. Where do we go from here?"

"He's not leaving this hospital," Neil said firmly. "And, in my professional opinion, he is not at this moment sufficiently rational to be answering your questions."

"What do you suggest?"

"Medically? I could sedate him, but if it was an IR it would likely make him worse and he still couldn't answer your questions. I think I'd prescribe a pot of tea, and discussing the weather until he's calmed down enough to start making some sense."

"He was making sense enough before," growled the sergeant. "We asked him about the death of Alison McAllister and he went for us with a broken glass."

It was near enough fair comment. You couldn't blame them for thinking it was cause and effect; maybe it was. I said, "I know what it looks like, but don't read too much into it. It could just be shock: sheer physical and emotional overload. This time yesterday I was trying to start him breathing. By any standards he's still a sick man."

Baker nodded stiffly. "We'll leave the rubber truncheons till later, then."

There was nothing more I could do. I had no right to be present: I wasn't Curragh's doctor, his solicitor or even a relative. The Oriental idea that saving someone's life makes you responsible for them has no reflection in British law, and if it turned out that Alex Curragh murdered Alison McAllister for fifteen thousand pounds in her will, I would be grateful for that. I backed towards the door.

Curragh's aching eyes stopped me. "Tell them." His voice was barely audible. "Tell them I didn't kill Alison."

I didn't know what to say. "I can't tell them that, Alex. I don't know that."

"You know," he insisted. "Tell them."

I shook my head and left. The hardest thing was, I did know. At least, I believed that he had loved and mourned her. I couldn't tell them that—it wasn't evidence. I had nothing to support my belief beyond intuition born of that intimacy of minds we had established when he was all but dead. But I believed that inner voice telling me he had been trapped by circumstances and didn't know how to get out.

I was halfway down the corridor, wondering why I felt like crying, when I remembered that Neil Burns had wanted to talk to me. I must have been halfway down the corridor when Neil remembered too, because as I broke stride and hesitantly turned, he came out of Curragh's room with a rush, looking round for me. We came together with a smile.

"That was quite something you did in there."

I shook my head. "He wasn't going to hurt me. He never meant to hurt anyone."

"Are you sure of that?"

I sighed. "Yes, but not for reasons I can explain. I got a message you wanted to see me."

It wasn't the smoothest change of subject anyone ever accomplished, and he looked momentarily surprised, but then he went with it. "Yes. I didn't want to tell the police until I'd talked to you. I mean, you know just how meaningless it can be, they say something and it sounds quite sensible but it comes from a dream or something that scares them or something they've seen on the telly—"

"Neil," I said, "what are you talking about?"

"The anaesthetic, when we set his arm. He came out of it talking."

There was nothing abnormal about that. Mostly when you come out of an anaesthetic you're surrounded by grinning nurses, but they know nothing you've just said bears any relation to reality. And they know better than to pass it on. I wondered why Neil wanted to share Curragh's ramblings with me.

"So what did he say that you've never heard before?"

He gave me a pained look. He'd come to me with this because he'd expected a more sympathetic, or anyway more understanding, hearing than from the police. I don't know why he didn't go instead to his chief medical officer. Perhaps he was afraid of starting something he couldn't afterwards stop, wanted to try it out for size first on someone with no clout whatever. Well, he'd come to the right place for that.

"He said," said Neil, " 'Your husband will kill us if he ever finds out.' "

II

Tuesday

I found a park and wandered round it. I looked in the windows of some shops. I went back to the hotel and hunched in an armchair, drinking coffee. I may have done other things too, I don't remember. Half the time I had no idea where I was or what I was doing, except that my brain was racing.

As Curragh's must have been as he surfaced from the anaesthetic. He'd babbled on as if language had just been invented. A lot of it made no sense, but Neil had understood more than just that one sentence.

It seemed he was eavesdropping on a conversation between Curragh and his mistress. He had no idea of the time scale—whether it was the last conversation they'd had or one of the first. Also, like overhearing a phone call, he'd heard only Curragh's side of the dialogue.

He had said, "Your husband will kill us if he ever finds out."

He had said, "I don't understand why you let him treat you like that."

He had said, "You don't need his money. I can look after both of you."

And, "What about my rights? What about how I feel?"

And Neil wanted to know whether he should break a confidence almost as sacred as that of the confessional to pass on what he had heard—whether I thought the contents significant enough to justify disclosure.

I couldn't judge their significance, except that to me they didn't sound like a young man talking to the woman he meant to murder. But I was sure he should tell the police. I didn't see how it could harm his patient; it might help him; more than that, it might help solve the mystery surrounding a woman's death. That took the highest priority.

Neil nodded. "Aye, OK." He left me without another word and

returned to his patient. I didn't expect him to talk to Baker there and then, but I thought he would soon.

I left too, walking aimlessly while my brain itched. For a couple of hours I worried at the problem like a terrier shaking a rat, but in slow motion; and when that time was up I had thrashed out a kind of explanation for what had befallen Alison McAllister and the *Skara Sun*. Not a definitive view of what had happened at the Fairy Isles, more an examination of what could have happened. When you work out how a magician could have done a trick, you're most of the way to knowing how he did it.

The problem was, I now had not one but two theories about what had happened to the *Sun*. One had Alex Curragh guilty of Mrs. McAllister's death, the other had him innocent. Both began with their affair.

I couldn't guess how or why it began. It seemed likely that she initiated it—a woman older than him, worldier and wealthier than him, a cripple's wife, her boat giving her a plausible claim on Curragh's time. It was less likely that he began it, simply because she would probably have walked away.

However it began, and however it ended, there seemed to have been some real affection in between. That was where his grief came from, and the memories he had babbled out under the anaesthetic. What mattered was whether the love or the affair died first, because that was where the two narratives split.

In the first, the affair grew cool long before the *Skara Sun* dropped anchor at the Fairy Isles. Alison McAllister had enjoyed her Highland fling, and the untutored urgency of Curragh's strong young body, but was beginning to tire—of the complications, of the time it was taking up, perhaps of the very lack of sophistication that had attracted her to him in the first place. The thing was become wearisome by contrast with the comfort and interest of her life in Glasgow. Perhaps Curragh himself, apart from his unflawed body, didn't measure up to Frazer McAllister as a companion. For whatever reason, Alison had had enough, and she told him.

I still found it difficult to accommodate the notion of a bequest rather than a gift, but that was what had happened so there had to be a reason. It may have started as a joke—"I'll leave you something in my will, darling!"—and seemed funnier to her to fulfil her promise than break it.

Indeed, she was so pleased with the joke that she told both Curragh and her husband, but probably neither of them laughed.

Perhaps McAllister had seen enough of the world to shrug off her infidelity with something approaching philosophy, but Curragh—who came from a small, remote village, was twenty-three years old and had seen very little of it—was consumed by anger and jealousy and a sense of having been used. At that point (in the first scenario) he decided that if money was what it was all about, he'd make sure of getting what he'd earned.

One of them had suggested a final weekend together. The Fairy Isles was a good place to say goodbye. When they saw the *Rubber Lion* already there, perhaps Alison wanted to push on and find somewhere they could be alone. But it would have suited Curragh to have a witness to the incident, someone to testify to the quiet companionship of the night before the cataclysm. So they anchored, made supper, maybe made love: the bunks on the *Sun* were undoubtedly more roomy than those on the *Lion*.

In the early morning, while Alison slept, Curragh returned to the galley. He deactivated the gas detector, then turned on either the stove or the cylinder so that the gas would build up in the nooks and crannies of the cabin, ready for Alison to strike a match and start breakfast. The smell wouldn't be very noticeable: some people can smell it better than others, but lying undisturbed around the floor-boats it would be hardly more obtrusive than the general fug you get from sleeping in a confined space. Waking blearily with the previous night's hangover, Alison was unlikely to realise anything was amiss in the minute or so before she lit the stove under the coffee-pot.

By then Curragh was on deck and ready to leave. A glance our way confirmed that no-one on the *Rubber Lion* was sufficiently awake to observe his activities, so there was no need to pretend an interest in the anchor-chain or the fishing when he climbed into the dinghy. All he had to do was rouse Alison, ask her for some coffee, and row away.

He miscalculated the extent of her hangover. She was out of her bunk quicker than he expected, and he was too close when the *Skara Sun* blew up. But for the proximity of the *Rubber Lion*, he would not have lived to claim his inheritance.

Fifteen thousand pounds. To a twenty-three-year-old on a boat repairer's wages, it must have seemed a fortune. I supposed it was pin-money to Alison McAllister, but it had cost her her life. If this first scenario was how it had happened.

The alternative had its appeal, too. In this one the affair was not petering out but still in full swing. "Your husband will kill us if he ever finds out," Curragh had said. McAllister had, and he had.

This time the bequest had been not so much a whim, a rich woman's joke, as an earnest of intent. She was committing herself to Alex Curragh. Her husband found out, and the man who was accustomed to being denied nothing that money could buy was overwhelmed by his fury.

For McAllister to take his revenge on his wife and the boy she had betrayed him with, he must have had an agent. Even if he could have got aboard unaided while the *Sun* lay at Oban, he would have been too noticeable a trespasser. Whoever doctored the stove had to be un-memorable and preferably both swift and agile. It would be best if the boat yard never knew there had been a visitor; failing that, he had to be someone they could not describe and would not recognise again. Yards attract hangers-on: boat fanatics, the innocently curious and day-dreamers as well as prospective thieves—there's a lucrative market in marine equipment. Because of this most yards are security-conscious and can protect their clients from casual theft and vandalism. But if McAllister hired a fixer there would be nothing casual about him, and probably the shore patrols at Holy Loch wouldn't have kept him out.

There were different ways he could have fixed it. He could have fixed the stove to leak, or one of the cylinders to leak. He could have planted a bomb. If I'd been writing it, I'd have had him substitute petrol or possibly oxygen for butane in one of the tanks, in which case events would have taken their course when the previous cylinder ran out, whenever and wherever that might be.

So he'd left his little surprise, and left the boat yard either unnoticed or unremarked, and collected his wages and vanished back into the underworld whence he came. And Alison motored the *Skara Sun* down to Crinan to meet her lover, and on their second morning together the bomb went off or the seal leaked or the doctored cylinder was con-nected and Alison struck the fatal match.

However the explosion was triggered, there was clearly a delay mech-anism, to ensure they were both aboard before it happened. McAllister wanted them both dead. But sheer luck had put Curragh on deck at the critical moment, and another mammoth slice of fortune had put

Harry and I close enough to help when the sea would otherwise have finished what the explosion began.

McAllister must have been furious to learn Curragh had escaped. But he thought quickly—all the indications were that he was a quick-thinking man—and found another way of exacting payment for the wrong he had suffered. Next best thing to having his wife and his wife's lover dead together at the bottom of Loch Sween was seeing Curragh rot his life away in Barlinnie Prison for a murder he didn't commit.

So as soon as the news came through he was at the hospital with his tale of Alison's bequest and his accusation, knowing that however wild it sounded, the police would have to investigate. The man who'd fixed the boat, or another like him, could fix him up with enough evidence to see the boy condemned. He'd still have achieved what he set out to, revenged on and rid of the wife who had cheated and the man who had cuckolded him, free to enjoy his wealth and his power and his son without—

Without, I thought then with the sudden grasp of a revelation, the risk of losing the child. That's why he needed Alison dead. Cutting her off without a penny wouldn't suffice: if she wanted to take the baby, custody was unlikely to be awarded to McAllister. "I can look after both of you," Curragh had said. He certainly wasn't referring to the sturdy Glaswegian. He wanted Alison to leave her husband and bring her baby and come to him.

McAllister was a man in his fifties, a rich man but a cripple. It had taken him until now to produce an heir. He must be aware that this baby might be the only one he'd ever have. A man like McAllister would not lie down while the courts took his son and heir from him. A man like McAllister would do what he had to in order to preserve his succession. He could even have done it still loving his wife.

Harry said, in the patient voice of a man repeating himself for the third time, "I said, Are you ready for lunch yet?"

My mind returned to the hotel room by degrees. For a few moments my eyes actually saw him blurred, standing in the doorway like a faintly woolly column of grey and white, rather than a middle-aged policeman in flannels and an Aran sweater wishing his wife had let him bring his suit on holiday.

I blinked and the woolliness dispersed. "What?— Sorry?"

He frowned. "Are you all right?"

"Yes, of course," I said. "Or rather, no. I've been thinking."

"Oh God," he groaned, "not again?" There was real pain in his eyes, as if I'd confessed to some dreadful vice he'd thought me cured of. "What have you come up with this time?"

So I told him, in a certain amount of detail—I seem to remember a glazed expression creeping over his face and halfway through he sat down on the bed to take the weight off his feet. But he listened without interruption until I had finished, which was as much as I had a right and more than I had reason to expect.

Then he looked down one side of his unshapely nose at me, a look in which I recognised affection and amusement and a tolerant disbelief at what he was married to. "That's it?"

I was a shade taken aback. "Well—yes."

"I see. You've spoken to both parties, and analysed both what they said and what they didn't, and you've come to the conclusion that Alison McAllister's death was probably murder and the culprit probably either her husband or her lover."

"Er—yes." Stripped of the detail, succinct and to the point, that was it.

Harry said, "CID came to the same conclusion yesterday."

It may have been no more than the truth but his manner stung and, rising abruptly from the chair and stalking to the window, I made no effort to disguise it. Perhaps I was dwelling needlessly on my fringe involvement in the matter. Perhaps I was presuming a role for myself that didn't actually exist. Perhaps there was an unattractive vanity in the assumption that I could think through motives and actions in a way that the professionals in the business couldn't.

But I'd had a difficult couple of days, trying in ways both physical and emotional, and if I had reacted oddly—an idiosyncratic response— I surely deserved better than sarcasm. I was forgetting that Harry too had had a difficult few days.

"Well, I'm very sorry," I said snidely. "Just for a moment I thought those posters they pin up in libraries between the literary reviews and the address of the VD clinic—you know, the ones that say the police force is *our* police force and only as good as the help it gets—actually meant something. I'd forgotten that the policing of my country is none of my damn business. Like its governance, except every five years when there's an election, and its judicial system, except that once in a blue moon I might have to lie my way out of doing jury service.

"Well, I have news for you, Harry Marsh. I don't operate that way. I happen to believe that government, and justice, and law and order are as much my business, and that of every other citizen of this state, as they are the business of those employed in our name to execute them. If I think the government is wrong I will say so, as loudly and persuasively as I can. If I see a miscarriage of justice I will denounce it and do all in my power to have it rectified.

"And if by chance I bump into the sort of bastard who thinks that other people's lives can be manipulated and ultimately terminated to suit his ego, his convenience, his ambitions or his mood, I will not abdicate—to you, or DCI Baker, or anyone else who keeps his sense of outrage tucked away in his warrant card and secretly feels that violent crime isn't wholly antisocial while it provides policemen with a decent living—either my right or my responsibility to do what I can to stop him."

"And you think you can do something about stopping this one, do you?" Harry's voice was rough; he was as incensed by my attitude as I was by his. He resented being lectured no less than I resented being patronised. "Make a citizen's arrest, why don't you? I'm sure you know the law gives you that right. Only you'd better decide which one of them did it—courts aren't much impressed by charge-sheets with the defendant's name a multiple-option question. Chinese?"

I stared at him, angry and without comprehension. Then I realised it was an invitation to lunch. I responded with about as much grace. "Indonesian."

We compromised. Harry had Chinese, I had Indonesian. In separate restaurants.

[2]

Of course he was right. I knew that even while I was shouting at him. I was right too, but Harry had practicality on his side. The police would always be in the best position to discover the truth. It wasn't the hundred-watt bulbs and rubber truncheons that made the difference, it was the access to facilities no well-meaning amateur could call on: the divers sitting out the storm at Loch Sween, the forensic scientists poring over the bits of twisted metal, perhaps most significant of all the infinite records held by officialdom on each one of us. If Frazer McAllister had ever been suspected of torching an unprofitable business, they would know. If Alex Curragh had been unwise enough to put down a small deposit on a large car in anticipation of good fortune, they would find out. I couldn't match that.

I didn't even want to. It wasn't my job and I didn't covet it; if I had left Harry with that impression it was because he'd rattled my cage until I squawked at him.

I didn't know whether McAllister or Curragh had brought about Alison's death, and I wasn't sure I wanted to. I had met both men. In so far as you can tell from a brief encounter, I had rather liked them both: McAllister for his strength, and Alex for that gentleness of spirit I had glimpsed through his suffering, which even the episode with the glass had not convincingly refuted. I liked them. I didn't want either of them to have deactivated the gas detector.

That detector, I found as I thought more about it, was more persuasive evidence against the lover than the husband. It would have offered no warning, on or off, against a bomb or a cylinder full of petrol. It presupposed a gas leak, which would have been very much harder to arrange from a distance. Curragh had only to turn off the detector, turn on the stove and go for a row before breakfast. McAllister, through his agent, would have had to rig some kind of remote control, because his last chance was probably at Oban before Alison went on board. If he wanted the woman and the boy both, an explosion the first time the stove was lit was unlikely to serve. In the event the thing didn't happen until the *Skara Sun* was forty-eight hours out of Oban. It wasn't impossible for a skilled technician to effect a time-delayed gas leak, but there had to have been an easier way. If McAllister was responsible.

If Curragh did it, of course, it was the easiest thing in the world, and the only trace would be that gas detector. Plus the fact that he'd been found floating beside the dinghy when he said he'd been leaning over the bows at the other end of the boat. Why would he risk lying about that? It was perfectly natural to row out for a spot of fishing or just a bit of exercise while breakfast was cooking. It might have seemed a lucky move but hardly a suspicious one. The lie was much more suspicious than the truth. If he had planned this—in the anger of rejection, perhaps, but in sufficiently cold blood to work out what needed doing and then to do it—why on earth had he made that particular mistake?

But it really was not my problem. It was a police problem, and the police would undoubtedly sort it out in their own way in their own good time. My efforts on their behalf, however well-intentioned, were surplus to requirements.

I thought I'd go shopping. My holiday packing had included nothing suitable for a night out and I thought I'd treat myself. I finished my meal with improbable Indonesian coffee and left the restaurant, turning back towards the city centre.

Almost at once I was aware that I was being followed.

It's an unbelievably vile sensation, knowing someone is on your trail like a dog. Thirty years of spy fiction had not prepared me for the sheer shock of realisation, followed quickly by a chaos of panic: fear in the heart, fury in the head, nausea in the stomach. I didn't know how to react. Half my mind told me to run, the other half wanted to know what from. I was surrounded by people in the heart of a major British city in the middle of the day: what secret harm could befall me here?

I was reluctant to make a scene, draw attention to myself. If I'd known which of the blank grey faces jostling round me belonged to my pursuer I'd have confronted him, but the feeling—the certainty—of being followed had come from some source other than recognition. The same problem made it difficult for me to seek help. I stood irresolute on the pavement, my back to a butcher's window, scanning the crowd wild-eyed for some clue to his identity, all my insides knotted up in a ganglion of sick anxiety such that I thought an overt threat, even an attack of some kind, would come as a relief.

The thing ended more quickly and more amicably than I could have imagined. One moment the street was a sea of alien northern faces, scurrying by on unknowable errands, remote and hostile and hardly less threatening than the spy hiding himself among them, and the next a rather plump, pleasant-looking man of about my own age, wearing a tweed jacket over a Fair Isle pullover, stepped out of their midst and stood on the pavement before me, smiled and said, "I'm sorry, I didn't mean to alarm you, Mrs. Marsh. I was hoping to have a few words with you."

His name was Duncan Galbraith and he worked for a Glasgow newspaper. I didn't have to take his word for that, he thumbed me his card. "I thought it was you in the restaurant, but I didn't want to interrupt your meal."

"How did you recognise me?"

He shrugged, a slightly foppish, elegant little shrug. "When we heard you were involved in the McAllister case we pulled your photo out of the morgue."

I didn't know whether to be flattered or horrified. "You've got my picture in your"—we doctors are sensitive souls, at least by comparison with reporters—"files?"

"Oh yes." I couldn't quite place the accent: Scottish but not local, it might have been an Anglified Edinburgh. He smiled again. His pink cheeks crinkled cheerfully round the corners of sea-grey eyes. "Our book reviewer ordered it, but I was in Edinburgh when you were instrumental in the arrest of a fugitive in a high-class nursing home there. I remembered you."

That was going back a day or two. It was soon after I lost Luke, just after I met Harry. I said, "It isn't deliberate, you know. I don't wake up one morning and think, God it's been a boring week, I think I'll go create some havoc up in Scotland."

His plump smile turned impish, the grey eyes twinkling. "Lots of our tourists take their main holiday abroad, come here for a second break. I expect you cause most of your havoc in Marbella, do you, only come here when you've a bit left over that you don't know what to do with?"

I started to grin, then to chuckle. I didn't know him from Adam, but he was the only cheerful thing that had happened to me since breakfast yesterday. We fell into step, walking down the broad pavement. "So, Mr. Galbraith, what did you want to talk about?"

It was a fatuous question, there could be only one thing, but he refrained from pointing that out. "I hoped you'd tell me what happened at Loch Sween yesterday."

"Haven't the police issued a press release?"

"Of course, and they'll issue a fuller one when they know a bit more. But they weren't there and you were. There's nothing like an eyewitness account."

"Earwitness."

"The explosion was the first you knew then?" He wasn't slow, my Mr. Galbraith. All the languour was on the surface, creating an impression which he enjoyed or which served him. His mind was quick and agile, and that one word was all the encouragement he needed. Before I knew it I was giving him an interview.

Harry, of course, would be horrified, but why not? If Alison McAllister had been murdered, there would be inevitable public interest in that; and if it turned out to have been an accident, it was very much in the public interest to publicise the dangers that even a familiar situation can hold for even a careful person. Besides, nothing I had seen or heard could be a point of contention; my own thoughts on the matter were and would remain private. With that proviso, I saw no reason to obstruct his efforts to report the incident.

I told him what I had heard and seen, and what Harry and I had done. He already knew who we were, so there was no point in withholding brief personal details. I included in the account the helicopter flight to Glasgow but nothing that had happened or emerged after I handed Curragh over to the hospital's care. For an update I referred him to Neil Burns, who had probably been told to say nothing but on whose list of virtues discretion figured less than prominently.

When I had finished, Galbraith put his notebook away but continued walking beside me, apparently half lost in thought. Finally, intrigued and exasperated in roughly equal proportions, I said, "Whatever's bothering you now?"

He shook his head. He looked troubled. He plainly considered for a moment before deciding to answer. "Off the record?"

That amused me. In my experience of the press, off the record is something that doesn't exist unless you have it in writing on the back of a Press Club wine-list. "Whatever happened to 'Publish and be damned'?"

His smile was wry, an uneasy shadow of its former self. "The publishers ended up in the High Court, and their legal bills meant selling their businesses for scrap and supermarket sites. The freedom of the Press is a Christmas-cracker motto these days."

"All right. Off the record."

"I would not care," he said carefully, choosing his words, "to be a young man of no wealth and no position coming up against Frazer McAllister in this city."

It seemed to be a warning, and if it was not for me it might still bear heeding. For the moment I skirted round it. "You know McAllister then?"

He looked at me in some surprise. Then he remembered he was talking to a foreigner, a tourist. "Oh yes," he said with a curious inflection. "Not personally, you understand. I mean, he doesn't invite me to his grouse moor, we didn't celebrate the Big Bang together or anything like that. But yes, I know him. He's a steam-roller. He goes over people. He leaves little flattened husks in his wake. He does this to people who stand between him and his profit, him and his plans, him and his self-esteem, him and his importance. I don't know what he'd do to some-one who came between him and his wife." His voice was bleak.

"There's actually no evidence," I reminded him gently, "that Curragh was aboard in any capacity other than as Mrs. McAllister's crew."

Galbraith smiled at that. "Indeed; so let the record show. But you and I know that whatever Alison McAllister needed, it wasn't help aboard her boat. I imagine McAllister knows that too. Have you met him?"

"Oh yes."

"Then you know what I'm saying."

"A forceful personality," I said judiciously.

"All of that," he agreed.

"How much more?"

His glance was both sharp and appreciative. "I came to wheedle an interview out of you, not to have one wheedled out of me."

I said with dignity, "I never wheedle. But I don't see how you can believe in freedom of information and refuse to answer my questions."

He grinned. "All right. Off the—er—?"

"Sure."

"OK. The bottom line is, Frazer McAllister has never been con-victed of anything illegal. He's never been formally charged with an offence. He's been investigated several times to my knowledge, and allegations have been made more often than that."

"What sort of allegations?"

Galbraith shrugged elegantly. "You name it, he's been accused of it. Everything but indecent exposure. All the business offences—income tax, VAT, insider dealing, fraud, corruption. None of it proved. Most of the thuggery ones—blackmail, extortion, assault and malicious damage. None of it proved. Then a couple of specials, like misprision of felony and perverting the course of justice. But you'll never guess . . ."

"I know, it was never proved. Who made the allegations?"

"Other businessmen mostly, if you use the term widely. Not many of them still around. Oh, I don't mean he disposed of them—what's the current term?—wasted them. But a lot of them ended up with no businesses and moved on."

"Sour grapes?"

"Undoubtedly a sour grapes element. But all of them, all those alle-gations? Some fire beneath all that smoke, I think. I don't know if it makes him an evil man, even as evil as some of the men he steam-rollered. It makes him a tough man, probably a ruthless one. Most of all, it makes him a powerful man, because neither you nor I—honest and lovable as we are—could sustain a barrage of accusation like that without being made to answer for it. That's what worries me. If he goes after Curragh, he'll hound him until he drags him down—and he'll do it just this side of any crime that can be proved. The lad's going to need friends, and in this city he won't find many. Even McAllister's enemies won't do him any favours."

"What about you?"

"Me?" He laughed, a sardonic little laugh. "What can I do? Even the truth I can tell is so hedged about with restrictions that it's hardly the truth any more, and that's just what the law says. When McAllister's had his say I'll be lucky if I can refer to the incident at all."

I didn't smile. If it was so, it wasn't funny. "Why are you telling me this?"

He shrugged, more awkwardly than before, even a little apologetically. "I wanted someone other than me to know."

"A problem shared is a problem halved? Why me?"

"You're a stranger, not involved in this city's power politics. I think McAllister may find you difficult to intimidate."

"More difficult than you?"

"Oh yes," he said with a wan smile, "much more difficult than me. You don't live here. You don't have to work here. Your evidence will be required any time this thing is discussed. This city is full of people who, for one reason or another—because of his money or his power, or because they owe him favours, or because he scares the crap out of them—will turn a blind eye to anything McAllister does that doesn't leave bloodstains on their carpet. If he goes after Alex Curragh, the people whose job it is to stop him will suddenly be busy elsewhere. I shall find myself despatched to Aberdeen to report some Heath Robinson idea for turning disused oil rigs into multi-storey car-parks. But you'll be here, and you'll be at the centre of it. I wanted you to know that nothing Frazer McAllister says can be trusted, unless he says it's raining. Even then you'd be wise to stick your hand outside the window."

Duncan Galbraith was afraid for Alex Curragh when he had no reason to suspect that Alison McAllister's death was other than an accident highlighting an indiscreet friendship. If he had known that there was a fifty-fifty chance that McAllister was not just a clever thug but a clever murderer, that he had killed his wife and tried to kill Curragh, and that under the guise of the wronged and grieving husband he was again conspiring at the boy's destruction, would he have left me then with a languid wave? Would he have said more? Would he perhaps have said less?

Perhaps I should have said more. I had the gut feeling that I could trust Galbraith: not only trust what he said to be true, but trust him not to turn everything I thought aloud into front-page headlines.

Harry would have been shocked at the very idea. But in Harry's world the police might be slow, might be unimaginative, might occasionally be wrong, but no-one ever accused them of being in somebody's pocket. For one thing, Skipley had no-one as rich as Frazer McAllister living there. Skipley had no three people as rich as Frazer McAllister. I didn't know if McAllister had any influence with his local coppers. Galbraith seemed to suggest he might have. Harry wouldn't believe that until he found a peaked cap on the back seat of McAllister's car.

But if the police investigation was going to be less than thorough, its findings less than reliable, Curragh's best chance of a fair hearing lay in public awareness of what was happening. Galbraith could maybe get him that, if I was frank with him. And if McAllister didn't get him dispatched to Aberdeen first.

[3]

I bought nothing. Though the Glasgow shops were tempting, I had suddenly gone off the idea of sampling this city's night-life. It seemed to have dark places enough in the daytime.

And waiting outside the hotel, taking up more space than two taxis but impressing the hell out of the guests, was a big dark car with tinted windows and a uniformed chauffeur. As I approached, the front passenger seat opened and the slick little item in the pin-striped suit got out and casually, carefully, barred my way.

"Sonny," I said heavily, "I am getting a little tired of tripping over you."

He looked surprised at that and a little put out. I think he thought he was a whole lot more alarming than he actually was. I could almost see him shrug the cloak of menace up under his chin. "Mr. McAllister's unhappy about the company you're keeping," he said.

The sheer impudence of it so astounded me that I let the moment for tearing his head off and kicking it across the street come and go. For a long time I held him in the baleful light of my What's-this-on-the-sole-of-my-shoe? glare, until he actually started to squirm. He was very young, I saw now, considering him as a person for the first time. It didn't excuse his manners, but perhaps it explained his lack of dimension. He was a bauble, all glittering surface and no substance.

When he was about as withered as he was going to get I said, very quietly, "What did you say? About Mr. McAllister?"

McAllister wasn't in the car. If he had been, this juvenile delinquent would have done a better job, or at least made a better show, of keeping his nerve. As it was, his fancy footwork subsided into a retreat if not a rout, and he glanced anxiously at the chauffeur for support. The studied smoothness of the Tartan Mafia accent gave way under pressure to his native Glasgow.

"He won't be happy you're hanging round with that hack Galbraith."

So McAllister hadn't sent him, didn't even know. I looked at the chauffeur, who very carefully didn't look at me. The peak of his cap pointing dead ahead through the windscreen, he was pretending he wasn't involved in this. I let my gaze travel back to the lad in the suit. "Sonny, what's your name?"

Half of him wanted to keep it secret, the other half to boast. Finally he said, "William Mackey." He tacked on a handsome grin that was a little too like a leer. He was about twenty-one.

"All right, William," I said. "Billy. I know you're doing your best, but you haven't quite got the hang of this game yet. Watch the grown-ups play a little longer and then have another go. With someone else." I turned away from him towards the hotel steps.

"Hey, missus," he hissed, colouring, and he reached for my shoulder.

It was a serious mistake. It would have been a serious mistake even if Harry hadn't been coming up the pavement the other way. He might have gone home with a black eye, even a marked disinclination to walk upright. But he probably wouldn't have ended up sitting on the pavement with blood pouring from his nose all down his pin-striped front.

Harry takes a lot of time about most things he does—at work, at home, even deciding whether to mow the lawn up and down or side to side. He likes to deliberate until the logic of a situation emerges to dictate its own solution. But occasionally, when a more expeditious approach is called for, he acts first and sweeps up the bits later.

Now he regarded William Mackey with a kind of grave concern for a moment, then offered him a clean handkerchief to deal with the consequences of his misadventure. Then he steered me gently past the small knot of staring bystanders and into the hotel lobby.

Back over my shoulder to Mackey as we climbed the steps I murmured, "See what I mean?"

Harry's lunch-hour had been less interesting than mine, though the coffee was probably better. Over it he began to suspect that we were both behaving rather badly, and afterwards he came back to make his peace with me. His arrival could not have been more opportune, but it left me with some explaining to do.

Actually, Mackey's intervention meant that Harry took Duncan Galbraith's warning more seriously than he would otherwise have done. When he heard the story, McAllister would know that. I wasn't sure the pin-striped suit would be worth cleaning after that.

Also, Harry had news of his own. He'd phoned the police station from the Chinese restaurant to say he'd be late back from lunch, and Baker's sergeant had said Baker was tied up at present anyway, talking to Alex Curragh in the interview room.

"Oh Jesus," I said in disgust. "The kid's sick. He's got a broken arm, his brain's still full of anaesthetic, only a few hours ago he threw a panic attack so bad I don't think he knew where he was. Now he's in a police station trying to justify his actions to a bunch of people who really rather hope he's a murderer. Couldn't it have waited?"

"His doctor must have passed him fit. He might as well get on with it."

"You think he did it?"

It was the kind of question Harry objected to on principle. He reminded me with a look of gentle reproach. "I think it's necessary to find out who did do it." It wasn't that he was reluctant to share his theories with me, more that he avoided theorising for fear that a favourite theory might some day obscure a less appealing truth. Harry reckoned that the time for theories was when no further facts could be dragged, kicking and screaming, from their hiding places in the fabric of an incident. It made him a very good policeman. It would have made him a terrible novelist.

He didn't go back to the police station after all, and in the middle of the afternoon the flowers came.

Harry's face was a study when he answered a knock at the door of our room and the porter thrust a bouquet of early roses into his arms.

I knew who they were from, of course, even before we read the card. Frazer McAllister might be many things—he was certainly a bully, he might be worse—but he wasn't crass. The roses were yellow not red, a vaseful not an armful, and the card was simply worded and addressed to Harry and I both.

It said: "I'm sorry about my nephew's behaviour. Thanks for putting him straight. I'd like to make amends: dinner at my house, about eight? My car will call."

No-one had waited for a reply. The card was hand-written and he hadn't appended his phone-number. No doubt we could have got it; equally clearly we weren't intended to. The item wasn't up for discussion; either we accepted his invitation or we rejected it. There was no mean course. That was clever too.

It was too tempting to refuse. Back home it would have been impossible, but Harry had no official function in this enquiry. We would be witnesses at any trial, but not against anyone in particular. There would be raised eyebrows and disapproving sniffs, no doubt, but we could cope with that if there were real gains to be had. Seeing McAllister on his home ground, learning that side of him, would be such a gain. I hoped Duncan Galbraith would understand that and not suppose I had been bought too.

I still hadn't got anything suitable to wear. But that troubled me less than having him think I'd dashed out and bought something special, so I put on my white jeans and my cleanest shirt, and put my hair up, and settled for sandals and no socks, and rather hoped we'd find him in white tie and tails.

But that would have been crass. He knew the circumstances of our presence in Glasgow, that we'd been interrupted in a sailing holiday. Our available wardrobe was necessarily casual. He greeted us on the steps up to his front door in a pale cashmere cardigan over a silk shirt, with a kerchief at his throat. As best I could judge his lopsided expression, he was glad to see us.

The smooth dark car had brought us westward out of the city, along the north shore of the Clyde until the Erskine Bridge faded behind and the signs for Loch Lomond proliferated ahead. Before we reached that over-hyped but still lovely lake, we peeled off the main road and up into the Kilpatrick Hills. McAllister's house was a small castle with the front door at first floor level, approached by a flight of well-worn and narrow stone steps.

The thing appeared to be authentic, though he could have commissioned that look. But if he'd built it the planners would have required a rail to guard those steps, which might have made them easier for a one-legged man to manage but would have ruined the impact of that lofty access.

Limping heavily, neither seeking help nor likely to accept any, Frazer McAllister ushered us to the eyrie that was his home. He sat us down in deep armchairs round a gently glowing log fire and put glasses in our hands. He sent word to his cook that we'd eat in half an hour. Then he set about apologising for the episode outside our hotel.

"My sister Sheila's a grand girl, nicest wee woman you could hope to meet. But she married a blockhead, and their boy William's going to be twice the dolt his father ever was. When he was twelve they took him to the flicks—Edward G. Robinson, George Raft or one of them, and the St. Valentine's Day Massacre. That was it. The wee lad's development stopped there and then. I swear, every time he blows out the candles on his birthday cake he wishes he was Jimmy Cagney."

I said, "He works for you."

McAllister shrugged. "Nobody but family would employ him."

That wasn't my point. "In the short time before he sat down on the pavement, he gave me to understand that you had something to say about who I meet and talk to."

He nodded. "It's like I told you, the wee lad's thick. Galbraith and I have had words before. When he saw you having lunch together he thought I'd be interested—"

"He thought *you'd* be interested?" Harry murmured softly, and I grinned at him.

"—and instead of coming to tell me about it he used his initiative and tried to talk to you first. I'm sorry you were bothered. It won't happen again."

"No?"

"I have an interest in a whisky distillery. He's on his way there now. It sounds a grand job but oh Christ, have you ever smelled one of those places?"

"I didn't have lunch with Galbraith." I'm not sure which of them I was explaining it to. "He introduced himself outside as I left and asked about the accident. I told him what I'd seen."

"You know," McAllister said quietly, "I really don't believe it was an accident."

"So I understand," said Harry. "Why?— Because she was careful?"

"Partly that. Partly the boy ending up beside the dinghy. Partly because he's told a different story every time he's been asked where he was, what he was doing. But also—" He made an angry, frustrated little gesture with his hand in the air. "Hell, I don't know. Alison—Alison was never going to die like that."

I don't think Harry knew what he meant. I did, but I'm not sure I can express it any clearer. It's as if destiny is a shopping-list containing a wide range of alternatives, and though you might not know which would be in stock at any given point, you'd know something was wrong if you came home with something that wasn't on the list at all. That was how McAllister felt: that his wife had somehow picked up the wrong shopping-bag.

Maybe it was the shock talking—it was still very soon after the event, too soon for him to have any kind of perspective on it. But there was a subtle difference between how he viewed Alison's death and how he viewed her infidelity which I found persuasive. It would have been easier to dismiss his misgivings if he'd insisted her liaison with Curragh had been other than it appeared. His candour on that score argued that his doubts were reasonable, even if he couldn't explain exactly where they came from.

Of course, he could still be wrong. Or lying.

I said, "How old is your son?" It sounded as if I was changing the subject. I wasn't.

He smiled. Nothing that ravaged face could do was handsome, but there was warmth in his smile. "Four months. He's asleep now, but if he wakes up later would you like to see him?"

Babies and bull terriers, they have to be yours for you to appreciate their charms. I'd never seen one of either that I'd even fleetingly wanted to take home. But you can't tell a fond father that. "I'd love to."

I waited while he refilled our glasses, then hit him with what I was building up to. "So you reckon this affair with Curragh started when Alison was seven months pregnant."

The silence gasped. Both men stared at me as if I'd said something unforgivable. I shrugged. "You told me she'd known him about six months."

His eyes were interesting. They could be frosty with umbrage at one level, blaze with indignation at another and still have enough scope left to register a kind of appreciation for a logic that unyielding. After a moment to marshall his thoughts he said mildly, "I could have been wrong about that, I suppose—the precise timing. There was an element of guesswork."

I chanced a guess that was a little more than a guess. "Her will predated your son's birth."

Harry too was looking at me with interest now.

McAllister nodded brusquely. "Yes."

"So she could have known him longer than six months but not much less. Could she have known him a year?"

He shrugged. "I suppose."

"Eighteen months?"

"No way!" The lion head came up sharply. "I'd have known."

I nodded slowly. He was reconciled to the fact that he'd lost Alison long before she and her boat were reduced to debris spiralling through the shallow waters of Loch Sween. But he was not prepared to entertain, even fleetingly, the idea that Alex Curragh might be the father of his son.

And was he? It hardly seemed to matter. He was the child of McAllister's wife, born in wedlock; McAllister wanted him to be his son, was raising him as such, wouldn't consider the alternative; and now Alison was dead the objective truth could be hard to discover. Every way that mattered, the baby was McAllister's.

I thought that was the answer to my question and was content to let the matter rest. But now Harry seemed to have been caught up by the implications. He let his gaze travel calmly round the room—not a big room, the space compressed by the four-foot-thick walls and the beamed ceiling. The walls were raw stone dark with centuries of smoke (or a good synthetic), hung with textiles—probably not priceles Flemish tapestries but giving the same effect. The beams too were smoke-blackened, but between them the high ceiling was plastered and painted in a fantastic bestiary of tiny golden dragons and gryphons and chimeras on a brilliant turquoise ground. That was almost the only brightness in the room. The carpet, like the hangings and the curtains at the two small, high lancet windows, was in brown and rich Turkey red, the three chairs in dark green leather, the two couches in burgundy velvet. The fireplace was made of the same stone as the walls, topped with a plank of the same wood as the beams.

On top of the plank were leather-bound books and silver-framed photographs. That was where Harry's slow gaze came to rest. "May I?"

I suppose it was hard for him to refuse, but McAllister looked as if he'd have liked to. "Help yourself."

Harry put his glass down and went over to the mantelpiece. For a moment I was afraid he was going to commit some terrible faux pas—"Look, darling, that's what the boat looked like before it blew up." But I misjudged him. He hasn't a lot of natural tact, my husband, but neither is he a thoughtless man. He smiled gravely at McAllister. "Is that your son?"

Our host squinted past him at the picture and nodded. "Aye, that's the two of them—Alison and the wean. I took that the weekend they came home from the hospital."

I looked too, craning to see. The woman's long fair hair was unmistakable, though here it was held confined by a scarf and the time-warp of photography, not streaming in the wind off Shuna Point. Her face we had not seen closely enough to recognise.

I looked at her now and saw a strong, firmly planed face, broad across the eyes and high in the brow. The eyes were cornflower blue, wide open and steady. Their clarity was a shortcut to her soul. Her mouth was wide and bent in the gentle curve of a smile: not the ecstatic, idiot grin of a new mum with her baby but the satisfied, knowing, slightly weary smile of someone who has completed a difficult labour. McAllister at the other side of the lens might have been beside himself with the joy of fatherhood, but Alison was just glad to have completed her pregnancy.

And I thought then that she had already decided to leave him. She was posing for his camera not so that she could flip back through the family album in years to come, but so that he'd have something of the child after she had gone. Gone to Alex Curragh, who wanted to take care of them both. Maybe the child was his, or at least he thought it was.

Or maybe it was Alison he wanted. I could see it, picture them together: the strong, knowing woman with her self-confidence born partly of money but also from living in a wider world than the boy from Crinan could imagine; and Alex, younger than she, at once urgent and innocent, with his strong young body and his yet untroubled soul. Each had offered the other things they needed and could have no other way.

Harry looked along the row of frames. "No wedding snaps?"

McAllister grinned fiercely. "Come on. I look in a mirror once a day to shave, I don't need any pictures round the place to remind me how I look. I've got one of Alison in her wedding dress somewhere." He looked at the fireplace as if it had been there once but it was gone now.

"When were you married?"

If he was finding this all a little personal, McAllister showed no signs of resentment, yet. "Four years ago. Man, she was bonny that day."

But he was already as I saw him now; those scars had to be many years old. I had assumed—for the moment I couldn't remember why—that Alison had been there when he met his accident.

A thin wail like a wet kitten's came from half the house away. McAllister had left the sitting-room door a little ajar when he sat us down, and now he was out of his chair before I had identified the sound as a baby. He grinned his gargoyle grin at me. "I might have known we'd hear from his lordship before this evening was much older. Come on up and say hello."

At some point the original staircase, which was probably stone and narrow like the one outside, had been replaced by something broader, in gothic-carved timber. The handrail was dark and glossy with use. McAllister led the way upstairs and I saw why: he hauled himself up, using the big muscles in his arm and shoulder to compensate for the lost muscles of his leg. It wasn't an elegant movement but there was nothing pitiable about it either. There was vigour and a great competence about everything he did.

As we gained the landing I said, "Will you get a nurse for him?"

"No, I don't think so. Alison was never that keen on the idea, and there's always either me or Mrs. Lilley here. I haven't had much practice, but she's raised four of her own. I think we can manage."

I thought so too. I also suspected that if the child required the experienced Mrs. Lilley's attentions at a critical moment, McAllister would take over cooking our dinner with no loss of dignity or flavour. Without really doubting what Duncan Galbraith had told me, I was finding it increasingly difficult not to admire Frazer McAllister.

The door of the little nursery was also ajar. He stepped inside and turned up the light, and bent over the high-sided cot, lifting the red-faced infant in his arms. I was sure it would redecorate his cashmere cardigan but he seemed unconcerned. He grinned daftly at it and jiggled it until it stopped whining. Then he grinned at me.

"Dr. Clio Marsh," he said, "may I present Mr. Peter McAllister?"

[4]

Halfway through the turbot I remembered why it was I'd thought Alison was there when McAllister met his accident. It was what Curragh had said: "She saw a boat burn up once, she didn't want to go that way." I had assumed that was how McAllister was burned, but perhaps I had assumed too much. I wanted to ask but couldn't imagine how to steer the conversation that way without being inexcusably rude.

Perhaps McAllister sensed my interest and decided, for his own amusement, to humour it. It may have been luck, or maybe he made a habit of dispelling the inevitable speculation at an early opportunity. I had just about persuaded myself that I couldn't broach the subject without causing horrible embarrassment all round, when McAllister broached it for me.

"There's not much comfort in all this," he said, his eyes distant, "but there's this: at least it's all over for her. I can't see Alison hanging round while they put what bits of her they could find together again. She's better out of it."

I couldn't accept that. It went against the grain of all I had been taught and had done, to think that some patients might be better off without medical intervention. Well, perhaps the very old and used up, perhaps the very young and unviable, perhaps the severely brain-damaged: these were issues you could argue about. But medical intervention, and infinite patience and skill on the part of my late profession, had brought Frazer McAllister back from the valley of the shadow of death, and he seemed to be suggesting that it hadn't been worth the trouble. I said, "Surely you don't believe you'd have been better out of it?"

He cast me again that sharp, appraising look. I think he enjoyed a good argument, and surrounded as he was by employees he didn't get many of them. "Not now, certainly. But the last time I nearly died of my injuries was eight months after the fire. All right, I came through it and I'm glad now that I did. But eight months is too much time and too much pain to invest if you're then going to lose. I wouldn't do it again, and I'm glad they haven't got Alison on a ventilator in the bowels of a big white hospital. If this had to happen, and she couldn't get away with a few broken bones or that, I'm glad it took her clean. When your number comes up, unless you can be pretty damn sure of fighting them off, you're better going when they call. There's no dignity in struggling till you're worn out and then being dragged away by your heels."

For a space none of us spoke. The turbot was gone and McAllister rang for the next course. When Mrs. Lilley had gone back to her kitchen I said quietly, "A fire, you said. What happened?"

He looked at me straight, his eyes not merely unflinching but holding a challenge. "I owned a chemical plant. I hired the latest thing in boffins. They devised the last word in new processes and brought me up to show me. They blew the place to smithereens. Long before I knew whether I'd live or die, I sacked all the survivors and sold the site for a rubbish tip."

It had the ring of a story he'd told many times before, and honed and polished with each retelling until now it had the edge, the cut, the sardonic humour of a flint skipping across waves. The pain was gone from it, even the memory of pain. That dwelt elsewhere, and he had buried it deep enough to think it lost until what happened to Alison dug it up again.

"When was this?"

"Twelve years ago. I wouldn't have been much older than you." Actually he'd have been younger than me, but there seemed no need to say so. I caught Harry smiling secretly at me and glared back.

But if it was not her husband's accident which inspired Alison's fear of fire, what was it? I thought that probably I would never know, and that anyway it wasn't important. In all the circumstances it was difficult to pump McAllister for any light he could shed on the matter.

With the woman only thirty-six hours dead and the remains of her body and her boat settling into the thick silt on the bed of Loch Sween, it seemed more natural to be talking about Alison and her sailing than carefully avoiding the subject. I said, *"Skara Sun*—was your wife from Orkney?"

"Aye, she was. Her family had a farm above Stromness."

"That would be where she got interested in boats, then."

He nodded. "Her old man kept a little fishing boat in the harbour there. He taught her and her brother both. The family were practically self-sufficient. Mutton and herring: she used to say she'd hardly tasted anything else until she went to university in Stirling."

We made small-talk then until, when we were sampling the cheese, McAllister suddenly stabbed the knife into a wedge of Stilton that was about ready to up and leave of its own accord, and looked up from it first to me and then to Harry, and said quietly, "Listen, I want to thank you people for coming here tonight. You probably thought it a strange request, even after—perhaps particularly after—the behaviour of the thuglet, my nephew. I'm awful glad you didn't do the sensible thing and ignore it."

He went on almost without pausing, pouring words like a tapped keg —not under great pressure but steadily. "It's been a weird couple of days, you know? I've hardly got speaking to anybody—the police, you, that cretin William, Mrs. Lilley who's been too upset to talk back and my son who's too young to. The people I employ have been going round with lowered eyes, and the people I call my friends have been so damn reluctant to intrude they've backed out of my life entirely.

"What do they expect?—that I'm going to start bawling into my whisky and embarrass them? They know me better than that. Any grieving I need privacy for I can do at night, in my own bed. Life goes on—but somehow they don't seem to want mine to. They'd be happier if I went into retreat for a month and needed expensive sessions with a trick-cyclist. That they could understand. They can't understand a grief worthy of the name not tearing a man apart. Damn it, if I let grief do that to me there'd be even less of me left than there is at present!"

I said gently, "Grief is what you feel, not what you do. Different people have different ways of handling it—none of them are either right or wrong. It's your grief, handle it how you handle it best."

He looked at me as if I'd given him permission for something he needed to do. "How come you understand what none of my friends can?"

I shrugged. "I'm bloody-minded too."

He grinned at that. But it wasn't actually a joke. There was something in me, and I recognised it in him too, that wasn't content to disregard public opinion but must confound and preferably scandalise it as well. From the outside such independence looked like strength; as an insider I knew it for a weakness, because letting your feelings and actions be dictated by other people's prejudices, even in order to outrage them, isn't independence at all, it's just another kind of confor-

mity. True freedom is doing what you think is right, even if that sometimes means doing what's expected of you.

We returned to the sitting-room for coffee, and soon after that but
still not much before midnight we started making moves towards leaving.

Harry has big feet. I'm not sure I've mentioned this before, but
being as he is a large person generally, it will not come as a surprise. So
as he turned on the Turkey rug, the long toe of one shoe went under
the corner of one of the couches, and a shimmering little rainbow
skittered across the carpet and turned my world upside down.

I don't know how I got outside but I did, somehow. I even managed
a fairly civil thank-you to our host. Then the smooth dark car took us
from the foot of the stone steps back to Glasgow, and still I couldn't
tell Harry what it was that had struck me like a fist below the heart. But
back at the hotel, while he threw himself on the bed with weary abandon and a slightly peevish expression, I sat carefully in the armchair
with my knees pressed together to still their trembling, and told him
where I had seen that child's toy before.

Bobbing on the afrighted sea at the Fairy Isles, a clear plastic globe
filled with coloured fancies that danced within it as it spun.

When I had finished he was sitting bolt upright on the bed, staring
at me with shock, alarm and that soul-raking disappointment, as if he'd
come home and found me swimming in a gin bottle. And I felt sorry
for him, because it was as embarrassing for a policeman to have a wife
who got involved in crime as it would be for a vicar whose wife tended
to manifest ectoplasm during the Benediction.

But it wasn't my fault. I did nothing to invite these revelations, and I
wasn't going to turn a blind eye to what I considered a material piece
of evidence however inconvenient it was for him. If the police could
make nothing of it, fair enough; but I couldn't just kick the glitter-ball
back under the couch and forget it.

To be fair, I don't think Harry would have wanted me to. Only
sometimes I'm sure he wished I wrote historical romances and only
thought I saw dangerous liaisons and aristocratic by-blows everywhere.

"What is it you're suggesting?" he asked. "That McAllister was
lurking behind a pine-tree all the time, detonator in hand, and after
we'd pulled Curragh out and motored off to Tayvallich he waded into
the water, picked up his kid's toy and came home?"

"Of course not. I don't know what I'm suggesting. Actually I'm not suggesting anything. But I saw that toy in the lagoon at the Fairy Isles, and it was under McAllister's couch this evening."

"It couldn't have been the same one."

"It was exactly the same. I was leaning over to pick it up when you spotted Curragh. I was closer to it than I am to you now. It was exactly the same."

"What happened to it?"

"I don't know! About then I had more urgent things to see to, yes? I let it go and I never saw it again. Until tonight."

Harry shrugged. "There must have been two. I don't suppose it was a unique work of art. There must be hundreds or thousands of the things round the country. The McAllisters ended up with two of them, one at home and one on the boat."

"Whoever buys two identical toys for their baby?"

"Maybe somebody gave them one."

"Then what was it doing on the boat? Wasn't this the first time she'd had it out this year?"

"That's what the boat yard said."

"She didn't bring the baby, and at the end of last season she didn't have the baby. How did one of its toys get on board? And how come it was still bobbing round after the explosion sent the boat to the bottom? The heat of the blast should have melted it, or so deformed the plastic that you wouldn't know what it was."

Almost against his will Harry was getting interested in this. "Then what do you think happened?"

"Harry, I don't know! I can't think of a single explanation—for any part of it, let alone for all of it at once. But I know what I saw."

He thought about it for quite a long time. His mind is more disciplined than mine, used to doing serious work at improbable hours when mine is turning to jelly. I left him to it and went to brush my teeth.

When I came back he said slowly. "Three things seem to have survived the explosion relatively unscathed: the boy, the dinghy and that toy. Suppose they were all together."

The image that conjured was even more unlikely than McAllister lurking behind a tree: Alex Curragh rowing like hell away from the doomed boat with his girlfriend's baby's toy on the boards between his feet. It made no more sense if it was his baby. Where had the toy come from? Why was he taking it? And how did it get back to McAllister's castle only thirty-six hours later?

"I suppose the likeliest place to get some answers is from Curragh," I said doubtfully. I wasn't confident that any answers he would give would be true ones.

"I'll talk to Baker in the morning, fix up an interview. Um—" Harry looked at me rather like a cat regarding a goldfish. "If I can square it, do you want to come too?"

"Me? You'll be doing well if Baker lets you see him. I don't think he'll extend visiting privileges to all your relatives."

"Probably not," agreed Harry. As we retired to bed I was aware that he was still regarding me as a cat regards a goldfish when he's just heard the front door close on the departing family.

[5]

It turned out to be easier than I had expected. The Glasgow police seemed to have accepted at face value Harry's contention that he was indispensable to their investigation, and hardly blinked when he requested an interview between himself, me and Alex Curragh. The fact that they hadn't been getting much sense out of Curragh themselves may have had something to do with it.

I was shocked at the sight of him. For a moment I thought someone had run out of patience and tried beating the answers out of him. But it wasn't that, it was the combined effects of his injuries from the Fairy Isles—reaching their glorious Technicolor peak after two days—and twenty hours of helping police with their enquiries. He would have had too much coffee and too little sleep, like the officers questioning him. His mind would be numb with the percussive effect of their voices.

The anaesthetic still circulating in his system would be contributing to the erosion of reality, as would this narrow, airless little room with no windows and only one door. The boy from Crinan must have craved blue sky and fresh air as if his life depended on them, must have been desperate enough by now to say anything that would bring them closer. But not yet ready, it seemed, to say what had actually happened.

For four hours, said DCI Baker, he had stuck to his story of checking the anchor-chain and being thrown clear by the blast. After that he accepted that no-one believed him and he stopped answering questions altogether. The only questions he had answered in the last sixteen hours, and answered consistently, were *a*, "Were you in love with Alison McAllister?" to which (after he gave up trying to persuade the police that he was no more than her hired crew with his own cabin and no claim on her but his wages) he consistently answered, "Yes"; and *b*, "Did you kill her?" to which he consistently answered "No." All that ground had been covered before Harry and I had sat down to our dinner with McAllister last night. None had been covered since.

"Visitors for you, Curragh," Baker said briskly, as he showed us in.

Curragh looked up from the table without enthusiasm, expecting more of the same. But his face changed when he saw me, his dull eyes brightening, life seeping back into his cardboard expression, animation into his slumped body. It struck me with a pang almost like guilt that I was the closest thing he had in this city to a friend and ally, and even I was half inclined to believe him a murderer.

I took the chair opposite him, another hard little kitchen chair designed for other purposes than comfort, and looked at him across the table. Every time I saw him I thought how young he was. Not so much in years, perhaps—twenty-three is a respectable tally, most of us have learned a bit of something by our mid-twenties—as in experience. There was a kind of innocence about him, as if he was unused, untried. It left him ill-equipped to cope with the events he had become involved in. He had no reserves, no philosophy, no fortitude. He was about as deep sunk in misery as a human being can get. But still obstinate. Obstinacy is one of the tools young men acquire early.

And now a tiny glow was creeping back into his cheeks because he thought I was here somehow to rescue him—a diminutive and middle-aged knight-errant assaulting the walls that held him. I wished I could. If I'd had the power to free him from the nightmare, whether it was of his own making or another's and whatever the form of release that might be appropriate, I'd have done it, confident that no act of mine could make him more unhappy than he was at this moment. But I didn't think I had that power. All I could do was ask the same questions he'd already refused to answer, and when I did the glow would die back out of his cheeks and he'd clam up on me too.

I thought I'd start with something uncontentious. I nodded at his plaster. "How's the arm?"

He looked surprised, as if he'd forgotten it. "Fine."

"Good. You're entitled to have it looked after, you know, whether you're here or at the hospital."

"They're taking me for another X-ray later today."

"Fine. How's your head?"

He touched his fingers lightly to his temple. He sounded puzzled. "My head's fine."

"I'm glad to hear it. It wasn't working the best last time I saw you."

He had enough colour now to blush with. "That's right. I'm sorry, I don't know what happened—I seemed to wake up in the middle of it with a broken glass in my hand. I didn't frighten you?"

I had to smile. "No." Would it reassure or offend him to learn how far from frightening he had been, even with an ugly weapon in his hand? I passed over it. "Alex, don't you want to get out of here and go home?"

His eyes kindled for a moment, fear and anger twisting in their depths like brown fire. "Of course I do."

"Then get it over with. Tell them what they have to know. Nothing can move forward until you do."

A weary indignation stiffened him, his long slender body coming almost erect in the chair so that he was looking down his nose at me. "They don't believe anything I say."

I sighed. "That's because you keep telling them lies. You lied to me, too—remember? At some point the truth will have to be told—it might just as well be now, before any more harm is done."

"I didn't kill her," he said. "I loved her."

"Actually, Alex, I believe that." At least I half believed it. "So what are you hiding? Why won't you tell us what happened?"

"I told them. I told you. I said—"

"You spun some cock-and-bull story about leaning over the bows when all the evidence points to you being in the dinghy when the explosion occurred. Where were you going? Why was it necessary to lie?"

"I wasn't going anywhere," he growled. All his young man's stubbornness glowered in his face, but so far as it went I thought it was the truth.

I pressed the tiny advantage that gave me. "All right, so you weren't going anywhere. But you were in the dinghy."

"I was—I wanted—" For a long moment he was so close to telling me that I could feel the words gathering in his mouth, struggling to free themselves. A kind of anguish joined the turmoil in his eyes. He hated the deception, ached to be done with it, was ready to take the consequences.

But then a shutter fell between his mind and his eyes, shutting him in with the secret he seemed somehow pledged to protect, shutting him off from me and Harry and the little room where we sat, and the hours that could run into days and weeks, and then possibly years before he would have his freedom again if he couldn't satisfactorily explain how he survived the going down of the *Skara Sun*. I felt him close, close enough to reach and touch, and then I felt him draw back behind this iron curtain of a shutter, and I thought he might never come within hailing distance again.

So I played the joker because it was the only face card I had. I lifted onto the table the paper bag I had brought in with me. "What do you know about this?" When I saw that I had his attention I up-ended the bag and let the thing inside roll glittering into his hand.

Harry had been right: the country was full of them. The second toy-shop I went in sold me one for just a few pounds.

I watched his face. His eyes widened, his jaw dropped, his lips paled and parted and a whisper of air came between them. He stared, unmoving, unblinking, as the bauble rolled towards him. Then a sudden spastic movement of his hand on the table-top captured it, his long fingers spreading round it protectively. He held it against his chest, his body curved round it, as if it might otherwise escape.

Finally he dragged his eyes away from it and looked up, and his voice when it came was thin and frail and half broken by emotion. "How—? Where—?"

Harry said quietly. "No need to ask if you recognise it, then."

The boy's eyes stayed on me. There was a shining there as of tears, as if after all the hours of dull and hopeless misery, this cheap toy had moved him, stirred the brew of emotions he had carefully battened down. But what I saw was not more pain, or grief or anger or fear. It might have been relief. His voice still thin but under some kind of control now, he said, "You know, don't you?"

"Some of it. Maybe most."

It wasn't true; it wasn't even necessary for him to believe that it was. It was the password he needed to let himself out of this prison he had built for himself. A permit, like the one McAllister had required of me. I didn't understand their need for the approval of someone neither of them knew. But then, my understanding was also unnecessary. The job of a catalyst is to facilitate a chemical reaction, not to understand the periodic table.

"Including Peter?"

It was a gamble. If I was wrong I'd lose him, and I'd never get him back again, and I believed absolutely that whatever he knew about the going down of the *Sun*—however much or little—he'd keep as a secret to himself probably for the rest of his life. But if I didn't take the risk I'd lose him too. I had to justify his trust in me, prove that he wasn't actually breaking the confidence placed in him.

I said, "Yes, Alex, I know about your son."

He sighed. The burden on him lightened visibly. "I promised I'd never tell anyone. I promised her that. It mattered more than anything to her."

"You didn't have to tell me. That much I knew."

He nodded slowly. He was ready to let go—let go of his secret, let go of Alison. "Then you might as well know it all. I've nothing to hide. We had nothing to be ashamed of. I loved Alison McAllister and she cared for me, but she was going back to her husband. He didn't have to kill her. She was going back to him, and nobody would ever have known he wasn't Peter's father. Not from her, and not from me."

And so it began to come, the story he'd pawned all his future to keep secret. And as it came I could see the tension and the weariness leaching out of him, the relief buoying him up.

"So you were in the dinghy when it happened. Where were you going?"

"I wasn't going anywhere. I was coming back."

He'd looked forward to the trip for weeks. Alison had promised that as soon as she had her boat in the water she'd sail down to Crinan to pick him up and they'd have a holiday together. Only when they were alone on the boat, lying at anchor that night at the Fairy Isles, did Alex learn it was to be their last time together. Even without the explosion. The trip was in the nature of a farewell present to him.

She had another parting gift. She confirmed what he had dared to suspect but never found the courage to ask: that he was the father of her child. He was like a child himself, stunned and excited at the news, and while he was celebrating with wine and song and a making of plans —making, too, the happy noise that had drifted over the still water to the *Rubber Lion*—Alison broke the rest of her news, that she was finishing with him.

"She said she loved me. She said she'd love me as long as she lived, but she had obligations that she couldn't neglect any longer. She said the time we'd known each other had been the best time she'd known but now it had to end."

At first he refused to believe her. Then he pleaded with her to change her mind, to bring her baby and come to him, at least not to shut him off from them. Finally, weak with beating against the palisade of her resolution, he had cried long and brokenly, and she had held him in her arms until they reached a kind of peace.

She wanted them to spend these last few days together but he couldn't face that. The thing was tearing him apart. When the dawn came, and she sleeping beside him, he rose carefully and quietly and got ready to leave. He wrote her a note saying she'd find her dinghy in Tayvallich, he would hitch home from there, and wishing her happiness.

So he took his pack and got into the dinghy, and rowed the couple of miles to Tayvallich, where he tied up the dinghy and went ashore. It was still desperately early and no-one was about. He thought he'd walk a long way before he got a chance to hitch.

By the merest chance then he found a group of people not only up and about but preparing to travel his way. He wasn't sure if they were gypsies or hippies or a bit of both, but they'd camped (quite illegally) outside the village and were now breakfasting before packing their belongings into the backs of two Ford Transits and an old school bus and heading north. They offered him a lift gladly.

They made their livelihood primarily by selling handicrafts and other trinkets from stalls which they set up beside the road, which they could strike with lightning haste at the sight of a police-car. They showed him the sort of things they sold, among them a cardboard box full of children's toys.

"When I saw them, I wanted to give something to my son more than I could remember wanting anything. I'd never know him—hold him, talk with him; he'd never know I so much as existed. But I could give him some little toy, and I'd know he had it and that would be a link of a kind. I bought this from the travellers and asked them to wait for me while I rowed back to the *Sun*. I thought I could be there and back in an hour. I hope they're not still waiting for me."

"They aren't," said Harry. His expression was rueful. "I got stuck behind them driving over here later in the day." He'd been as close as one bumper can safely be to another—probably closer, knowing Harry —to Alex Curragh's alibi before we even knew he needed one.

I was thinking that it said more about Alex Curragh, his simple nature and his backwoods upbringing, than almost anything else could have: that he had had his pick of a gypsy hoard of curios, and many would be handmade to secret and arcane designs passed down through generations, full of skill and interest and history, and he had chosen this mass-produced little plastic gew-gaw because of the glittering colours that danced at its heart. He probably thought it was beautiful and special; and who was to say he was wrong?

So he'd returned to the dinghy and rowed back up the loch with the toy and a scribbled explanation on the boards between his feet. He didn't think Alison would have missed him yet and he didn't mean to wake her. But as he pulled between the fringing rocks and past the *Rubber Lion,* glancing round to check his bearing he saw the shadow of movement in the cabin. He was going to have to say goodbye after all. But it was worth it if Alison would pass his gift on to his son.

He pulled up to the *Skara Sun* and shipped the oars, and reached out with the painter to make fast. And then the world turned inside out through its own navel, with a roaring and a screaming and birth pangs like fire and salt, and he fell slowly through air and water watching the disintegration of half the universe like the whirling, glittering, colourful chaos at the heart of his child's toy. That was all he remembered, and all he knew. He didn't know about the bequest until the police told him.

"That's it?" I was angry with him. I couldn't believe he'd risked everything to protect a really rather ordinary little secret like that. "You were willing to stand trial for murder, conceivably be convicted, rather than explain what happened?"

"I promised." All the obstinacy of the twenty-three-year-old male was grained in the creases round his eyes. I saw something else there too: a certain pride, a dignity, a nobility even. Dear God, he still thought his word to a dead woman incapable of being injured further was more important than his liberty. "Alison: I promised her. It mattered to her that no-one should know Peter wasn't McAllister's son, so I promised no-one would hear it from me. It was almost the last thing I said to her. I couldn't break my word."

Break his word: as if they were school-kids and he'd told her mum she'd been doing homework when she was out late dancing. He could have spent the rest of his life paying for that promise.

"You didn't have to lie," I snarled. "You could have told the police you were in the dinghy. You didn't have to tell them something that the sheer physics of the situation prevented them from believing."

He shrugged. He still didn't think he'd had any option. "They'd have wanted to know why I was in the dinghy. Someone would have asked in Tayvallich, traced the gypsies and found out what I'd bought from them. It would have been the same as telling them about Peter. Nobody rows five miles in a tender to buy a toy for another man's child." He spread his fingers and looked at the bauble nestling there. "I never even wondered what had happened to this. I thought it was gone."

"The one you bought is. I bought that one this morning. But I saw the one you had, bobbing round in the water after the explosion, just a moment before we spotted you." I wondered if I should tell him about the third one, saw no reason not to. He might even find an odd comfort in it. "Actually, Peter has one too. Either his mum or his"—I had to change that quickly—"or McAllister must have given it him. We saw it at the house last night. I couldn't understand it. I knew they wouldn't have got him two the same. I never thought of you."

The glow was back in his face, heightened and intense. His words stumbled. "You've been to Alison's? Did you—?"

I knew what he was asking. I smiled gravely and nodded. "Yes, I saw Peter."

"I saw a picture once," he said. There was a shy longing in his eyes. "But—what's he like?"

What was he like? He was like every other baby I'd ever seen—well, like the large proportion of them that were white, well-fed and healthy. I couldn't have picked him out of an identity parade of half a dozen such. Babies?— He'd asked the wrong person.

Or maybe not. I lie for a living. I invent whole families, whole towns, out of nothing: what was one more baby? So I made up what I hadn't noticed, and spun him a tale about his child that brought tears to his eyes.

[6]

But where the hell did that leave us? Curragh's behaviour had been that of a guilty man and had given some hope that the investigation could soon be brought to a conclusion. The one piece of forensic evidence yet dredged from the bottom of the loch, the gas detector that had been switched off, seemed to point more to Curragh than anyone else.

And now? When the travellers were found and asked, they would remember Alex and what he had bought, and not even Frazer McAllister would believe in his guilt after that.

Or perhaps McAllister never had. Because if Alex didn't murder Alison, the logical alternative was that her husband did. I had that awful wearisome feeling of having been here before.

Alex was taken back to the hospital for his X-rays. Harry and Baker and I were discussing the new state of the union over a pot of cooling coffee and a cellophane packet of Nice biscuits. There are few occasions more intrinsically sordid than morning coffee in a police station.

"Suppose," said Baker, obviously reluctant even to suppose it but biting the bullet manfully, "that McAllister wanted his wife dead. How would he have done it?"

"Loads of ways," said Harry. He is not a vague man, particularly where his job is concerned—he meant it literally. "A radio-controlled detonator would be the best way, probably. It's a bit technical, but McAllister could get that kind of help. The receiver would have been planted on the boat before she left Oban, and somebody watching for them on shore with a transmitter.

"It could have been an honest-to-God bomb, but that would leave traces. If he wanted it to look like an accident—and remember, he wanted Curragh dead as well—it would be better if the signal set off the gas cylinder. That way there'd be precious little for the divers to find that would argue against an accident. If Curragh had died too, that's the way we'd have read it."

I squinted at him. "If he was watching them from the shore, how come he waited until Alex left the *Sun?*"

"I don't suppose he meant to. But he couldn't blow it in the middle of the night—gas explosions happen when people are lighting the gas, mostly. He was waiting till breakfast-time, but Curragh was away at first light. He wouldn't know what to do then—this is McAllister's hired help, remember, not McAllister—so he waited to see if Curragh would come back, and an hour later he did. Our friend on the shore was so bloody relieved to see him that he jumped the gun, rather. He wasn't going to risk him rowing away again, so as soon as Curragh reached the *Sun* he pressed the button."

"Who turned the gas detector off, and why?"

He scowled at me. "I suppose—when he went on board at Oban, our friend turned it off in case gas leaking while he was working at it triggered the alarm and brought half the boat yard down on him. When he'd finished there could still be gas around, so he left it off and Alison never noticed."

"She was a careful woman. She was on board two days."

"She was saying goodbye to her lover. She had other things on her mind."

It was possible. If it had been done that way, they'd have to strain the bed of the lagoon through a sieve to find the fragments of a radio receiver that would prove it.

Baker was watching me, eyes shrewd over his moustache. "Why, how do you think it was done?"

"I know nothing about radio-controlled bombs," I said, "but I do know something about boats. One of the biggest mistakes you can make when you're cruising, and people go on making it though they don't often make it twice, is to confuse the containers in which you keep the petrol for the engine and the paraffin for the stove. If you put paraffin in the engine you wreck the engine. If you put petrol in the stove you wreck the boat, the crew and anyone passing along the tow-path at the time. You have to keep them separate, store them in different places in different-coloured cans.

"Alison wouldn't make that mistake. She had no petrol on board— her engines were diesels. She wouldn't think she had anything but cooking gas—butane—in the cylinders. But if someone wanted her dead they could substitute something more volatile, knowing that sooner or later she'd connect the new cylinder, turn it on and put a match to it. It couldn't go off accidentally while they wandered hand-in-hand along a twilight shore. It would probably happen at a mealtime when they would both be on board and at least one of them in the galley.

"As it happened, because of precise circumstances which could hardly have been predicted, only Alison was on board, but she was in the galley. She woke and found Alex gone. She found his note. I doubt if she felt like breakfast then. But a little later she looked out the window and saw him rowing between the rocks, coming back. She did what nine women out of ten would have done at that moment: she went to put on the kettle. But the gas wouldn't light, the cylinder was empty. She changed it. As the dinghy reached the *Sun*, she went to light the stove."

We sat a moment in a silence filled with the echo of the explosion. Then Baker said, "Would there be anything left to show it wasn't butane in the cylinder?"

"I don't know. Ask your forensic people."

Harry said, "A gas leak would explode in the bowels—"

"Bilges," I corrected him. God alone knows how I knew what he meant.

"Right, whereas a doctored cylinder would explode at the stove. That might be detectable, if they find enough pieces. There's one problem."

"Yes?"

"Who turned the gas detector off, and why?"

I glowered at him but his face remained straight. "The same person who turned yours off, and for the same reason—he was handling gas cylinders, he didn't want a minor leak to give him away." It was plausible, but it wasn't enough. "Maybe he thought it would warn her in time to blow out the match." It wouldn't have done though. She never turned the gas on until she had a match lit and waiting. Alex told me that.

"All right," said Baker. He slid another biscuit from the pack and nibbled it contemplatively, the crumbs frosting his moustache. "So McAllister could have done it. Why might he have done it?"

The obvious answer was unlikely to be the right one. Infidelity provokes murders enough, but most of them are committed in the shock and fury of the moment. This killing, whoever did it, was too cold-blooded for a crime of passion.

Harry said, "Clio has a theory," as if it was something indelicate and a little humorous, like crabs. Baker looked at me with interest and foreboding; he looked he was ready to duck.

"If McAllister killed her," I said, "the child was the reason. I doubt he married for love, and I don't think he'd see infidelity as reason enough to risk his liberty. No-one likes feeling betrayed, but I can't see McAllister killing his wife for dirty weekends on her boat with Alex Curragh.

"I think the reason McAllister married, and married a woman twenty years younger than himself, was to get an heir. They were married for three years before anything happened; then Alison announced she was pregnant and in due course young Peter arrived. McAllister's heir. But not McAllister's son. Before she sent Alex away, Alison told him the baby was his. If it wasn't true it was vicious, and I don't think she was a vicious woman. I think Alex made her pregnant after her husband had consistently failed to, and if she was so sure who was the father I dare say McAllister had a good idea too.

"He thought she was going to leave him. He could have borne that philosophically enough, but if she went she'd take the child with her. If he tried for custody she'd tell the world the baby wasn't his—that he hadn't been able to father his own heir. He'd lose his wife and his dignity, but most of all he'd lose his son. I've seen him with that baby. I have no doubt he'd kill to protect it."

"But she wasn't leaving him," objected Harry.

"No. Perhaps she'd only just decided. Perhaps she hadn't told him, or he hadn't believed her. She was setting off to meet Alex, and he was young and strong and undamaged and also the father of her child: perhaps McAllister couldn't believe that, given that choice, she'd stay with him. He's not inured to what happened to him, to the state it left him in. He's made a pretty good adjustment—being clever, ruthless and filthy rich may have helped—but he's very aware of the fact that he's a physical wreck. One of the reasons the baby means so much to him is that it's perfect.

"Because of what happened to him he was in his late forties before he married, turned fifty before she provided him with an heir. That's a lot of years he has invested in them. If Alison left, he could lose a lot more looking for someone he'd care to marry who'd care to marry him, and even then he couldn't be sure of a child. If Alison died, at least he'd be left with his son."

"Is that what you believe?" asked DCI Baker.

I don't know why he thought it mattered what I believed. "I think it's likely. It's consistent with what we know, and what we can guess. Yes, sitting here talking to you, it's what I believe. But if Frazer McAllister came through that door and sat down with us, I'd start doubting before he opened his mouth. He's an enormously powerful character; if you take him before a jury you'd better be sure you have him neatly packaged and all your facts sewn up, because he's a hard man to discredit, and he would be if he hadn't got a penny to his name."

You know what they say about speaking of the devil. We heard doors bang, raised voices, then Frazer McAllister was looming monstrously over our table. I had thought the ravaged half of his face incapable of expression, but it could manage rage.

Baker got to his feet quickly, Harry slowly. I stayed where I was, the table between us.

McAllister bellowed, "You've no' let the wee shite go?"

I looked at him as calmly as a woman can when she's sitting behind a table and flanked by two strong men, and said, "The wee shite didn't kill her."

His eyes and even his nostrils flared at me, but he heard what I was saying. "Then who did?" There was anger in the gravelly voice, and hubris, but also something like fear. It was unmistakably a challenge.

DCI Baker rose to it magnificently. He seemed to grow two inches. His moustache had never bristled so impressively. "I'm glad you came in, sir," he said. "I wanted to talk to you about that."

I left then. Harry stayed.

I waited in reception for about half an hour, but when there were no signs of any of the three of them emerging I thought I'd go back to the hotel and freshen up before lunch. But as I got to my feet the phone rang, and the desk sergeant answered it and looked quickly at me and away again. So I made an excuse to hang around a little longer, routing through my bag for something I hadn't lost and was therefore in no danger of finding. Sure enough, when he put the phone down the sergeant came out from behind the desk and over to me.

"Mrs. Marsh, you know Alex Curragh, don't you?"

My heart sank. "I've got to know him in the last few days."

"Only we sent him back to the hospital for an X-ray and he's gone AWOL. You wouldn't have any idea where he'd be?"

My God, I thought, for an innocent man he certainly does a good impression of a guilty one. It was the broken glass all over again. "No. But I could make an educated guess where he'll be heading—home, to Crinan. How would he do that—without a car?"

"Beats me," said the sergeant feelingly. He found maps and time-tables under the desk. "Well, he could take the train to Oban, though he'd see half the west of Scotland before he got there and he'd still be thirty-odd miles from Crinan. He can get there by bus, but it'll take him most of the day." He folded away the sheets. "Well, I'd better get someone organised to watch the bus and train stations. We'll maybe pick him up soon enough."

Actually I didn't think they would, because actually I didn't think he'd go anywhere near public transport. He was used to hitching, and even then there were two ways he could go.

But none of this was altogether relevant. I said, "Before you organise anything, get it approved by your chief. The last I heard, Alex Curragh was no longer a suspect in the murder of Alison McAllister, in which case he's free to go home any time he wants to, and though I don't think it would occur to him to sue for wrongful arrest, you never can tell."

I left him worrying about that and went back to the hotel. I was still wondering what I should do next when Harry came in. He threw himself into the chair that had previously proved equal to the strain and stared glumly at his left knee for about a minute before speaking. Then he said lugubriously, "This is all your fault, you know."

It was too preposterous even to take offence. "Mine?"

"Yes. Twenty-four hours ago we had one crime and a prime suspect who was going nowhere. Now we've got more theories than you could shake a stick at, two suspects—neither of whom is assisting noticeably in our enquiries—and now one of them has disappeared and the other is threatening me with his lawyer, his friend the Secretary of State for Scotland, and something called a Procurator-Fiscal, and I don't know whether I need a bullet-proof vest or a clove of garlic."

At least he was hanging onto his sense of humour. Mind you, nobody but me would know. "Would it be helpful if you found Alex? Or would it be just as handy if he stayed out of sight for a few days?"

Harry was watching me, his grey eyes steady. "Do you know where he is?" He hadn't answered my question.

"He's hitching his way home. He may be going by road but I doubt it. The Clyde is still one of the great rivers of the world, and Glasgow one of the great ports. Alex has worked with boats since he was a kid, there's damn all else to do in Crinan. It's my guess he's on one now, watching Gare Loch and Loch Long and Holy Loch slide gently by to starboard."

"When will he get to Crinan?"

"Depends what kind of boat he's on, and which way it's going, and whether it's making any calls along the way. He could be there tonight, it could be the middle of next week."

Harry nodded slowly. He didn't seem altogether displeased. "There's one thing to be said for it. If we couldn't keep him in custody—and after today, barring something new, we couldn't—a boat at sea is probably the safest place for him."

"Safest?"

[7]

They had been unable to find any grounds on which to detain Frazer McAllister. They had questioned him at length about his relationship with his wife and he had replied fully, frankly and with obvious resentment. His answers left no apparent gaps to be queried and quarried, they were unable to catch him out in either general or specific untruths, and in due course when they had asked all the questions they could think of they had to thank him for his time and show him to the door.

Yet Harry and Baker both, two experienced detectives, were left with the faint, persistent feeling that the full and frank answers had served only to cover up a deeper truth which they could suspect but not yet even glimpse. McAllister was hiding something, and doing it so well they couldn't see the cracks, let alone force them. They hadn't given up, of course, but for the moment and until they got more evidence or more ideas, they had gone as far as they could.

It would surprise no-one who knew him that Frazer McAllister had almost as many questions to ask as the police. Particularly he wanted to know why Alex Curragh had been returned to the hospital and left there without so much as a police guard when it was as obvious as sin that the man was a murderer.

Harry told him what Curragh had told us, which explained his improbable survival when the *Skara Sun* blew up and also the ill-considered lies he had told hoping to protect Alison's confidence. While he was talking he watched McAllister closely for a reaction that might cast light on his own role. But McAllister's expression barely flickered—not when he spoke of Peter's paternity, not when he said Alison had decided to end the affair.

When he finished, McAllister said only, "And you believed the wee shite?"

"I wasn't sure what he meant by that," Harry observed reflectively to his left knee.

I didn't understand. "Isn't it obvious?"

"It wasn't. The way he said it—the inflection, the look in his eyes—I wasn't sure if he was telling me it was unbelievable, or asking me if I thought it was true."

"What did he say about the baby?"

"Very little. The idea didn't seem to come as a shock; I think he must have considered it before now. He said it's a wise father that knows his own child and only Alison knew for sure. He really didn't seem that troubled. He was much more upset by the idea that Curragh had hoodwinked us."

About then the news reached them that Alex had had his X-ray, that it had proved satisfactory, and that instead of returning to his room off Neil Burn's ward as agreed, he had climbed back into his borrowed shirt and walked out of the hospital into the anonymity of the city.

At that point Frazer McAllister's temper, just about under control throughout the interview thus far, hit the fan. He swore terrible oaths —against Harry, against Baker and his colleagues who couldn't solve their own crimes without involving foreigners, against me—absence failing to make the heart grow fonder—most of all against Alex Curragh.

He wouldn't accept that there wasn't evidence enough to arrest him twice over, and if there had been inadequate grounds for holding him before, he was adamant that the boy heading for the hills clinched the matter utterly. He wanted an APB issued; he wanted helicopters and tracker dogs; he wanted guns and stun grenades and lots of men on the ground, and he saw no reason why he shouldn't provide anything the police were short of.

That was why Harry considered Alex was safer at sea. "You think if you don't find him, McAllister will?"

He grimaced. "I think there's a serious danger he may try."

"You warned him off, of course."

"Of course. You can imagine how deeply impressed he was."

Quite. The niceties of the law would seem a poor reason to McAllister for doing anything. Also, he had powerful reasons to deal with Curragh himself. If McAllister had murdered his wife he needed to dispose of the boy while he was still a credible scapegoat. Alex had played right into his hands; the last thing he wanted was for the boy to come to his senses and turn himself in. If McAllister's people found Alex first, he'd be dead before anyone else got to him.

And if McAllister didn't murder his wife, he must feel sure that Curragh had. With the police apparently disinclined to arrest him, there was again the substantial prospect that McAllister would take the law into his own hands, extract his own vengeance. If Alex was never found we would probably never know for sure which of them had done it, if it was Alex and he had escaped or if McAllister had finished the job begun at the Fairy Isles.

Harry sighed and stretched his feet out to the hearth, though it was June and there was no fire burning there. "I'm going to fly up to Orkney this afternoon, talk to Alison's mother. As far as McAllister knows she's the last of the family still living there. I don't know if she can cast any light on this, but it might be useful to hear about Alison from someone other than the two men suspected of killing her. Do you want to come?"

"Yes, sure." Whatever I thought of how it was turning out, this was likely to be the only holiday I'd get this year. Meeting a murdered woman's mother mightn't compare with breaking the bank at Monte Carlo, for instance, or wind-surfing in the Bahamas, but at least Orkney was somewhere I hadn't been before. "Didn't McAllister say there was a brother too?"

"He did, didn't he? Maybe he's moved away. The father died several years ago. Mrs. McKeag, that's the mother, lives in Stromness."

. . . In a street of little houses that looked they had grown somehow organically out of the rock of the island, a narrow street of stone sets and cobbles, with barely room for the car we had hired in Kirkwall. The street flowed like a river over the contours of the shoreline and round the curves of the harbour, and a hundred yards in any direction started to take you out into the country again. Small green fields confined by stone walls hemmed in the little town, kept its face to the sea. The harbour with its long pier seemed almost larger than Stromness itself.

Mrs. McKeag might have been sixty, though she looked older. The wild North Sea winters had kept her indoors, or within the shelter of that maze of narrow streets which was the next best thing, for chunks of her life months long, and it showed in her skin: soft, almost white, with a surface texture like talcum powder. She was a pretty woman, prettier than Alison, with fine features instead of her daughter's broad ones, and delicacy where Alison had strength. I presumed Alison took after her father.

She was in the kind of mourning you seldom see in England now: black dress, black stockings and shoes, even jet pins to hold her silver hair. The room she showed us to was half in darkness, a linen blind drawn over the window. Black crêpe framed a photo of Alison she had on the little dresser.

Everything in the room was little. The notorious weather of the Pentland Firth had bred a race of troglodytes to survive and prosper through it, and the most effective way was to build houses like caves, with thick walls and low ceilings. The small rooms were easy to heat, but I imagine most of the furniture had to be specially made. The doors were low and the window behind the blind not much more than a porthole.

But within those limitations it was a comfortable little house. The furniture was good, there was silver and china on the dresser, and a thick-piled carpet soaked up the draughts. It was a modest way of living, but not an impoverished one. Of course, Alison's father had owned land and a fishing-boat; there was no reason his widow should live hand-to-mouth.

She sat us down in the living-room, excused herself for a moment and returned with a silver tea-set on a big silver tray and a plate of substantial scones.

Harry had already introduced us and expressed our condolences. She received them graciously and without obvious distress. It occurred to me that it might have been some time since she saw Alison, so when we were supplied with our tea I asked.

It didn't take her too long to get at it. "She was home for George's funeral. That's six years now."

"Did you go down for her wedding?"

"No, I did not." She spoke slowly but without frailty; it was obviously the natural tempo of the islanders. "It was the middle of winter, so that was difficult. And then, it was a very quiet wedding they wanted. The registrar it was, not the minister."

It didn't take a great detective (much less two) to deduce that Mrs. McKeag had not approved of her daughter's match. That wasn't altogether surprising, in spite of McAllister's wealth: he was a lot older than Alison, and a cripple, and then there was the matter of the registrar. I wondered which had disturbed her most but found it difficult to ask.

Harry didn't. He's had a lot more practice than me. "Did you like Frazer McAllister?"

She pursed her lips. "I never met him. I was not particularly anxious to."

"Why was that?"

She had Alison's eyes, steady and knowing. "I did not approve of the marriage. I thought neither my daughter nor my prospective son-in-law were behaving either wisely or well." She stopped there, waiting to be asked to elucidate.

"You didn't think they'd be happy together?"

She sniffed. "Happiness was never an issue. She married him for his money. He married her for her womb. The only thing to be said for either of them was that they were honest about it. They never pretended to be in love."

I said, "How did they meet?"

Mrs. McKeag looked me straight in the eye. "They didn't meet, exactly. He advertised and she applied."

It really had been as simple as that. He had put a notice in the "Personal" column of a Scottish daily paper, describing himself as a rich man in need of an heir, and Alison had taken a long cool look at her job as a solicitor's clerk in Stirling and decided that while the wages of sin might be death, the hours were better.

They exchanged two or three letters. With the second, McAllister told her who he was and enclosed a photograph. It was a brave move that paid off, because it gave her time to come to terms with the idea before either of them was committed even to a meeting. With equal frankness she replied that she had seen his advertisement as a commercial proposition and, as long as that was his feeling too, she saw no reason why his misfortune should be a barrier. It would be no obstacle if it was anything else she was offering to sell him.

Plainly he appreciated her businesslike approach. They discussed what each might bring to the partnership and what dividend each might expect, and arranged to meet in Edinburgh, on neutral ground.

McAllister wanted an heir—a son or daughter. If Alison proved infertile she would co-operate in divorce proceedings, in return for a generous settlement to be specified, exactly, in a prenuptial contract.

What Alison wanted was the kind of lifestyle she could enjoy as McAllister's wife, far from the solicitor's office in Stirling and from worrying about the HP payments on her car. She would quite like to be a married woman and a mother; she could settle contentedly for being a rich divorcée if that was how it worked out. She saw no problem about a marriage of convenience, so long as it was convenient to both of them and neither of them expected it to be anything more. She rather hoped they'd get to like one another.

So it was done. The rich, damaged man married the twenty-seven-year-old girl with the broad, child-bearing hips, and it seemed to Mrs. McKeag from her daughter's letters that they had got to like one another quite quickly. Neither of them spoke of passion but they seemed to achieve an easy, comfortable relationship that was friendship or maybe a little more, and after nearly three years of marriage Alison wrote to say she was pregnant.

North of Stromness the road divided, the eastern branch heading back to Kirkwall and the little airport. The signpost for the northern branch numbered among its destinations Skara Brae, and I wondered if anything useful could come of visiting the place Alison had named her boat for. It was only a mile or so, so we followed the sign.

But instead of taking us anywhere it stopped us at the roadside, within sight of the sea but nothing else, and enjoined us to take a walk along a pale sandy footpath down towards the shore. Harry and I exchanged puzzled glances but we were in no particular hurry so we left the car and took the route indicated. While we walked, scuffing up puffs of sand, we talked.

I said, "Do you get the feeling we're missing something?"

"Like what?"

"I don't know. What went wrong? They were two such sensible people—cold-blooded if you like but sensible—they each knew what they wanted and four months ago they both had it. Even if one of them had had enough, they were cool enough to sort it out without bloodshed."

"McAllister wasn't going to risk losing his heir."

"It hadn't come to that. In fact it never would have come to that: Alison entered into a contract and she was going to honour it. Another man might have panicked and jumped the gun, but McAllister? It seems out of character—not so much the murder as misjudging the need for it."

One of Harry's eyebrows climbed. "You're not telling me you think Curragh did it after all?"

"No, I don't think he did. I think probably McAllister did it. I'm not convinced we have the right reason yet. And another thing—"

The other thing died on my lips as we breasted a grassy rise and
Skara Brae spread out before us. I had expected a village of low stone
houses like those in Stromness, huddled together against the North
Atlantic wind; and apart from the fact that no-one lived here now and
most of the roofs were gone, that was what we found. The difference
was that Skara Brae was built and occupied maybe four thousand years
before. It was older than Mycenae, not much younger than the pyramids of Egypt.

We wandered in silence over the turf which had grown over Skara
Brae. Beneath us, circular stone-walled homes displayed their square
stone furniture—a dresser here, a bed there, something that could have
been a sink close by the hearth, a quern, and niches everywhere to take
a wealth of Neolithic possessions: knives, fish-hooks, needles, scrapers,
maybe a string of beads and a few pots. Between the houses ran little
streets, shoulder high and not much more than shoulder broad, with
low lintels that even I would have had to crouch under. When the
whole thing was roofed over, streets and all, it would have been as
impervious to the outside elements as a badger's set or a mole's run.

Or the McAllisters' marriage, I thought then, sitting on a turf-
topped wall with my legs dangling in the street. All there was to be
seen of Skara Brae, before first a storm and then the excavators
breached its age-old integrity, was a low mound of rabbit-cropped turf
close above the beach; but underneath the turf was a warren of remark-
able and unexpected things, a secret world of deep complexity where
lives could be lived and children born, and murders done, quite unsus-
pected by those dwelling in, and attuned to the customs and parameters of, the open air. Different rules applied down there, because different things were important.

McAllister and his contract bride had grown fond of one another
over the space of four years. It wasn't love, but they liked each other:
the marriage wouldn't have survived three childless years if they hadn't.
By one means or another, then, she had contrived to produce a baby.

Perhaps Alison had loved Alex Curragh, at least for a time. Her life
under the turf mound had been warm and comfortable, untouched by
the hot and cold winds of passion and disappointment, but it was
natural for a young woman to wonder if she had made the right choice,
to long sometimes for an uncontrolled blast of fresh air.

But she hadn't left the Stirling solicitor to settle for life as a boat-
man's wife in Crinan. She was never going to leave Frazer McAllister

for an attractive, ardent, impoverished boy any more than McAllister was going to throw her out over one. He was an interruption in the even tenor of their lives, like one of them getting flu: something to put up with and get through, and not talk about too much. It was something they would not allow to dominate their lives to the point where either of them might see it as a serious threat to their future. What they had together suited them both: too well for Alison to throw it away for a late-firing adolescent fling. And too well for McAllister to hit the panic button and assume that she would, when all his experience of her must have told him her head was screwed on as tightly as the fourth wheel-nut on a flat tyre halfway up a motorway on a wet night.

And if Alison wasn't going to leave and take her baby with her, and McAllister wasn't going to jump to unwarranted conclusions, then he had no reason to kill her. So maybe he didn't.

"What was the other thing?" When Harry sat beside me and dangled his legs, his feet almost reached the flagstones.

I cast back, remembered. "That will. It's crazy. I haven't made a will. How many women of thirty-one have?"

"She took a very practical view of money."

"She had an affair, she ended it, she felt she owed the boy something —so she included him in her will? No way."

"But that's exactly what she did do."

"There had to be a reason—a proper reason, something that makes sense. I know what solicitors tell you but nobody under the age of forty makes a will."

He looked surprised and slightly affronted. "I did."

"Harry, you're the exception that proves all sorts of rules. The only young people who make wills are hypochondriacs."

I said it without import, almost as a joke, but as soon as it was out in the salt air and the sunshine between us, we both knew we could have struck pay-dirt. I felt my brain move up a gear. "Harry, could she have thought she was ill?"

[8]

After the ancient quiet of Orkney, arriving back in Glasgow was like visiting a madhouse. I thought at first it was the contrast, but actually the city—at least, those parts of it which concerned us—was in uproar. The police station was at the epicentre, and we got an explanation of a kind when DCI Baker stopped rushing round like a decapitated hen long enough to accept a cup of tea and a chocolate biscuit.

"That bastard McAllister," he gasped then. He was perched on the edge of the table as if sitting in a chair would take up too much time. "He's put a price on Curragh's head."

"What?" I couldn't believe what I was hearing. We were a long way from home, but not that far.

Harry said, shortly and with uncharacteristic savagery, "Sling the sod inside."

"It's not that simple." Baker was beginning to look frayed at the edges. "I put it to him straight and of course he denied it. He said what he'd done was ask that anyone who could help the police find a missing witness should do so, and he'd reimburse any expenses incurred. There's nothing illegal in that. I can't even do him for obstruction.

"But you know and I know, and everyone in his employ knows, and probably by now every cowboy north of the border knows, exactly what the old bastard wants and is willing to pay for. He wants Alex Curragh found and brought back, and he doesn't give a monkey's what state he's in. None of the people that reward is geared to will ask the kid politely more than once. Some of them won't ask him once. If he's dragged in here black and blue, I shall reckon we've got off lightly. It could be worse than that."

"Surely to God," I whispered, horrified, "he can't offer a reward for a man dead or alive?"

"He doesn't have to," said Harry. His lips were tight. "If the reward's there, there'll be people prepared to go to any lengths to get it. If they try too hard and he ends up dead, they're no worse off than if they never found him or they couldn't bring him in. They'll just roll him into the nearest bog and go home, and we'll never know. If he ends up hurt enough to send them to prison they'll do the same thing. Christ almighty, McAllister might as well declare open season on him. If we don't find him first, he's liable to end up dead."

"Is there no law against it?"

"Oh yes. But he's a bit of an expert, isn't he, at staying just the right side of laws." He had a thought then. I saw it strike him, saw the ripples of it in his eyes, guessed what it was and wondered if he'd have the nerve to come out with it.

He didn't have to. The same idea had occurred to Baker, and he didn't have to worry about facing me over the breakfast table every morning if it didn't work out. I am not at my sweetest and most generous best in the mornings.

Baker said, "Mrs. Marsh, you and McAllister understand each other pretty well. I think he listens when you talk, and that's more than he does for me. Will you talk to him?— Tell him we'll find Curragh, bring him back while we get this sorted out, but if he doesn't call his dogs off he's apt to be responsible for an innocent man's death. Hell, you know what to say to him. Will you go?"

I had no option. I didn't know if Frazer McAllister was more likely to listen to me than an officer in his city's police force. I didn't know if this understanding Baker spoke of amounted to anything, or if it was just some residue of good manners that prevented McAllister shouting as loudly at women as he did at other men. It would be interesting and possibly useful to talk with him again now I knew more about his marriage than he had volunteered, but even that was a minor consideration.

The seminal point was that a man could get killed, and though it might be I couldn't prevent his death, I could at least prevent myself feeling responsible for it. If Alex Curragh died—or disappeared, and we never knew for sure if he was dead—and I hadn't done everything I or anyone else could think of to stop it, the next several months would take a lot of living through. Harry would be in for some pretty miserable breakfasts.

But it was Harry who made the token protest, which I appreciated. It wasn't much more than a token, designed not so much to obstruct as to put on record the unease that probably all three of us felt. "You're not forgetting that McAllister is a suspect in the killing of his wife? If he did it, he's hunting Curragh not to bring him back but to silence him. If he did it, nothing Clio can say to him will make him less determined, but she could put herself in danger as well."

Baker nodded. "I am aware of that. I'm not suggesting she goes alone. If she's willing to, I suggest the three of us go together—and immediately afterwards, whatever you decide to do yourself, sir, I think Mrs. Marsh should go home."

Harry looked at me askance and there was a glint almost of humour in his eyes. "Well, dear, what do you think?"

He wasn't asking whether I'd talk to McAllister for them, but that was the question I chose to answer. "Come on, then, let's get it over with. Which den do we beard the lion in?"

McAllister was at home. A terse phone call from Baker ensured that he would stay there until we arrived.

Most of the way up I was wondering what I was going to say, rehearsing arguments and even emotions before rejecting them as trite and inappropriate, even unworthy. Finally I decided that anything worth saying and worth hearing would come of a dialogue, not a prepared speech, and stopped rehearsing and watched the scenery instead.

Because the best hope seemed to lie in a dialogue, and if all three of us marched in there it would develop into either a committee meeting or a slanging-match, when we drew up on the gravel beneath the front door of McAllister's castle I asked Harry and Baker to stay with the car and went up alone.

I wasn't present when Baker phoned him, but from his surprised expression I gathered McAllister hadn't been led to expect me. He looked past my shoulder to the granite steps. "Where's—er—what's-his-face?"

I didn't believe that, after a number of meetings and one protracted interview, he had forgotten DCI Baker's name. It was part of the game he played, of bolstering his ego by diminishing other people's. It was only a game—no ego ever needed less bolstering than his—but it had become a habit.

I declined to play it with him. "Down below, with the other wee plod. It's me he wanted you to talk to. Well, listen to, actually."

He had already recovered from the surprise, and acknowledged with a quirk of the lip the failure of his great-man-impressing-the-peasants routine. Now, his eyes warming but still guarded, he stood back and ushered me in. Mrs. Lilley must have been busy with the baby—I doubt if he'd have answered his own door otherwise, not in all the circumstances.

He showed me into the sitting-room, offered me a drink, poured one for himself when I declined. "What did Mr. Baker"—a fractional emphasis on the remembered name—"want me to listen to you saying?"

"Call off your dogs. Alex Curragh didn't kill Alison, but you're going to get him killed if you put a price on his head." Whatever else it was, it was to the point.

The warmth died out of his eyes. He was used to being the most outspoken member of any company. Also, he didn't much like being seen as a gangster except at his own invitation. "If he didn't kill her, why did he run?" The gravelly voice was harsh, cold.

It was hard to explain. I thought I understood the state of mind which the last few days had induced in him, and which had made him react in that dangerously irrational way, but it was hard to find the words to describe it. But McAllister was waiting, so I tried. I told him about the episode with the glass.

"Why did he hold a broken glass at my throat when he'd no intention of hurting me? Because he's very young and very scared, and because nothing in his life till now prepared him for what has happened to him, physically and emotionally, during the last week. He understands almost nothing of what's going on: not what happened at the Fairy Isles, not the accusation that he killed Alison, not how the police work—not even how the city works, that's home and second nature to you and me.

"He's lost here. He understands the sea, maybe the forest and the moor, but stick him down in Sauchiehall Street and he can't remember which way to watch for traffic. He feels desperately vulnerable here, prey to forces beyond his control. So when the opportunity presented itself, he took it and got out. He isn't going far. In a day or two he'll turn up back home, and by then and in his own surroundings he'll have his head together enough to give the police all the co-operation they need.

"Unless some cowboy out for the bounty you've posted hammers the living daylights out of him, in which case he'll die on some bleak fell for no better reason than that he loved your wife. And if that happens, a lot of people are going to need convincing that wasn't exactly what you had in mind when you offered this reward for him."

"You seem to be suggesting," McAllister said softly, "that I should feel some sympathy for my wife's murderer because of his bereavement."

"I told you, Alex didn't kill Alison. He was returning to the *Skara Sun* when she blew up. He'd bought a toy in Tayvallich. For his son." I told him the rest of it, all that Alex had told me.

He was watching me very closely, like a dog watching a rabbit. It might have been unnerving but somehow it wasn't. My husband and his colleague were only the thickness of a wall away—a castle wall, admittedly, but at least there was no moat. More than that, McAllister's interest, while acute, wasn't threatening. I felt myself in no greater danger than when Alex Curragh fended me off with his broken glass.

"You think you know, don't you?" he said. "About Peter. About Alison and me, and her affair with Curragh. How?"

"Harry and I flew up to Orkney earlier today."

"Ah." The breath ran out of him slowly and there was comprehension in the sigh. "So you were talking to her. The Iron Maiden."

I didn't quite manage not to smile. "Alison's mother, yes."

"She reckoned to know about us, did she?"

"Alison kept in touch. She didn't approve of your marriage. I suppose you know that."

"Oh aye, I knew that. She told you it was a marriage of convenience, I suppose. What else?"

"That she got the impression from Alison's letters that you were both pretty happy anyway."

McAllister's eyes glimmered with what could almost have been unshed tears. "So she knew that. I'm glad. What else?"

I wouldn't necessarily have told him, but in fact there was nothing else. "That was all."

He nodded slowly. "Alison mustn't have told her. I don't blame her. But I'm going to tell you. I never meant to. We never meant to tell anyone. For all our sakes—mine, Alison's and Peter's. The world's a narrow-minded place, and anyway it had no business knowing. But if it's made up its mind that Alison betrayed me, and maybe I killed her because of it, I guess I owe it to the three of us to put the record straight.

"Alison took up with Curragh for one reason and one reason only: to give me a child. It wasn't her fault she wasn't getting pregnant, it was mine—the echo of that damn chemical explosion still reverberating round my body. Ending our marriage would have gained me nothing. So she didn't have to do it. She did it for me, for love."

They could have gone through the normal medical channels, joined an Artificial Insemination by Donor programme. But neither of them was enthusiastic about channels of any sort. Alison objected to the clinicality of it. McAllister disliked the idea that a record might exist into the future showing he was not the father of his child. They talked long and seriously, and decided there would be less trauma, fewer long-term repercussions, if they set up a channel of their own and got Alison pregnant without medical intervention.

They chose Peter's father together and very carefully. From Alison's point of view, it was necessary that he be someone she could like. Both of them wanted to be sure the baby wouldn't inherit any health or character defects, so it seemed best to select someone Alison had known for a little time and got on well with. They opted for a younger man in the belief that the ties between him and Alison would be flimsier. Alison knew why she was doing this; if the man looked on it as the one-night-stand of a rich, bored woman the risk of emotional complications should be minimal.

Crinan was a regular port of call for Alison. She'd had work done on her boat there a couple of times when she'd struck a problem too far from Oban to limp back, and she'd talked boats to the back of a young man's head while he tinkered in the bowels of her engines. McAllister didn't want to meet him, but agreed that he was a good choice.

The next stage was accomplished easily enough. Alison was an intelligent, sophisticated, not insensitive woman who had her heart and mind set on seduction and the confidence to carry it through. Alex was twenty-one, all he knew of the world was Crinan and the boats that passed through it; if he wasn't still a virgin he might as well have been. He was easy prey for the McAllisters, a young man bowled over by the flattering attentions of an attractive older woman.

She said one engine was running rough and asked him to come out in the *Sun* and listen to it. They motored round Danna Island and up Loch Sween, and dropped the hook in the Fairy Isles lagoon. It was the middle of the day and still only April, there was no other vessel there. They made love in the cabin with the reflected brilliance of the water dancing in splashes of light on the coach-house ceiling.

A month later she made another excuse to take him out and the same thing happened. Shortly after that a pregnancy test proved positive.

McAllister was both thrilled and relieved. It was what he wanted, why he'd gritted his teeth while his wife went to another man. But it had been harder on him than he had expected and he was immensely glad it was over.

And Alison? He found it hard to judge how Alison felt. Clearly she was happy to have achieved what she had set out to. She seemed glad she wouldn't have to see Alex again, but more as if she felt badly about using him than about being used. She grew listless and moody, then restless. She said nothing, but gradually McAllister realised what the problem was. Alison had fallen in love with her stud.

108 *The Going Down of the Sun*

He tried to talk to her about it. She denied it. He said it was natural in the circumstances, she mustn't feel guilty about it. She said there was nothing to feel guilty about, it was just her hormones affecting her moods.

He thought that part way through her pregnancy she started seeing Curragh again. He couldn't be sure: he asked, she denied it, he wouldn't interrogate her. He felt to blame.

He was hurt too, but not so terribly surprised. He hoped and believed that it wouldn't last, that the novelty of having a perfect body in bed beside her would wear off and she'd tire of a young labourer who had nothing else to offer her. He watched, patient and anxious, for signs that she was coming back to him—not physically, she had never been away that often or that long, but in spirit and mind. He missed her. From the pain it was giving her, he thought she missed him too.

He blamed neither Alison nor Curragh so much as himself, his own egotistical wants. It had been a calculated risk; they had played with fire and they'd got burned. He still hoped that once the baby came they'd find their way back to an equilibrium, in which case it would all have been worthwhile, even the hurting.

Perhaps they would have had fewer problems if they'd been a bit less careful in selecting a father for Peter. But they didn't want just anybody with rough and ready ways and a dirty-weekend philosophy. They looked for someone kind and caring, and when it came to the point Alex Curragh cared enough to want to make a future with the woman he loved, and was kind enough for Alison to recognise that she would lose something valuable whichever way she chose.

Right up to word of the explosion coming through, McAllister expected to get her back. He knew she was going to Curragh; she'd said goodbye to him as if she meant it. He didn't know until I told him that she had decided to end their affair, but he believed she would, if not soon then sometime.

The news that his wife was dead, rolled by the salt tide with the rest of the debris from the *Skara Sun*, at first struck him to his knees. Then the anger which had served him before surged again to save him from the dissolution of grief. It carried him forward through the days, reinforced at intervals by the failure of the police to make the man he blamed accountable, finally overflowing in a vicious cateract at the discovery that Curragh had evaded custody and disappeared back up country. His response had been typical of the man: pragmatic, ruthless and fast.

[9]

I had no idea how long I had sat there listening to him talk. Only when the low, gravelly voice rumbled into silence and the parade of powerful, disturbing images rolled to a halt did I remember the two men waiting in the car outside, their ears cocked for sounds of mayhem. There wouldn't be any but they couldn't know that; however long we took they'd sit there worrying, but I wasn't going to sacrifice McAllister's confidence in order to put their minds at rest. While he would talk, I would listen.

Except I wasn't here to hear his tragedy but to prevent another, and however much light was being shed by his narrative it wasn't lessening the danger he had whistled up for Alex Curragh.

I said, "Nothing that happened was Curragh's fault. You used him when it suited you, thought you could dump him when you'd finished with him. Now you've put his life in danger. Why? Because he loved Alison? You *wanted* him to love Alison. Or because she loved him? She wasn't an automaton—you can't turn emotions on and off like a lightswitch. Neither of them was to blame for what happened."

"I could forgive him for loving her. But he killed her. Damn it, woman, I know Ali's feelings got the better of her. We risked that from the start, we both knew it, we were ready to cope with it. But she didn't deserve to die for it, and I'm going to get the wee shite that killed her."

I shook my head in despair. I just wasn't getting through to him. So much depended on my being able to convince him—too much, and I'd almost nothing left to say. He knew everything I knew now, and he still believed Alex had blown up the *Sun*. I couldn't prove that he hadn't, only repeat it. "That isn't what happened."

Angrily he turned on me. "That's easy for you to say. You always thought I did it—because of Peter, for fear of losing him. Well, I know I didn't, and that leaves Curragh."

It wasn't as easy as he thought. I found his account pretty convincing too. But I've never believed in passing maniacs, and the accident theory just didn't stand up. Not with the gas detector switched off.

"I don't think he even knew about her will."

"Well, he would say that, wouldn't he?" And of course he would.

"You knew. But she didn't throw it at you in an argument, did she?"

Again the shrewd glance out of the tortured face. His emotions moved as quickly as his mind. "No, that was a lie. She wanted to do something for him. He hadn't much; he was trying to get the money together for a boat of his own. She didn't think he'd accept it as a gift, thought he'd be offended if she offered. So she made it a bequest."

"She was thirty years old. He'd have had to wait forty years."

"That must have worried him too."

It wasn't his thinking that concerned me, it was hers. If you want to help someone do something with their life you don't wait until they're sixty years old. "When did she make the will?"

"The bequest to Curragh she added as a codicil after she was pregnant. The will itself she made after we were married."

"That didn't strike you as odd?"

Clearly it hadn't. Of course, he was a man to whom the moving around of money was second nature. "A marriage revokes an existing will."

I stared. "You mean, as a single girl of twenty-six working as a clerk in Stirling she had already made a will?"

He nodded, surprised at my surprise. "She worked for a solicitor, you mind. And then, she had a little capital of her own. The family farm was sold after George McKeag died and her mother bought the house in town. Some of the money from that came to her, and she had a half share in her father's boat. It must have added up to around . . ." He paused for a moment, calculating.

I knew what it added up to. "Fifteen thousand pounds." That was the money she had bequeathed to Alex: her own money, the money she'd brought to her marriage. At last the amount made sense. She had wanted to thank Alex, not reward him. She wouldn't pay him with McAllister's money. Her own was hers to give with honour.

McAllister nodded slowly, thoughtfully. He hadn't appreciated the significance of the figure until just then. It confirmed something he had always known. "Aye. She was some lady, my wife."

I was still thinking about what he'd said. It seemed curious that the McKeags, with their history of self-reliance, would sell the family farm. "Alison had a brother, hadn't she? Wasn't he interested in farming?"

Again McAllister looked faintly surprised. "He was of course. He ran that place of theirs for nigh on ten years after the father died, and worked at the fishing too. But Alison's mother couldn't manage alone, and Alison had no mind to go back to the island, so they sold up."

Dates and figures danced like spots before my eyes. I couldn't get them to agree. There was something here that I really wasn't understanding. "Alison's father's been dead over ten years? Mrs. McKeag said she was home for the funeral six years ago."

McAllister saw my problem. "So she was. But it wasn't her father's funeral. That was when George died."

Comprehension dawned. "George was the brother?" Mrs. McKeag never said otherwise, I'd just assumed she was speaking of her husband. "And he ran the farm for ten years, and then he died too. Was he a lot older than Alison?"

McAllister shrugged. "A few years. About eight, I think."

He'd only been thirty-three when he died. I had the sudden dreadful urge to comment that, while losing a daughter in her early thirties could be construed as misfortune, losing a son young as well smacked of carelessness. I fought the urge and thank God it passed. "What was it, an accident?"

"Aye. At least, the family always believed it was. The insurance company wasn't so sure. They paid out on Alison's share of the boat but they wouldn't meet the claim for George's interest."

The blood within my veins seemed to run slower, and cool. In the snug room, insulated from the real world by four-foot walls, time seemed first to stand still and then flip backwards. I said, very carefully, "Boat?"

McAllister nodded, unperturbed. "That fishing boat they had from the old man. George was working on her in the harbour one night. There was a fire; George was killed and the boat was gutted."

Two things staggered me to my heels: that both George McKeag and his sister should have died in catastrophic boating incidents six years apart, and that McAllister seemed to have read no great significance into that. Not enough to mention it to the police. Not even enough to keep it from me, though it had only come out because I chanced to ask the right question.

He'd even told me that the insurance company refused to meet the claim of George's estate, and I could think of only one reason for that. The premiums were paid or they wouldn't have entertained Alison's claim as joint owner. They believed George had started the fire himself, deliberately.

And Alison had seen it. Her mother said she was home for the funeral, but she must have been on the island some days before. I found a voice from somewhere. "Alison was in Stromness that night, wasn't she?"

"That's right." He was watching me in some puzzlement. Astute as he was, he still couldn't see where I was going and so didn't understand the hollowness in my face and voice. "She was home visiting for a week or so. There was a dance that night in the Stromness Hilton." I had noticed the hotel overlooking the harbour. I couldn't remember the name, but it wasn't the Hilton. "When the fire started they all went outside. She'd been watching for a couple of minutes before she realised it was their boat—hers and George's.

"It wouldn't have made any difference, there was nothing anyone could have done. It burned to the water-line. It was after that they sold the farm and the old lady moved into town." Mrs. McKeag may have been ten years his senior, not more. The puzzled frown between the remnants of his eyebrows deepened. "Did she tell you this—Alison's mother?"

"No, Alex Curragh did. He said Alison saw a boat burn once, that was why she was so careful. She didn't want to die the same way."

Even the purple side of his face turned pale. He ground out, "The bastard!"

I shook my head. "McAllister, I know it's hard but face the facts. Alison's brother committed suicide, and he did it by setting fire to his boat. I don't know why, we may be able to find out. Six years later, when she'd been under enormous stress for fourteen months, feeling herself ripped apart by her feelings for two men and a baby, Alison took the same way out. She said goodbye to you, she said goodbye to Curragh and sent him away, and when she thought she was alone she turned off the gas detector—in case it should wake Harry and me in time for us to stop her—turned on the gas, closed all the vents; and after a time she struck a match."

He threw me out. Not quite bodily, though I think he would have done if he'd had to.

It quite simply hadn't occurred to him that Alison's death was suicide, and when I put it to him he wouldn't consider it. I tried to reason with him. He would not be reasoned with.

He accused me of collusion, of trying to protect Curragh at the cost

of Alison's memory. He accused me of being infatuated with him myself. I pointed out, with what dignity I could muster, that I was ten
years older than Alison and old enough to be the boy's mother. In view
of the fact that McAllister was old enough to have been Alison's father
it wasn't the most tactful thing I could have said. It was around then
that he showed me to the door.

Mindful of the unguarded steps beyond, I didn't continue the argument over the threshhold. I turned and came down, and both Harry
and DCI Baker, who had heard our voices raised in dispute and were
on the points of intervening, were out of the car and waiting for my
report.

Before I could catch my breath and explain, Harry murmured, "You
talked him round, then."

I ignored him. "Alex didn't kill Alison. I don't think McAllister did
either. She killed herself, and she did it that way because that was how
her brother did it six years before."

"Why?"

It was two possible questions. I answered the one I had an answer to.
"Because she loved two men and one baby, and she couldn't resolve the
dilemma without hurting someone she cared about deeply. Because if
she left Alex she expected to spend the rest of her life wanting him;
and if she left Peter with McAllister she'd spend the rest of her life
wanting him; and if she took Peter away from McAllister she'd spend
the rest of her life hating herself. She saw no way out except a Viking
funeral."

I told them what McAllister had told me and what I had pieced
together for myself. I believed I had finally got it right. They listened in
silence. Once Harry looked up at the little castle looming greyly over
us. Once Baker kicked unhappily at the tyre of the car.

When I had finished, Baker said, "Will he call off the manhunt?"

"I don't know." Suddenly I felt weary, a deep weariness of bone and
spirit. "If he believes me when he calms down enough to think about it
he will. He's not a vicious man. But he'd much sooner not believe it,
because it makes him and his need for an heir the reason for Alison's
death. If he can persuade himself that I'm wrong, he won't lift a finger
to help Alex. We have to find him, because wherever the hell he is
there'll be someone who can get to him for enough money."

Harry was looking away now, over the hills. He said quietly, "When
Alison made her will, she wouldn't expect to be in that quandary twelve

months later. This was the very start of the enterprise, remember, before the emotional entanglements began to hurt. All right, she wanted to thank Curragh for her baby. Was she really content for him to wait forty or fifty years for the expression of her gratitude to reach him?"

He was absolutely right. If I hadn't been side-tracked by the role and fate of her brother George I'd have spotted it earlier. She hadn't spent twelve months planning her suicide, at least not for the reason I'd come up with. I said, "Shit," with feeling, and from Baker's expression that shocked him more than anything that had gone before.

"Or were you right," Harry went on, "when we talked about this at Skara Brae and you wondered if Alison thought she was ill? Maybe she half expected to die young—not necessarily at thirty-one but in middle-age. If so, the bequest to Curragh makes a lot more sense."

So did other things, not least her marriage to a man sh.e hardly knew. She would have worked her way out of Stirling if that was what she wanted, found a man to care for and had a family. But these things take time, and if time was her enemy she would have been looking for shortcuts.

Baker was flicking his eyes between us like a man sitting too close to a Wimbledon final. Then his gaze settled on me. "You're a doctor. How do we check that?"

With difficulty, I suspected. So much depended on what it was she thought she had. "The autopsy will give the definitive answer—when they find her, if there's enough of her left to work on. If she was seeing a doctor about it there'll be a record of any tests that were made and their findings. Failing that, the hospital that delivered her baby may know something."

Baker looked glum. "I know doctors. They won't want to talk about it."

I know doctors too. I said sharply, "They don't have any choice. Their patient is dead, and a man's life could depend on establishing why. Put them on that spot and they'll talk."

Harry said, "Somebody had better talk to Mrs. McKeag again. If her son killed himself for the same reason her daughter expected to die young, that's a family problem and she's the only family remaining. Nobody's more likely to know about it than her."

"According to McAllister she never accepted George's death was other than an accident."

"She may have to accept it. The stakes are too high for people's sensibilities to be humoured."

"OK," said Baker briskly, "so what are we doing? I'll chase up Alison McAllister's medical record, see if there's anything there that'll help."

"I'll go back to Orkney," said Harry. "Clio, do you want to come with me? Or can she be more help to you, Chief Inspector?"

It was possible, but the Glasgow police must have had more expert witnesses than me to call on. But I wasn't going to Orkney either—Harry needed no help that I could give him in questioning a stubborn old lady with her family honour to protect.

I said, "I'm going to look for Alex. I'll start in Crinan—I don't think he'll be a million miles from there. Once he's safe we have all the time we need to work out what happened."

Baker looked doubtful. "As you think best. But half the police on the west coast are looking out for him—I don't know what you can do that they can't."

"Probably nothing. Except that Alex will be looking out for them too, and he may not go to the same lengths to avoid me."

It was a long shot, I knew. It was more that I wanted to be doing something useful rather than trailing round after either Harry or Baker, waiting to hear the worst. Also, all those summers sailing had given me a familiarity with the fine detail of the area Alex Curragh would make for that perhaps even the local police couldn't match. Alex was a sailing man: even if he was on foot he'd make for the shore, and there wasn't a beach or a cove between Ballachulish and the Mull of Kintyre where I hadn't dropped anchor sometime in the last fifteen years. If he went to ground, and unless they put the Army in, I had as good a chance of finding him as anyone.

After a moment Harry nodded. "Yes, all right. Just remember there may be others looking for him, besides you and the police."

I dropped Harry back at the airport and kept the car. But I didn't go straight to Crinan. I went first to Duncan Galbraith's newspaper.

Their star reporter was hunched over a notebook an inch thick, filled with tightly packed scrawl that made doctors' handwriting look like copperplate. It was shorthand, of course, though that didn't occur to me until I'd spent half a minute trying to decipher it over his shoulder.

Then he looked up with a harrassed grin. "Sorry, I'm with you now. If I'd lost track of what the defence counsel said the prosecution witness had said to the defendant about the defendant's wife, I'd never have made sense of this if I'd lived to be a hundred." He'd spent the day in court. I gathered it was a way of keeping him out of Frazer McAllister's hair without actually sending him to Aberdeen. "What's happening? What have I missed?"

"Nothing, yet. Do you want a story?"

"Of course."

"You know Alex Curragh's missing? I'm going to find him. Do you want to come?"

"Yes."

As quickly as that we fixed it up. He needed an hour to finish his court report. It was already evening, it would be dark before we could reach Crinan anyway, so that was no problem. I went back to the hotel to throw a few things into a case; Galbraith it seemed, like many a hack reporter with pretentions, habitually kept an overnight bag in his office. I picked him up an hour later and we took the Loch Lomond road, and only then did I tell him exactly what we were doing and why.

It was a calculated risk, but not much of one. If he'd leapt out at traffic lights and dashed for the nearest telephone, probably his paper's lawyers would have squashed the story before it ever saw a compositor. It was still nearly all speculation; McAllister had ways of discouraging speculation about him. Galbraith might have had more luck with the London papers, but I couldn't see him doing that while he had an exclusive shot at the full, unexpurgated, inactionable story. And in fact he never so much as tried the door handle when we stopped for petrol. So as we travelled north and west the day ended.

Around Inverary, Duncan Galbraith said thoughtfully, "We know why I wanted to come. Why did you want me to come?"

I said, "I'm after your body," thinking it was a good job Baker wasn't with us, and we both giggled.

"Seriously," said Galbraith.

"I want a witness. Oh, I'm glad of your company, and I may very well be glad of your help, but mostly I want a witness. If anybody starts playing silly buggers I want it to be more than his word against mine. And if McAllister is calling the tune, I want him to know he could get famous quite quickly by pushing us around."

In the faint backwash of light from the instruments he looked doubtful. "If you're planning on threatening him with me, I think you could be disappointed."

"If you get a story, you'll get it published, one way or another. He knows that."

"Are you sure you've got the right chap?"

"Why did you leave Edinburgh?"

He blinked. "I got another offer."

"A better offer?"

"Not exactly." He grinned. "The guy I'd spent the last six months slagging off bought the paper I was on."

"He sacked you?"

"No. But I didn't want to work for him."

"You wanted to go on slagging him off?"

"I wanted to be free to." There was something odd about how he said it, a hint in his manner and his voice that there was more he wasn't saying.

I said, "I got the right chap."

"You reckon?" He looked at me sideways, and the green glow put a hungry cast on his ample cheeks. "The man who bought my paper was Frazer McAllister, and when I came to Glasgow he bought a good slice of the one I'm on now."

While Duncan was taking rooms for us at the hotel I went round and introduced myself to the local constabulary. I told them who I was and what I was doing, and referred them to DCI Baker if they had any problems with that. I can't say they were wildly glad to see me, but nor did they raise any particular difficulties. They had, of course, been watching for Alex Curragh since about midday; they hadn't seen him or found anyone who had, and they didn't think it likely that I'd succeed where they had failed. I didn't think it all that likely myself, but it was something else to try and Alex needed people working on his behalf.

The Crinan police had also been warned about McAllister's bounty, and were watching out for anyone who might be interested in that. But it was the tourist season, strangers in cars and on boats would be drifting through Crinan with no obvious purpose from now until September. The only way a bounty-hunter would be different would be when he started asking questions in the local pub.

Which is where I wanted to start, but the pub was closed now. I dragged the manager of our hotel away from his TV, gave him a potted version of my talk with the police and asked what he knew, but though he was civil enough and willing to help, he actually knew very little. He wasn't a local man, and though when the television news carried a photograph after the explosion he had recognised Alex Curragh, he knew nothing of his haunts and habits.

It wasn't far short of midnight now. I phoned our hotel in Glasgow but Harry wasn't back yet. Duncan Galbraith and I shared a supper of coffee and sandwiches, then went to our beds.

III

Thursday

The sun rose early. So did we. We met briefly over breakfast, then Duncan went to see the people at the yard where Alex worked and I drove south into the crowding green of the Knapdale Forest on a narrow little road that brought me at length to the little stone house where his father lived. From the map I judged that the Fairy Isles, where all this started, were only a couple of miles away, but most of that was dense woodland. I couldn't see the loch, let alone the islands.

I had felt guilty about calling at this early hour but I needn't have worried. Sinclair Curragh hadn't slept last night and I doubt if he'd slept the night before. The police had visited him several times since the explosion, including once about three o'clock this morning when they very gently and politely insisted on seeing every room as well as the outbuildings.

More disturbingly, he had also had two callers asking directions. One produced a map, and while Curragh was showing him a route he got the strong impression that the other was looking in at the cottage windows.

"But Alex hasn't been here, has he?" I couldn't imagine it. If he was hiding he'd do it properly. If he came back he'd go to the police.

Sinclair Curragh shook his head. He was a short, stocky man, much shorter than Alex, with grizzled hair and a weather-beaten face. He might have been a shepherd or a trawlerman. He was Frazer McAllister's age but he looked older. It wasn't the weather on his skin that had done that but the fear in his heart.

"I told the sergeant," he said. "Alex hasn't been home since before . . ." The explosion. The echo of it was still audible as a tremor in his voice. "I heard it. I didn't know what it was. I didn't think for a minute . . ."

I said, "Mr. Curragh, we don't think Alex was responsible for that. We don't think he's done anything wrong. But there are those who blame him for what happened, and we have to find him before they do. Can you help, at all?"

I met Duncan back in Crinan, beside the little harbour. He looked he'd been waiting a while. In his tweed jacket and his Fair Isle pullover and his journalist's regulation suede shoes, he looked just a little out of place.

"Any luck?"

He rocked a hand. "Some. Nobody's seen Alex or heard from him. Nobody knows where he is. But the feeling is he's back in the Sound. A sailing boat went missing from Machrihanish last night and the smart money says Alex took it."

I unfolded the map, found Machrihanish near the end of the Kintyre peninsula. Any boat leaving Glasgow for the north or west would pass within a few miles. It was maybe half a day's chugging from the Clyde, and he could have been landed there any time after nightfall and no-one any the wiser.

It was entirely in character that he would find a boat to continue his escape. He was probably under sail at first light and well into the Sound of Jura by breakfast-time. Right now he could be only a few miles away, cruising easily on the steady breeze, or more likely beached in a cove somewhere with his sails struck and maybe his mast shipped to avoid being seen. If he could live off the land he could stay out of sight for as long as he cared to.

"Do the police know about the missing boat?"

"I got the impression that maybe no-one had got round to telling them yet."

I wasn't surprised. These were small, close-knit communities— they'd back one of their own against the authorities any day. They couldn't know that closing ranks this time could get their boy killed.

I said, "What about our boat?"

Duncan looked unhappy. "They're getting it ready now. Are you sure you know how to handle it?"

It was a good question. If it had been a sailing boat I'd have had no worries: if it sails I can sail it. But sails wouldn't cover the sea-miles quickly enough to find Alex Curragh before the ungodly did. I'd asked Duncan to hire us something with speed and range, and we went back to the yard now, via the grocer's to take on supplies, to see what he'd come up with.

The *Fairy Flag* was the child of an unnatural union between a drag-racer and a landing-craft. Her cabin may have started life as a potting shed, her hull as an ice-breaker. She looked like a cow, she smelled like a cow, and when I took her out into Crinan Loch it came as no surprise to find that she also steered like a cow. But on behind were two big, strong engines, and tanks filled to capacity would take us halfway round the British Isles. A thing of beauty she was not, but she'd do our job.

Half an hour out, with the sun high in a blue sky and the waters of the Sound gone in laughter-wrinkles from a friendly little breeze, Duncan retired to the potting shed with white knuckles and a pale green complexion. It hadn't occurred to me to wonder if he was a decent sailor. It hadn't occurred to me that he'd need to be to ship as supercargo aboard a big sturdy cruiser in inshore waters in June. I wondered how he'd cope if we had to row ashore in the rubber dinghy.

I left the wheel just long enough to dive below and drag him out. "That's the last place you want to be if you're feeling off-colour. What you need is fresh air and a job to occupy your mind."

"What I need," he replied faintly, "is somewhere quiet to die."

I tried to get him scanning the shore, but using the binoculars made him worse. Studying the map made him worse still. So I put him on the wheel and made him steer. "It's just like a car." Except that she was longer, pivoted in the water about a third of the way down her length, and you steer from the back rather than the front. On the other hand, there are no pedestrians. "That's the compass. We're running south-west—there." I showed him. "Keep her head about 220 degrees, that'll keep us parallel to the shore. If any islands get in the way, feel free to deviate; ditto any small boats full of screaming people."

Actually I didn't intend to abandon him utterly to the erratic mercies of this creature of his nightmares. Beside him in the wheel-house I could keep an eye on his progress without it occupying all my time and attention. These I turned on the shoreline running along our flank and the occasional small island occulting it. The binoculars didn't make me feel sick.

I had assumed Alex could be nearly home by now, but when I thought about it that didn't seem too likely. If he'd taken the missing boat at first light, he might have sailed for four or five hours but then the risk of being spotted would send him under cover. Also, by then he'd be ready to sleep. Five hours of the kindly south wind we'd had all morning might have brought him just north of Gigna, if he'd used every minute and every breath. More probably he was ashore somewhere south of a line drawn through the island to Clachan on the Kintyre peninsula and Ardmore Point on Islay. We wouldn't reach that line for a couple of hours.

Navigation was the saving of Duncan Galbraith. With his attention divided between the wheel, the compass rose and a narrow channel of sea a few points either side of our bow, he hadn't the leisure to feel ill. The roses returned to his cheeks, the sun began to burn his nose and the breeze blew his thinning hair about in an engaging fashion. Before long he looked he was enjoying himself, albeit in a rather daring, dangerous sort of way.

I wasn't enjoying myself. The sun and wind were pleasant, the surroundings as spectacular as ever, the *Fairy Flag* an acceptable if not ideal access to them. But it needed more than the wonders of navigation to take my mind off what was bothering me. I was worried—about Alex, about the men who called at his father's house, about what McAllister was doing now. I wished Harry was nearer than the Orkneys.

As the day warmed up we found ourselves with company on the Sound. Two pocket cruisers, obviously travelling together, passed us northward bound off Loch Killisport. A handful of sailing dinghies wove intricate patterns like bright-winged butterflies up in West Loch Tarbert. Twice we were buzzed by a little red speedboat, and just north of Gigna we crossed the wash of the Islay ferry. I saw nothing that fitted the description of the missing boat, a fifteen-foot day sailer with a clinker hull and tan sails. But then I didn't really expect to. It wouldn't be as easy as that.

Once the long narrow island of Gigna came up on our bows, I began searching in earnest. It was one of Alex's haunts, according to his father. With the engines throttled back and Duncan steering closer inshore than he really considered safe, I ran the binoculars over every foot of every beach and bay, looking for a small boat anchored or hauled up, or signs of a camp on the shore. I had hopes of the little anchorage at the north end of the island where fingers of rock reached into the sea and defined a couple of well-sheltered bays, but we found only a cabin cruiser in one and a tent pitched beside the other.

We cruised clear round the island, poking our bows into every nook and cranny, but unless he'd scuttled his transport Alex wasn't there. Perhaps Gigna was too close to the mainland for comfort. So we motored across the Sound to Islay, ten miles away.

For the rest of the day we puttered round the southern half of Islay, the deeply indented coastline folded into miles of shore. Yet much of it would have offered little to tempt the fugitive: the main tourist road ran beside long stretches of it, and there was water traffic too in Port Ellen and Port Askaig. We searched carefully round the strange, remote, almost circular southern peninsula called the Oa, and again along the eastern shore where there were few dwellings and fewer roads. But we found nothing, and that evening, with the sun slipping behind the shoulder of Bein Bheigeir looming over us, we found a decent anchorage and dropped the hook.

I explained the situation to Duncan. "We could go on to Port Askaig and get rooms for the night. But by the time we got there, and got in somewhere, and got ourselves settled in, it would be time to move again in order to be back here about dawn, which is when he'll do most of his travelling.

"So we're sleeping here, on the boat. You bridle your lust and I'll bridle mine. If the wind blows up during the night the sea will get a bit choppy and the boat'll move around some. This is nothing to worry about; it is most specifically nothing to wake me up for. If you feel the need to call Hughie on the great white telephone, over the stern's your best bet—the bows will always be pointing upwind. I'll be on deck about four. Be ready to leave any time after that."

He had only one question, and he posed it diffidently. "Who's Hughie?"

The travel alarm woke me half an hour before dawn. The potting shed was cold. I hadn't taken that many clothes off to bunk down; now I scrambled back into them as quickly as I could, and pulled the spares from my suitcase on top of them. I stumbled round in the dark until I came across the galley and the box of matches. Mindful of why we were here, and not wholly confident of the *Fairy Flag*'s plumbing, I had a good sniff round before striking one.

By the time Duncan Galbraith was re-entering the land of the living, assisted by the smell of coffee and a couple of hefty kicks to the side of his bunk, there was a perceptible lightening of the sky eastward towards Kintyre. Wrapped in three sweaters and two pairs of socks, my gloved hands nursing a mug of hot coffee, I went on deck and watched the day come.

Somewhere near, I thought, Alex Curragh was waking and warming his hands, and watching the same sky pale over the same Kintyre uplands. And when the oyster streaks spread down to the horizon and bled into the sea, he'd hoist his tan sails to the stirring breeze and resume his private journey up the Sound of Jura.

I'm not sure, now, why I was so confident he was here. The only evidence was a missing boat. It could have been Alex who took it, landed nearby from a vessel outward-bound from Glasgow, but it didn't have to be. I don't suppose straightforward theft is a crime unknown in Scotland, even on the wild and picturesque west coast.

Even if it was Alex, no natural law said he had to come this way. If he was anxious to stay out of sight, the islands to the north of Islay and Jura offered more remote and less accessible anchorages still, and were well within the scope of a fifteen-foot sailing boat in competent hands in settled weather. Beyond Islay lay, effectively, the Atlantic Ocean and as many chances to lose himself as even a private man could want. By comparison the Sound of Jura was a big boating lake, three-quarter land-locked, heavily trafficked and easily observed.

Yet I was sure he was coming home. He might take his time about it, give himself space to think and come to terms with what had happened. But after that, where was there for him but Crinan, where he lived and worked, where he had friends and people he trusted as he could not understand or trust the city-dwellers? He had nothing left to hide; sooner or later he would let the police know where he was and let the thing get finished. I thought he would be making his way home by easy stages, not fleeing into an unnecessary exile.

Apart from all of that, I could almost feel the nearness of him. In this extraordinarily barren beauty of heather, rock and water, where he and I might be the only wakeful people watching the sunrise in a hundred square miles, I was conscious of something faint, electric, intangible, that said he was close. It was an awareness a woman might have of her lover, or a hunter of his quarry. I *knew* he was there— invisible, out of reach, probably out of earshot though sound carries across still water in that quiet hour after the dawn: it was not impossible that if I hailed him he would hear. I toyed with the idea but reluctantly dismissed it. I was more likely to scare him off than bring him out, and there was still the risk of attracting the attention of someone whose interest would be better avoided.

So I sat hunched up on top of the potting shed, six feet above water-level, folded round my coffee with the binoculars on the roof beside me, watching the light colour first the sky over the hills, then the hills themselves, finally run down the hillsides to touch the water with blue and silver. The water was like a mirror, the breeze not yet firmed up enough to ruffle it. As soon as the light touched it, the whole flat sheet of it from the Mull of Kintyre to the funnel at Luing was ablaze with the pale brilliance of shot silk; for just a few glorious moments.

Then, as it were out of nowhere, mists began to gather. The long view up that highway of bright water lost its brief sharp clarity as if a curtain of faint translucent gauze had been drawn between. As I watched, shores which had been clear first softened and then vanished behind the gossamer veil. Thickening even as the sun rose, it shrouded the contours of the land and filled the little bays with a vapour so fine it was impossible to see where it was coming from. There was a breeze, just, that brought me the scent of the land and caressed my cheek with soft misty fingers, but it wasn't enough to blow holes in the opacity and dispose of the shreds. My guess was that it wouldn't clear before mid-morning.

And just then, as the mist closed in, moving outward from the shore in slow-motion billows like frosty breath, not a mile away I saw it—a gunter mast carrying a tan sail. The mist had already swallowed the hull. He was clearing Ardmore Point, or where the Point had to be, and setting north. God knows how he could see where to steer. I suppose he couldn't, and sheer familiarity with the Sound kept him clear of its rocks.

I had his sail in view for two or three minutes. If I'd had the courage to weigh anchor and feel my way through the mist in his wake, I would have caught him in ten minutes more, and then it would all have been over and we could have gone safely home. But I couldn't do it. I knew these shores and waters, but not as intimately as Alex did. I couldn't find my way blind. Maybe I hadn't his skill either. Certainly the *Fairy Flag* was ill-designed for feeling her way—at least under sail you have a chance of hearing breakers before you hit the rocks they're breaking on.

Anyway, I couldn't bring myself to follow him into the pale oblivion, and even with hindsight I don't think it would have been sensible to do so. I sat on the potting shed watching the tan sail slip gently northward and the mist swallow it from the reefing points up, and then I went below again.

Duncan was dressed and warming himself at the stove. He looked up as I swung down the companionway from the wheelhouse. Then he looked again, startled. "Whatever's the matter? You look you've seen a ghost."

"I've seen him," I said, keeping my voice low and the emotion out of my eyes. "Alex. He just sailed past us not much more than half a mile away, and there's barely enough wind to keep him moving, and if I was half the sailor I think I am I'd pull up the hook and follow him, but I'm not and I shalln't."

Duncan moved sharply to the window and looked out as if he might catch a last glimpse of the tan sail. Instead he saw mist all round. "I should bloody well hope not," he said feelingly.

[2]

We had porridge for breakfast. It was that or baked beans, and would be for as long as we were on board. While we ate, I was studying the chart.

"We must have sailed right past him. He must have been in here"— I stabbed my finger into the chain of tiny islands with romantic names like Eileana Chuirn and Eilean Bhride—"it's the only place close enough for him to have got here since sunrise. We must have passed within a few hundred yards of him. He's only been a couple of miles away all night!"

Duncan was peering at the chart with me, struggling to relate it to the world of rock and water outside. He frowned. "That's the lagoon just south of here. We went in there."

Indeed we did. Perhaps we were getting tired and not looking as carefully as we should. Or perhaps he had out-thought us. With the boat beached, the sails struck, the mast shipped and the keel rolled up she could have looked very like another rock—particularly if, to go with his tan sails, her owner had tarred her bottom. Alex could have slept under her all day with almost no risk of discovery unless someone was prepared to walk every beach in the Sound. But when he was ready to move he could rig her fit for sea in a matter of minutes.

The breath of air that carried Alex Curragh into the safety of the dawn mist began to firm up around eight, and by nine the combination of sun and wind had reduced the miasma to a mere haze, a shimmering of the air. The water was losing its glassiness now that the breeze was kicking a sparkle into it. The breeze had veered from the south round into the west.

By then Duncan had the anchor on deck and I was taking the *Fairy Flag* out of Claggain Bay and heading north for Jura. I guess that Alex had already reached whatever haven he meant to pass the day in, and secreted his boat as well as he had yesterday. He might have had five hours' sailing. For much of that time the wind had been breathy light —the tide pushing up the Sound would have contributed as much to his progress. He might have got fifteen miles. Unless he was prepared to risk being spotted as day began in the civilised world, I doubted he could have got much further.

I looked at the chart. There were eight miles of crags, islets and coves along the eastern shore of Jura that he could have taken his pick from by nine o'clock. Admittedly the road—*the* road, the only road on Jura—ran along the shore for maybe half that distance, and he might prefer not to camp that close to even Jura's meagre traffic. On the other hand, the cluster of small islands moored half a mile out would be an ideal alternative. Any way you looked at it, Duncan and I had eight miles of fine-tooth combing ahead of us.

It took us six hours. Four times I left Duncan on *Flag* and rowed ashore in the rubber dinghy because rocks on the shore showed an improbable symmetry. Another time I rowed ashore and the long low shape was indeed a boat turned turtle on the beach, but the couple sheltering from the sun on the landward side had anticipated no pursuit, unless possibly by her father.

By early afternoon, with the sun already past its zenith and about as warm as it would get, the long stretch of the Sound was dotted with pleasure craft. Multi-coloured sails stretched to the freshening breeze, multi-coloured hulls dipped and spun on the dancing waves, and the little red speedboat we'd met off Kilberry head raced past us again, this time heading north, carving a bright wake that *Flag* trod underfoot with barely a nod of acknowledgement.

The sheer scale of this body of water, surrounded by land on three sides but still unmistakably an arm of the sea, was more emphasised than undermined by all this activity. We could count the boats, esti-mate their size, guess at the number of people afloat that afternoon, yet what the eye saw essentially was a great stretch of water, hemmed in by dark hills, flecked by occasional islands, with the coloured dots small enough and far enough apart to look lonely. Where they crowded together it seemed to be for company in a void big enough to ache. Worrying about the impact of pleasure craft on the Sound of Jura was like worrying whether the butterflies in Kew Gardens were leaving enough room for the plants. It was a big place. Searching it was a big task.

But a little before three it crept up on me again—a little like subliminal music, a little like indigestion—that quivering in the nerves, that quickening of the blood that said the quarry I sought was near. I'd felt it before, and too late to do anything about it I'd been proved right. I was right this time too, and now I had time and daylight on my side. I called to Duncan to throttle back and move inshore, and from my perch in the bows—as his seamanship improved I had abandoned first the wheelhouse and then the well it opened into—I raked the rocky coast with the binoculars. I saw nothing, but I could almost smell him.

Quite suddenly then I knew where he was. Nothing I could see, or smell, confirmed it but I knew as surely as if I had been with him when he went in there. It was perception of a kind, but hardly extra-sensory. He was there because logic put him there. It was about as far from Islay as he could have safely sailed: he needed to have those noticeable tan sails stowed by nine when the mist was beginning to yield to the firming breeze. Tomorrow he would sail into Crinan, and what happened after that would be out of his hands, so this last quiet time would be important to him, important enough to protect. I couldn't think of a beach within ten miles where he could feel safer than Lowlandman's Bay.

It's a strangely bleak place. Dark rocks tumble to the water's edge, enclosing a perfect pocket of a bay. A long causeway runs across from a little promontory on the north side, all but completing the stone circle. The narrow mouth keeps it safe from any sea and almost any wind, though sailing in and out can be tricky. The winds are not wholly to be trusted, either in force or direction, spilling as they do off the shoulders of the twin mountains looming above the beach.

On a clear day the Paps of Jura are visible from all over the Sound, the sharply thrusting breasts of that old warrior the Earth Goddess, who held sway in Scotland long before the Kirk cast its grey shadow of sanctimony and disapproval. You could identify with a goddess like that, all rounded contours, breasts and hips carved out of the living land, wearing green for summer and in winter white. You could see her gather the weather about her, clothe herself in storms, press not milk but rain from her erect nipples. It didn't take much faith to believe in a deity like that. The idea of an invisible, intangible, unknowable and male God came later, marking the movement away from the warm-hearted, hot-tempered, loving, bloody earth-mother and towards the distant, unapproachable, cool and intellectual sky-father. But a majority of the world's Christians still crave the return of their own little earth-mother as intercessionary.

I was worried that the sound of the engines might send him scurrying for cover. If he'd been ready to give himself up he'd still be sailing towards Crinan. I dropped anchor on the north side of the promentory and rowed ashore, and walked across the spit of land to look over the bay.

For a minute I couldn't see anything out of the ordinary: the little crescent beach, the jumbled rocks to either side, the hills rising steeply beyond. Then I saw it. He hadn't even turned the boat over. He'd pulled her onto the shingle hard by the rocks, and shipped her mast and spread her tan mainsail over her, and from here she looked almost exactly like another rock. I picked my way over the broken ground towards her, at the same time picking over the fragmented emotions in my mind.

I was glad that I'd found him, satisfied to have achieved what I set out to. I was glad that he would soon be safe and the matter capable of a final resolution. But I was sorry to be the means of wresting him—if only temporarily—from this beautiful bleak world where he was at home, master of his own destiny. Born here, he might well mistrust cities and city people. Here the living was as simple as learning to use wind and tide with authority and respect. Causes and effects were clear, above-board. There was no need, and no room, for deviousness. Alex Curragh in Frazer McAllister's Glasgow had been an up-country lamb to the slaughter.

But not here. I had made no sound in approaching: perhaps the odd scuff of deck-shoe on rock, the occasional hiss of breath in the unfit throat. But he had heard or seen, or sensed, me coming. By the time I reached the draped hull and lifted a corner of the tan fabric he was gone. Disbelieving, I tugged back the sail as if I might find him tucked into a corner between the tiller and the transom. He had been there. A blanket lay abandoned on the boards, a rolled-up jersey still bore the imprint of his head. But Alex was gone.

Disappointment stabbed and I stumbled back a step. The rocky cirque slipped out of focus and I blinked a surprising tear away. "Oh shit," I muttered, and my voice creaked.

A hand lit on my arm. I startled as though I had thought myself alone on the island. I hadn't heard him, had had no sense of his closeness this time. A shade bashfully he took his hand back. "I'm sorry. I didn't mean to frighten you."

I wasn't sure if I was frightened, or angry, or just relieved to see him. "Alex, you've had us all worried sick."

"Worried?" He was surprised at that. "I'm sorry. I couldn't stick it any longer."

"So you just walked out? Have you any idea what that looked like?"

That certain stubbornness crept back into his face. His face was dirty. It was two days since he'd washed with soap and hot water, and he hadn't shaved in that time either. The plaster on his right forearm was streaked with mud and salt. I couldn't imagine how he'd manhandled that boat around literally single-handed, but the first thing we were going to do back in Glasgow was stick his fracture under the X-ray machine again.

He said, "I suppose if you didn't know better it might have looked I was running away."

"That's exactly how it looked."

"Except that you knew better. So did the police."

"McAllister has a price on your head."

That shook him. His jaw dropped, his eyes hollowed. He looked round him uncertainly as if bounty-hunters might lurk behind every rock. Finally, his voice strained, he managed, "The police let him do that?"

"As a matter of fact, no. We went and read him the Riot Act, but whether he'll call his people off, or even be able to reach all of them, remains to be seen. Some men called at your father's house—asking directions, but maybe looking round too."

Through the shock a coal sparked angrily in his eye. "He's all right, is he—my da?"

"He's fine. He didn't know there was anything suspicious about his callers—he gave them their directions and they went away. Maybe they were lost. But the sooner we get you back to Glasgow the better, for all concerned. I've got a car waiting in Crinan. We can be there by tea-time."

He looked startled. "Not in my boat we can't."

"In my boat, towing your boat, we can. It's got the engines of a destroyer and the superstructure of a Blackpool tram."

Recognition dawned. "You've not brought the *Fairy Flag?* Holy God, I thought we'd sold her to the Iranian Navy."

"I thought you'd bought her from them. She's anchored over the point. I'll give you a hand with your dinghy—well, somebody's dinghy —and we'll pick up my inflatable on the way out to *Flag.*"

He looked at the shrouded hull, made no move towards it. "I'm not sure I'm ready."

"You were heading for Crinan, weren't you?"

"I suppose so. But—not yet."

"Listen, Alex," I said. "We have to get this sorted out. Yes, it'll mean going back to Glasgow, for a day or two. Then, as far as I know, you'll be free to come back here or go anywhere you want. I know you feel lost in the city. A lot of people who feel at home there would feel equally vulnerable out here. McAllister's one. The yard in Oban call him the Supercargo."

He smiled at that. He was getting used to the idea. He knew he had to go back, the only question was when. He'd expected a little more time to himself first. Healing time.

Another thought came into his eyes and he frowned. "I don't under-stand. Why's McAllister after me? He knows I didn't kill Alison. Christ almighty, does he want me dead?"

I took a deep breath. I'd hoped to put this off—a bit like Alex delaying his return to Crinan, knowing I had to do it but reluctant to get it done. "Alex, McAllister still blames you for her death. Because he knows he didn't kill her, and the alternative was no easier for him to accept than it's going to be for you."

I think he guessed what I was going to say. His eyes went deep and unhappy, pleading with me not to say it. But both of us knew I had to, and I did. "Alison fixed the explosion herself. She said goodbye to her husband, she said goodbye to you. She thought you were safely away. Then she turned off the gas detector, turned on the gas and—" I stopped, only just in time. He knew what had happened then. I didn't have to spell it out for him in biological detail.

He didn't deny it. He wasn't used to being lied to, as McAllister probably was. He'd never got in the way of moulding fact to his convenience, as McAllister undoubtedly was. So he believed it for no better reason than that I told him it was true. Very softly, as if to himself, as if his heart was breaking, he murmured, "Alison." Then, to me, "Why?"

I told him what I believed, beginning with why she had seduced him. That was a rough thing to tell a man, that the woman he loved had wanted not him but the fruit of his loins, but it was necessary to explain the dilemma which I believed led to her death.

"If she hadn't loved McAllister, she'd have left him for you. If she'd cared mostly about his money, she'd have ditched you. If she'd cared only about the child, you'd never have seen her after the day she found she was pregnant. She loved you and McAllister both—perhaps in different ways, but deeply enough that she couldn't choose between you. Post-natal depression may have played a part.

"I think she found it increasingly difficult to contemplate any of the alternatives—life without you, life without McAllister, life alone, or stumbling along from day to day with her emotions torn between you and no clear view to an easier future. Suicide must have seemed the only way out, her only prospect of peace. She'd been under a lot of stress for over a year. She was worn down, worn out. She wasn't altogether rational when she did it."

"That's not true," said Alex. We were walking slowly, side by side. It was easier to talk that way than face to face. But now he laid his good hand on my arm again, quite roughly, and stopped and made me face him. "She was completely rational. She was calm—more than me." He snorted a terse little laugh, remembering. "Much more than me. She was in control."

Privately I thought that was Alison's tragedy, that she had always been in control. She had controlled every facet and detail of her life, left no room for sentiment or spontaneity. Then when she made demands on herself that even her well-schooled psyche couldn't contain, the power of repressed emotion bursting through had been devastating. She hadn't known how to cope. In the end she had exercised the only control left to her. She'd pressed the self-destruct.

I tried gently to explain. "She didn't want you to know how desperate she was. She couldn't tell you why, and anyway she couldn't see how it would help. You weren't the problem. The problem was how she felt about everything. She couldn't see that changing, whatever you or McAllister did."

"She told me about Peter."

"Only that you were his father. Not—" Again I stopped myself just in time.

Alex slowly smiled. He'd done a lot of growing up in the last few days, and most of it he'd done out here, alone with his thoughts and his memories and the sea and the wide canopy of the sky. Horizons were broad out here. It was possible to start seeing even personal tragedies in a global context. He said quietly, "Not that I was picked out of a stud-book. Maybe I should be flattered."

"At least you shouldn't be bitter. However it started, she came to love you."

"I know that," he said, almost indignantly, his jaw lifting. "Do you think I need you to tell me that—you who never even met her? I know how she felt. And I know you're wrong. She wasn't torn, or mixed up or desperate or any of that. I'd have known if she had been. She was calm —sad, aye, because we cared for each other and we were parting, but not distraught, not irrational. She'd thought it through and decided what was best. I don't believe she killed herself because between us we'd messed up her mind."

I didn't argue with him. I thought it was just his way of holding it at arm's length until he came to terms with the part he had played, albeit unwittingly, in Alison's death. It never occurred to me that he could be right.

I helped him rig the boat. Her name, he said, was *Maebh*. I wondered how he knew—it wasn't inscribed on her anywhere. By way of explanation he said, "I took her from Mr. Murdoch's cottage at Machrihanish." From the way he said it, he knew every boat on the Sound.

He didn't need much help with the rigging either. Even one-handed he was surprisingly strong. Of course, he was used to hauling boats about. But also he was bigger than I had realised. Until today, at every meeting we had had, he'd been in a position of disadvantage—uncon-scious and drowning in the loch, weak with pain, shock and drugs in a hospital bed, under interrogation at the police station. It had all con-spired to diminish my perception of him. I knew he was tall; I had not realised that physical labour had grafted a useful musculature onto those long bones. But he hauled *Maebh* down to the waterline by means of the painter over his shoulder as if he was auditioning for the

Paul Robeson part in *Showboat*. I followed with the bundled-up sail, feeling slightly superfluous.

It would have been quicker for me to walk back to where I'd left *Flag*'s inflatable while Alex sailed round the spit. But I hadn't chased him this far, and spent so many uncomfortable hours aboard a smelly, noisy old scow with the personality of a garbage lighter, to have him change his mind and sail off down the Sound while I was waiting for him to appear round the point. So we went together in the little boat with the tan sails, and put ashore long enough to take the inflatable in tow for the last leg back to the *Fairy Flag*.

Beside me at the tiller Alex gave a low chuckle. "The old cow never looks any better."

I thought Duncan might have been looking out for us but he was below—maybe brewing up, I thought, or catching up on lost sleep, or calling Hughie to tell him about the short choppy motion you tend to get while riding at anchor.

We made *Maebh* fast astern, with her spar and sail down and stowed, then lifted the inflatable over *Flag*'s transom. When that too was lashed I went through the open wheelhouse to the cabin door to look for Duncan.

As I reached for it he opened it and stepped through. He'd done something to his right hand. His handkerchief was bound round it and blood was seeping down the nails. Something had also happened to his face, which was white and drawn in a way that even sea-sickness would not explain. His eyes were blank and looked right past me.

Suddenly he stumbled forward as if pushed. And indeed, level with the small of his back was a chunk of black iron too big and too ugly to be anything other than what the TV-trained mind said it looked like but couldn't possibly be. A hand-gun.

[3]

You can get guns small enough to fit in a woman's clutch-bag, and very useful they are if what you're after is essentially the nasty pop. If you really want to shoot someone you'd need their co-operation—unless they stand still and very close you could be on your third clip before you got near enough to worry them. Real guns, for shooting people with—and I'm drawing here purely on my research as a crime writer—tend to be both bigger and heavier than you expect.

This one was very big and obviously very heavy, and the rather small hand that held it couldn't cope with the weight well enough to stop it wandering all over the wheelhouse. I froze rigid when it wandered over me. It was no comfort to realise that it was pointing at my navel inadvertently: someone that bad with a gun could quite accidently shoot my guts out, and that was the weapon to do it with. I could only hope that the trigger was as heavy as the rest of it.

When Duncan took another step forward the gun, the hand and the man behind him came up out of the cabin. I sighed. No surprises, not even the blue and white matelot outfit that had replaced the pin-striped suit.

I said, "Billy Mackey. Still playing grown-ups' games?"

And he hit me in the face with the muzzle of the gun.

I didn't lose consciousness, not quite, but I went down, and from the soft elastic collision of my body with the boards a good share of my awareness was taking time out.

I made no effort to rise, just lay there among the feet on the bare wood and let my senses find their way home. Predictably, pain came first. Every tooth in the left side of my head howled in protest, and there was a stinging and a coolness under my eye that suggested he had laid my cheek open. None of it was as serious as it was unpleasant. It would pass.

Much more serious was the fact that Frazer McAllister's gangster nephew was after his uncle's reward, was tooled up in pursuit of it and had already crossed the shadow-line between using a gun as a threat and using it as a weapon. That nobody had been shot yet was almost incidental. The willingness to hurt was all. He'd hit me with the gun because he was confident of his superiority; any time he felt threatened he'd fire it just as easily. Indeed, the first shot could be fired quite casually, and into any body including his own, if he persisted in using the thing as a truncheon.

Confident. He didn't get to feel that confident, even with a gun in his hand, from standing up alone against three people on the deck of a boat he'd just pirated. He had company. Without moving my head I screwed my eyes round, looking for a pair of feet I didn't recognise.

I found them, in elastic-sided suede shoes that he'd never get the salt out of, but not in time to do me any good. Mackey must have got tired of looking at me curled up on the deck. He said irritably, "Get her up," and a pair of hands like props from a Hammer movie picked me up in one easy movement and restored me to the vertical. He must have thought I was taller than I am, though, because he held me for a moment with my feet dangling off the floor and couldn't seem to work out what the problem was.

The senses I had been carefully shepherding home took advantage of this development to break for the hills, but they didn't get far before I started rounding them up again. I found Alex close beside me and leaned against him for a little extra support, hoping the need for it wasn't too obvious. After a moment he put his arm round me and held me while my muscles and nerves got themselves organised.

I knew then what had happened to Duncan's hand.

There were just the two of them, but Mackey had that big gun and his company was built along the same lines as a Mulberry harbour, so they probably thought it was enough. I thought so too. Besides, the little red speedboat tied up against *Flag*'s seaward side, out of sight as we approached from the shore, wouldn't have taken any more. It wouldn't have taken the two of them if Mackey hadn't been as slight as his friend was hefty.

I had been about to ask, when I got my head together enough, where they had sprung from. Now there was no need. That little red mosquito had been buzzing round for two days, never out of sight. They'd found Alex by following me. I had thought I could help him in ways no-one else could, and in my arrogance I had led them straight to him.

"There's no need for that," Alex was saying, his voice tight with anger. "It's me you want. I'll come with you. But leave them alone."

Mackey shook the gun in his face. I'm not sure he meant to shake it, perhaps he just meant to point. It illustrated graphically the danger of being on the same boat as William Mackey.

He said, "You're coming, all right. We're all going. Mr. McAllister can decide what he wants done with the bunch of you." There was real malice in his light voice, and a kind of indecent hope. I think he genuinely expected to be asked to gun us down and chuck us into the Clyde with our feet encased in concrete.

Mumbling round the ache in my jaw, I said, "I've seen your uncle since you have, Billy. He's not after blood now—not Curragh's, not mine." I hoped it was true, but didn't very much care if a lie would serve as well. "Call him up. The reward's been withdrawn."

He couldn't and I knew he couldn't. His toy boat didn't run to a radio, while *Flag*'s had long ago been cannibalised to keep something more profitable seaworthy. Mackey must have seen the state it was in when he was waiting below.

He shrugged. "It doesn't matter. I'm not doing this for the money." He got a surprisingly sharp look out of the broad face of his friend which suggested that this was news to him. But Mackey didn't notice or anyway didn't respond.

"Had enough of the smell of raw whisky? Sonny, if you embarrass him any more he's going to buy a sewage farm solely for the pleasure of having you manage it."

He drew himself up to his full five-foot-six. He really did look very silly in blue and white stripes. He said with dignity, "I need no advice from you on my dealings with my uncle."

"You think not? You think attacking me and a representative of the Press with a weapon you've almost certainly got no licence for was a good career move?"

Mackey's big friend was growing visibly uneasy as the conversation progressed. Now he said, "Hell, William, I don't know—if Mr. McAllister's pulled his money out, maybe we shouldn't be going on with this." So while he may have looked like Godzilla the man was no fool.

Mackey turned on him waspishly. "Listen, Barry"—I couldn't tell if it was his first name or his second, decided Jimmy Cagney would never have addressed a henchman by his Christian name—"I won't tell you how to work a fork-lift if you won't tell me what my uncle wants and doesn't want." He jerked the gun my way again. "She's all talk, her. She'll say anything that suits her. I'll answer to my uncle. You answer to me."

Barry was definitely no fool. "What if there's no money?"

"There is money!" shouted Mackey. "He'll pay, all right, when we give him what he wants. But if by any chance he doesn't, I'll pay you. Out of my own pocket. All right?"

"What is the going rate for a sewage-farm manager?" I murmured.

I'd pushed him too far. He was already on edge, too nervous about what he was doing to take baiting in his stride. He swung back to me, his eyes vicious, the gun in his hand swinging quite deliberately. If he'd hit me in the face again he'd have broken my jaw for sure. I shrank against Alex's sleeve, too sick-scared of what he could do to me to care what I looked like, a grown woman turning for protection to a boy hardly yet come to manhood.

I had a split-second in which to despise myself, not long enough to acknowledge that natural imperative for self-preservation which demands we take what help we need where we can find it. Then the hammer-blow landed, with a crack like a breaking spar. I'd screamed a little breathless scream into Alex's shirt before it occurred to me that the blow hadn't landed on me.

His voice low and quiet, his words as near a threat as you'll hear an unarmed man address to a man with a gun in his hand, Alex said, "I told you to leave her alone." The quiet anger in the depths of his voice rumbled at me through his chest wall.

Not quickly enough for my self-respect I peeled my face off his shirt and looked round. The well of the *Fairy Flag* was littered with little white chips. For a crazy moment I thought there'd been a sudden hailstorm while we were otherwise engaged. But they weren't chunks of ice, they were flakes of plaster. Alex had fended the blow with the plaster setting his fractured arm.

I gazed at him in horror, but there was no reflection in his face of the hurt that must have run through his torn nerves and muscles like an axe tipped with acid. His face was stern, like these Scottish hills that spawned him: stern, enduring and unyielding. There was a strength in him, like the strength of rock under the summer green of this ancient Argyll forest, that he had from his ancient and troublesome Argyll forebears who yielded neither to Rome, nor to the Saxon or the Norman or even the English, though they bled and starved for it.

A boy not yet come to manhood? Alex Curragh had been a man from the age of fifteen, and earlier if called on—up to two thousand years earlier. I still hadn't made allowance enough for the differences between urban and rural breeding. The city makes people hard on the outside, the country makes them tough on the inside, in their bones and sinews and souls. Except that he had Sam Colt in his corner, William Mackey would never be a match for Alex Curragh, and he would never understand why.

Which was perhaps understandable, in view of his age and his background and his sex. But I wondered fleetingly what my excuse was. I had thought, because I had seen him cry, that I had the measure of Alex, knew the depth and breadth of him. I had failed to recognise that all his tears were for Alison. He saved none for himself. You wouldn't wring self-pity out of him if you nailed him to the wall. It was a matter of honour.

Mackey too was shocked by what had happened: partly by what he had done with his swinging weapon, perhaps more by the lack of any obvious consequence beside the brief flurry of plaster snow. He stepped back, off-balance, and a tiny breath whistled between his teeth. For a long moment he couldn't seem to drag his eyes off the plaster, crazed like old china under the gauze, and his gun hung a dead weight at the end of his arm.

Then he pulled himself together, hauled it up and pointed it at Alex's chest. He still couldn't hold it steady; or his voice. "Inside," he hissed, jerking his head at the cabin door, and when no-one else moved I gently separated myself from Alex and led the way. I'd started enough trouble for one day. After a moment Alex followed me and Duncan Galbraith followed him, and the door slammed and the latch snapped, locking us in.

At least we were alone, free of the ungodly. I steered Alex to a bunk and sat him down. "Let me see."

As the weight came off his feet he let go, and I saw the colour drain out of his face and the hurt pool in his eyes. I thought he might faint but he didn't; soon he began to rally. "I don't think there's much damage," he said. His voice was a little thin, that was all. "I didn't feel the bone move."

If he was right I'd do more harm than good getting the broken plaster off. Even if he was wrong, we'd be back in Crinan by evening, where presumably Mackey would hand him over to the police, and a proper job could be done. In the end I took all the crêpe bandage out of the First Aid kit and strapped it tightly round the jigsaw of plaster pieces. Held together like that, it gave him most of the support and protection of the original.

When I'd finished I rocked back on my heels and looked him in the face. "That was a crazy thing to do."

"He could have killed you."

And when I thought about it he was right. If my head had stopped that blow, twelve feet of crêpe bandage would have done me no good at all.

It was a bit sobering; that. Not just my narrow escape, though it was enough to chill the blood, but the implications for an ending to this which, if not exactly happy, we could at least all walk away from. Alex's shattered plaster he could just about get away with—the police might frown on Mackey's behaviour but he could reasonably expect McAllister's gratitude to be adequate compensation. But what if the blow had landed where it was aimed? Facing a charge of murder, even one of GBH, there was the very real possibility that Jimmy Cagney would cut his losses and get out.

Cutting his losses in this case meant not only foregoing the reward but disposing of the witnesses. Another boating accident wouldn't be too hard to arrange, and even if the coincidence was more than a shade suspicious, there would be nothing to point to William Mackey's involvement. In the long expanse of the Sound of Jura it was probable that no-one had noticed the little red speedboat rendezvous with the *Fairy Flag.* It offered, in any event, a better prospect of avoiding prison than sailing into Crinan with one or more of us seriously injured, or worse.

Duncan had been thinking along similar lines. When I had finished with Alex's arm and turned my attentions to his hand—there was nothing broken, only the skin ripped off the knuckles—he caught my eye and said, with the utmost seriousness, "You know, don't you, that we'll all end up dead if we don't do exactly what they want precisely when they want it. However much it goes against the grain, we have to co-operate."

It was me he was warning, not Alex. Alex might have taken the blow that could have cost us all our lives, but I had provoked it. He thought he could trust Alex to husband his anger against a more suitable time, and he had the strong suspicion that he couldn't trust me. I don't know what kind of an irresponsible idiot he took me for, but now I knew what we were up against I was too damn scared to step out of line again.

I finished binding his hand and gave it back to him, meeting his gaze as I did. "Is that how you got that?" I asked, straight-faced. "Co-operating?"

He grinned his chubby, boyish grin and chuckled down the front of his Fair Isle jumper. "Not exactly. I tried to warn you, after they came on board. We were in the wheelhouse. All the time they were talking I was working out which of the buttons on the dashboard was the fog-horn. When they ordered me below I made a dive for it."

"I take it you didn't reach it."

"I reached it all right. It wasn't the foghorn. A quick flick of the windscreen wiper doesn't have the same impact at all."

"It's the thought that counts," I assured him; but of course it isn't or we wouldn't have been sitting there in the *Fairy Flag*'s potting shed like three refugees from an out-patients' department.

Alex touched his fingertips to my face. A nerve leapt. "Put a dressing on that," he said, "before the salt gets at it." I had forgotten the cut on my cheek. Lacking a mirror, I got it covered up with a little help from my friends. I'd have let one of them do it but neither had two good hands.

About then I remembered they hadn't actually met, so I introduced them. Duncan knew who Alex was, of course, but Alex had no idea who Duncan might be. He was amazed to learn he had a natural ally against Frazer McAllister.

Soon after that, we heard the latch and Mackey pushed open the door. He crouched in the rectangle of daylight, still pointing the gun. "You: out here." He was pointing it at me.

I started to say, "Why?" then remembered what we'd agreed and got to my feet. "Coming."

Short people have a tremendous advantage aboard boats. We're not forever having to duck—under booms, through hatches, under the low coach-house roof which minimises windage and helps a racing boat keep her end up. So there was no necessity for me to pass between my companions bent low, with a hand on each man's knee. It was to remind them, if they needed reminding, that co-operation was the order of the day, and for them that meant sitting there. Regardless of what was coming.

Mackey backed away as I climbed up to him. He had no intention of letting me within grabbing range of his gun. In fact he had nothing to fear from me, but it was rather heartening—if rather dangerous—that he thought he might have.

He jerked his head at the console. It had been bastardised off a U-boat, I think, and a good half of the instruments had no function aboard *Flag*. Those that had were mostly duplicated, for the two big engines. The effect was arcane and intimidating.

"Can you sail this thing?" From the tone of his voice he might have been asking if I could levitate.

I nodded, casually. "Of course."

"Do you need any help?"

It was tempting but I resisted. "Someone to pull the anchor up, just."

He looked relieved. "Barry can do that. OK, get us back to Crinan. And see, I don't want any trouble with you."

I gave him my most reassuring middle-aged-lady voice. "Nobody wants any trouble, William. Everybody wants to get back to Crinan. McAllister and the police can sort out between them where we go from there."

So I made the speedboat and *Maebh* fast astern, and started *Flag's* big noisy engines. Mackey covered me with his gun, and his big friend Barry hauled up the chain and the anchor, hand over hand, covering himself in mud and sweat as he did so. It was sheer malice on my part that I omitted to tell him about the winch.

[4]

We had about twenty miles to go. Even towing two boats, *Flag* could have done it in ninety minutes—it was a straight run on a slack tide, and the wind on the beam offered scant resistance. Out of deference to Duncan Galbraith's shaky sea-legs, knowing the effect that being battened under hatches would have on them, I notched the throttles back a few pegs. I couldn't see that another half hour would matter. With the benefit of hindsight, though, it was a bad decision, even from Duncan's point of view.

The afternoon was drawing in by now. There were noticeably fewer boats on the Sound, and most of them appeared to be making for shore. The breeze had firmed up to a delicious Force 4 that made me resent more than ever the stench of petrol and the thunder of the engines. I found the constant vibration more tiring than short tacks.

Actually, though, the smell of petrol was not without compensation. It masked, more effectively than anything else would have done though still not totally, the stench of the mud Barry had transferred from the anchor-chain to his person. He was dabbing at it ineffectually with a handkerchief as he sat too close behind me, where the wheelhouse opened onto the well. The smell was a perpetual reminder of the future I had predicted for Mackey.

I think it reminded Mackey too. Even as the tension between us fell —with a common goal that was drawing nearer with every revolution of the big engines under our feet, it seemed that the drama was over—I could feel his animosity towards me mount. He sat in sulky silence to my right, hardly looking at me as I helmed *Flag* homeward, and while you couldn't say his gun was on me all that time, the restless obsessive way he played with it was a constant threat, not only to me.

His malodorous friend Barry also found it disturbing and twice told him to put it away. The first time Mackey grinned at him, rather too vividly, and drew a bead on an imaginary apple balanced on my head. Quarter of an hour later his response was less good-natured. He just about looked up from his almost indecent caressing of the thing, and his eyes were narrow and blood-dark, an unhealthy gloom vibrant with anger and resentment, and he growled, "Fuck off," in a low toneless whine.

I don't know what it told the big man he'd roped into this doubtful enterprise, but it told me that young Mackey was losing his grip on reality by the minute. This exploit of his had been ill-conceived but in fact he'd carried it out successfully, gambling that I would find Curragh before anyone else and arranging to take over when I did. I'd even been conscious of that danger, but still he had been more effective in using me than I had been in thwarting him. We had gamed for Alex Curragh and he had beaten me.

It should have gone some way towards restoring the self-esteem that Harry had so casually deflated by knocking him down. But anti-climax was setting in, aggravated by the time he now had for thinking. I don't know what thoughts were going through his little gangster mind, but they didn't seem to be soothing him. Probably he was beginning to suspect that he'd misjudged the situation, gone in like the Green Berets where he should have tip-toed, and that whatever his uncle may have said in grief and rage, he was unlikely to be grateful to have his enemy delivered into his hands in an indivisible package with a newspaper reporter and the wife of a detective superintendent. The smell of the sewage farm became more overpowering with every mile. By the time the little community of Tarbert Bay was sliding down our port side, Mackey's hostility was as present and animate as another person beside me in the wheelhouse.

The bottom line was that he was a seriously unbalanced young man, armed with a big gun and held back from profound violence by natural and social inhibitions worn to the denier of gossamer, and that he blamed me for most or all of his problems. A very small push could take him over the brink into mayhem. Almost nothing at all might do it: an unwise remark, a smart reply, even a look of a kind he didn't like. His tolerances were paper-thin. I swore to myself by all I held most dear—

principally Harry and my publisher's next advance—that I would not
be the means of unleashing his tiger.

What happened next was an accident.

The heat had gone out of the day now, though the sun was still high.
Neither Mackey nor his big friend must have spent much time afloat
prior to this because neither of them was dressed for west-coast sailing.
Mackey would have looked chic on a cruise liner in the Cyclades;
Barry, I think, had his gardening clothes on. Force 4 is a steady wind,
and Scottish winds are never warm, and both men were beginning to
feel the chill in the three-sided wheelhouse. I saw no advantage in
having them more uncomfortable and therefore more irritable than
they already were, so I suggested that Duncan make some coffee.

When it was ready he rapped on the door and Barry opened it and
took three mugs from him. We had no milk with us so it was black and
very hot. I wedged mine in the fiddle designed for the purpose and left
it to cool for a minute.

I don't know where the baulk of wood came from. One of the local
boat yards possibly, though it was a big lump of timber to have any
function in the building or maintenance of pleasure craft. It could have
been drifting about since the last big ship was launched on the Clyde,
working its way slowly round the Mull of Kintyre, getting more water-
logged with every tide and every mile. From how it lay in the water,
practically awash with glassy ripples silvering the square-hewn black
surface, it could have been around long enough.

Because so little of it showed above the waves the wind was kicking
up, and because *Flag*'s wheel was a long way back from *Flag*'s high
flared bow, we were almost on it before I spotted it. If we'd hit it
travelling at that speed, even *Flag*'s substantial bottom would have
suffered a nasty prolapse—I couldn't judge exactly how big it was, or
how heavy, but those little waves were breaking glassily over it rather
than bearing it with them. I did the only thing I could do: take imme-
diate avoiding action.

The old girl might steer like a cow but her reactions were lightning.
The big wheel was spinning in my hands even as I shouted a warning,
and before the words were out, the big blades shovelling the water past
the rudder had *Flag* digging one shoulder into the sea and throwing the
other at the sky in a steep banking turn she might have learnt from a
Spitfire. We missed the log, God knows how, and *Flag* crashed through
the next three waves sending salt water in a high fan across the potting

shed and over and partly into the wheelhouse, where the raked sides gave only partial protection.

Only when I had *Flag* back on an even keel did I realise I'd heard someone yell. With my luck it had to be William Mackey, and William Mackey it was.

The sudden crisis had caught him with his mug to his lips, and the violence of my manoeuvre had sent the scalding liquid slashing into his face and down his front. To add insult to injury, the subsequent inrush of sea had soaked his sailor-suit from collar to turn-ups. He looked like a drowned pierrot.

I knew that laughing could get me killed. I said, "Sorry about that. There was a damn great block of wood in the water. Is everyone all right?"

William wasn't. William was wet through, and his face stung with hot coffee and cold salt spray, and the eyes he lifted slowly burned like pitch, smouldering pits of a hatred so profound it amounted almost if not entirely to madness.

"You did that on purpose," he said, and his voice was quite without inflection, sexless and thin. Then he screamed it. "You did that on purpose!"

It wasn't true, but if he hadn't seen the wood he couldn't know how much worse than a hot and cold shower I had saved him from. I shook my head. "No." I turned my attention back to my steering.

He had lost his temper and his dignity, his self-control and arguably his marbles, but of course he still had the gun. He waved it in my face as if trying to shove the barrel up my right nostril. He had his finger on the trigger: if it had gone off it would have blown half my head away. There was no comfort in the knowledge that it would be mostly an accident.

It's never nice to be held at gunpoint, but an incompetent gunman is infinitely more terrifying than a cold-blooded pro. The latter will almost certainly succeed when he decides to kill you while the former may miss, but the chances are the nerd will pull the trigger from panic or by mistake before he has to or even wants to. Also, being killed by a bad shot hurts more, relying as he does on quantity rather than quality of marksmanship.

Improbably, one sliver of my brain remained cool enough to consider all this even while I was sniffing cordite and gun-oil. In that calm oasis I was also aware that if I tackled him now, while he was shaking with fury and his movements barely co-ordinated, I could probably wrest the weapon from him and drop it in the Sound. But I couldn't do it, couldn't bring myself to take the risk. Smothering initiative as the desert smothers the oasis, fear held me paralysed. It was as much as I could do to keep from whimpering.

Behind me Barry, whom I was increasingly coming to think of as my ally rather than Mackey's, said tersely, "For God's sake, put that cannon away before somebody gets hurt." He sounded deeply uneasy. He hadn't expected things to turn out quite as they were doing. Alex was one thing, but Duncan and me being here changed the nature of the game and he was worried that Mackey didn't seem to accept that.

For a moment longer my face was full of the gun; then, abruptly, Mackey backed off. The heavy muzzle dragged down my lip before it disappeared into his belt. I dared the briefest glance at his face; his eyes were unspeakably vicious. Then he too disappeared, behind my back. I could only have kept him in view by turning away from the wheel, which seemed unwise on two counts: because it would let him know how much he scared me, and because there could be other hazards to navigation floating around.

So I didn't see him reach behind me to take my mug, still almost full, from the fiddle at my left elbow which had held it safe through *Flag*'s acrobatics. The first I knew was the tap on my right shoulder, and as I turned automatically he threw the half-pint of hot dark liquid into my eyes.

After that a lot happened in quick succession, though I saw none of it. I howled in shock and pain, and staggered back from the wheel clapping my hands over my eyes. The scalding heat burned my face and lanced my eyes like acid burning a track into my brain. Blind, rocking in agony, I lurched around the wheelhouse until big hands that had to be Barry's brought me to a standstill and held me with just a suspicion of concern.

Meanwhile I was dimly aware that the *Fairy Flag* was taking advantage of my absence to do some lurching around of her own. She slid sideways off a wave and pitched her shoulder into a trough before Mackey—it had to be him; Barry was holding me—grabbed the wheel and tried to haul her back on course. She responded to the crudity of his touch by oversteering and sliding off the other way, burying her bows in a welter of sea. He cried, "Leave her—give me a hand here," and there was mortal terror in his voice.

Before the words were clear of his throat I heard the crash of wood that was someone kicking open the potting-shed door, and then the clatter of feet on the companionway. Duncan Galbraith cried, "What have you done to her, you bastard?" and his mild voice was thick with uncontainable fury.

I knew what was going to happen. I did all I could to prevent it. I pushed myself out of the big man's grasp, using mostly my elbows, and turned my face towards Duncan by homing on the sound of his voice. By force of will, and it took almost more than I had, I lowered my hands from my flayed eyes and tried to open them. "It's all right, Duncan—I'm all right." The shaky little whimper was unconvincing.

But I could actually see. Not brilliantly: streaming tears filmed the scalded cornea so that the pictures swam, but there was a picture and it was good enough to suggest that, pain apart, no serious damage had been done.

I could see Duncan coming towards me with his arms out. I could see the flush of anger and the twist of anxiety in his gentle face. Beyond I could see Alex framed in the cabin door, his long legs out of sight down the steps. He was watching Mackey and Mackey him. William was trying to steer *Flag* with one hand and train his gun on the three of us with the other. *Flag* had her nose sometimes on Beinn Sgallinish on Jura and sometimes on the Knapdale coast across the Sound.

I said, very clearly and distinctly, "Please, Duncan, don't start anything. I'll be all right in a minute."

Mackey said, "You two, get below."

Alex ignored him. "What happened? We heard you shout."

I wasn't going to tell him. Barry did it for me. "The Boy Wonder threw coffee in her face." Contempt dripped thickly from his tongue.

Mackey said again, "Get back inside. And take her with you." His voice was rising.

Alex regarded him for a long time without expression. Then he said, "All right." He put his good hand out to guide me, and I picked and stumbled my way through the half-seen doorway onto the steep steps into the cabin. Alex's hand on top of my head kept me clear of the low lintel, and I climbed awkwardly down into the gentle half-light. The tears were already beginning to abate, and I thought the danger was over.

At the bottom of the steps I turned back to the door. "Duncan, come inside now."

I saw him move towards me. His rather bulky figure in its Fair Isle jumper was stiff with anger. As he drew level with the wheel he paused and his eyes flicked sideways. At the same moment, *Flag* lurched askew off a wave-crest and Mackey turned his mind and both hands to getting her straight again.

It wasn't even half a chance, but I knew a split second before he did that Duncan was going for it, and I shouted at him. But I wasn't quick enough. With an unlikely agility born of desperation, Duncan threw himself at Mackey and pinned him to the wheel, his hands scrabbling between their bodies for the gun.

His greater weight, and the element of surprise—nobody expects to be mugged by someone in a Fair Isle jumper—gave him the advantage, and he would have succeeded in disarming the little thug he had pinned at the console. But when push came to shove, Barry remembered whose team he'd been picked for and—possibly reluctantly but anyway effectively—weighed in on the side of his boss's nephew. One stride took him to the wheel and a seemingly casual swipe of one ham-sized fist knocked Duncan clear across the wheelhouse and tumbled him helpless in a heap under the horseshoe lifebelt. He lay half dazed, all arms and legs, and Barry moved patiently to pick him up.

Mackey moved too. To me he looked quite deranged with anger. His encounter with Duncan had earned him a bloody nose, and it ran red over his mouth and chin as he abandoned the wheel entirely and hurled himself across the wheelhouse, the gun in his hand swinging mightily.

Duncan was halfway to his feet, aided if not actually lifted by Barry's big hands, when the first blow of the heavy weapon smashed across his head from behind. He pitched sideways and Barry, astounded by the attack, reacted instinctively to keep him from falling. And while Duncan hung senseless in the big man's grasp, William Mackey hit him again and again.

[5]

The breath hissed through Alex Curragh's teeth and he tried to push me away from the steps, looking at me startled when I wouldn't go. But if he'd got up there in time to do anything for Duncan, the situation as a whole could only have gone from bad to worse. Numerically we had the advantage but in practice—with Alex one-handed, me half blind and Duncan bloody and unconscious on the deck—no intervention by us was as likely to help Duncan as it was to get him and all of us shot and tipped over the side.

I was gambling, and the brief moments before I knew if I'd got it right were among the longest in my life. Then, to my profound relief, and also before either Alex or I could have reached them, Barry put a stop to it, letting Duncan slump bonelessly to the boards and interposing his own big body between the injured man and the crazed one.

All he said was, "That's enough," and he didn't even shout. But it would have taken a bigger man than William Mackey to elbow him aside. He backed up a step. He wiped the back of his hand across his mouth, gazing savagely at his own blood. There was blood on the gun too: in a gesture of unbelievable callousness he bent and wiped it on the cuff of Duncan's trouser leg. Then he stuffed the weapon back in his belt and returned to the wheel. It occurred to me that for the last half-minute the *Fairy Flag* had been sailing herself better than Mackey had been sailing her before, and not noticeably worse than I'd been sailing her for the last two days.

Close behind me, his voice low, Alex muttered, "If that had gone on much longer, you'd have had a man's death on your conscience."

It wouldn't have been the first time, but there was no point telling him that. "Then I'd have had to carry it." I'd been lucky: I'd been right. Contemplating the cost of being wrong was a chill whisper up my spine. But actually none of us was safe yet and I was just beginning to realise it.

Barry lifted Duncan off the deck, his limbs trailing, and passed him carefully to us through the cabin door. "It's as well you're a doctor," he said to me. His voice was quiet, his eyes appalled. "Do what you can for him. I'm sorry that happened."

"Thanks for stopping it."

We eased him onto a bunk. I mopped my eyes with cold water from the sink before I began, and using my fingertips with more than usual sensitivity to supplement my defective vision, I examined him.

There wasn't much I could do for him—not because he was past help, or needed none, but because the treatment he needed involved facilities I couldn't begin to improvise. I loosened his clothing, got him flexed on his side in the recovery position and covered him with a sleeping bag. It was literally all I could do.

Alex looked at me as I straightened up. "Will he be all right?"

I shook my head and sighed. "No. Not unless he's got to a hospital."

"For God's sake, woman, you're a doctor—there must be something you can do."

It was so bloody unfair. If there was anything to be done, didn't he suppose I'd be doing it? "That's right," I snapped back, "I'm a doctor —not a miracle worker." Even that was an exaggeration: I *was* a doctor, once, years ago. The only surgery I'd performed in more than ten years was an emergency tracheotomy on my brother-in-law. "He has a depressed fracture of the skull—there's pressure on the brain and probably some bleeding—subdural haematoma. Without X-rays, EEGs, a CAT-scan, I can't judge what the damage is, how urgent it is or how to tackle it without making matters worse. Even if I had those things, I'm not and never was a neuro-surgeon.

"What do you want me to do—operate with a knife and fork on the dining-table, while Barnacle Bill up there throws us from one wave-crest to the next? Well, I may have to do that, if it's his only chance of living long enough to reach a hospital. But since I'm as likely to kill him as save him, and I can't even see what the hell I'm doing, as long as he's anything like stable I'm not touching him with a barge-pole, let alone a knife!"

Alex stared at me a moment longer, anger and incomprehension clouding his eyes. Then he bowed his head and exhaled slowly, letting the air run out of him. With it went the tension and rage that had built in him when he'd had to watch Duncan Galbraith beaten bloody and senseless and I had prevented him from intervening. He had resented that almost more than the attack itself. With the return of a kind of sanity, he saw how unreasonable that was. When he looked up his eyes were clear, the planes of his face still and calm.

"I'm sorry," he said. "I've no right to blame any of this on you. If anyone's responsible—besides that animal at the wheel—it's me. The only thing you did wrong was pulling me out of Loch Sween when it would have been better for all concerned if you'd left me there." There was neither bitterness nor irony in the way he said it. It was just a statement of opinion.

It wasn't an opinion I shared. I shook my head vehemently. "Nothing that has happened, nothing that might happen now, will make me regret having been close enough to do something useful when the *Skara Sun* blew up." It was almost true, and anyway worth a small lie for the look on his face. It was as if I'd given him life all over again.

"Thanks," he said softly. Then he looked down at the bunk. "I doubt he'd agree with you, though."

I looked too. Duncan Galbraith's slightly thinning brown hair was thick with his blood, and his plump cheek white for the lack of it. His eyes were closed, long lashes dipping onto the cheekbone like a sleeping child's. Under the thick quilt of the sleeping bag he might have been asleep, except for the blood in his hair and the soft rattle of breath in his throat that was nothing as innocuous as a snore. He was on his left side with his right arm crooked in front of his face. I felt for the pulse at his wrist, found it as thin and thready as before, went on holding his hand long after it had told me all it was going to.

Then I looked at Alex and shook my head again. "He'd be with me. It's why he's here. He cares about people, about injustice. It was him warned me about McAllister." And it was McAllister in the end who had done this to him—in spirit if not in person. The old Roman had crucified kindness again.

"And is he?" asked Alex. "Anything like stable?"

"Not really." I could have been more specific but not more accurate.

Alex moved away from the bunk, pacing his confinement like some long-limbed animal, his eyes tracking from one little square window to the next along the length of the potting shed. There was nothing out there to warrant such attention so I assumed he was thinking, and maybe avoiding looking at me.

And indeed his gaze was still on the sea when next he spoke, softly to carry no further than the cabin door shut and barred behind me. "You know we have to take this boat back?"

For a moment I didn't understand him. I thought he was anxious about restoring the *Fairy Flag* to her owner, his employer. Then I realised what he meant: take back command of her. I stared at him as if he was mad. "Don't even think about it."

"We have to. It's his only chance." He looked at Duncan, then at me. "Ours too, probably."

He was wrong. He was going to get us all killed. I left the bunk and strode forward, and glared into his face from a range of inches. "Don't you dare start anything. We're on our way to Crinan. Even with Mackey at the helm, we'll be there in an hour. That's Duncan's only chance, and even if you didn't have a broken arm and I wasn't seeing in triplicate, it still wouldn't be worth the risk to get there ten minutes earlier."

He shook his head and explained it carefully, as if to a backward child. "We're not going to Crinan. Not now. How can they go to the police with a man half dead from a pistol-whipping and two people who saw it happen? They'll do time for what they've done here. If anybody ever finds out."

I knew what he was saying: that the cost of keeping us alive had just become too high to be worth any reward they might expect from McAllister. With us dead it had been only a couple of wasted days; with us alive, it would be wasted years. I'd worked it out for myself earlier when it didn't matter quite so much. Now it was fundamental to any future we had, I was afraid to face it. I murmured hesitantly, "Barry—?"

"Barry helped Mackey hijack this boat for money. He knocked Galbraith down, and he held him while Mackey hit him. He knows we saw that and no-one else did. If he helps us, he might do less time than Mackey but he'll still do time. If he helps Mackey, he gets to walk away. When it comes to it, he'll do what Mackey wants."

In my heart and soul I knew that he was right: it was just my head that kept shaking, my lips mumbling, "No, no." Fear like cotton-wool was clogging the machinery of my brain.

Alex reached out his good hand and took my arm in a grasp of surprising strength. Because he was too tall to stand upright in the cabin, our eyes were on much of a level and his poured urgent determination into mine, willing me the courage to believe and to act. "What do you think they're doing up there? Discussing the weather, where to tie up in Crinan, and whose ten-penny piece they'll use to call the police? They're working out where to scuttle *Flag*, and you, me and Galbraith with her."

We had a little time to think because they wouldn't want to do it here. It's a big body of water, the Sound of Jura, but sailors sail it and houses overlook it and roads run beside it. On a clear afternoon there was the serious risk that someone would see them drive their little red speedboat away from the sinking *Flag*, maybe even in time to rescue the survivors. No, they'd do it at dusk at the earliest, and preferably somewhere quieter than this.

Like, for instance, the Firth of Lorn. On the far side of Islay and Jura lay an even broader expanse of water where Loch Linnhe emptied into the Atlantic. No roads overlooked it. There were no centres of population and few houses. Only the fishing boats offered a realistic prospect of our murder being witnessed, and they weren't so many they would be hard to avoid. Once through the Sound of Luing into the broad Firth, our chances of making a safe landfall would diminish with every mile, and *Flag* could cover a lot of them in a couple of hours. Even if Harry guessed what had happened, in that waste of water even a full-scale search would never find our grave.

I made a positive effort to pull myself together, to husband what nerve remained to me. I nodded. "All right."

"All right what?" He wanted me to say it, to make the commitment, so there would be no wavering when the going got tough. Well, tougher. Anyway, less wavering.

"All right, let's take our boat back. How do we do it?"

He grinned. It was mostly relief that he didn't have to fight me too, but in the dim of the potting shed it had a radiance that was partly childlike, partly vulpine. It was a revelation, that grin. It told me I had been premature in deciding Alex Curragh was no killer. He was no murderer, but in fact this hard land where his ancestors grew up had bred him hard enough to do whatever was necessary. He'd kill if he had to, if he got or could make the opportunity, if the alternative was submitting to his own destruction. Caught momentarily in the pagan brilliance of that grin, I thought I'd sooner be me, locked below decks in a doomed boat with him on my side, than William Mackey at *Flag*'s helm with his big gun and his bigger friend. It wasn't rational, but it wasn't that crazy either.

"God only knows," said Alex.

While he was staring out over the running sea, grasping for the straws of a solution, I turned back to Duncan. He might have been a little better. His pulse had firmed up, and while he was still a good way off there were signs that he was groping his way back towards consciousness. There was some eye movement, the fingers of his hand made slight, unco-ordinated gestures beside his face and tiny regular moans were audible in his breathing.

There were almost no conclusions to be drawn from that. Duncan had a serious head injury, and that was all I could say for sure. It might kill him, or cripple him, or he might make a spectacular recovery. It was impossible to know. But I knew how much better his chances would be in hospital.

Quite a while afterwards Alex said, "Corryvreckan." He was still at the port-side cabin window, bent under the low roof, his chin resting on his forearm on the sill, his nose against the glass. He must have been standing like that for half an hour.

I thought he was rubbing it in, making sure I knew he'd been right. Because on a passage from Lowlandman's Bay to Crinan, even allowing for Mackey's steering, we should never have seen the narrow strait between Jura and Scarba opening up. The land should have appeared continuous, one blue hill blending with the next. If he could see through the strait to the Firth of Lorn beyond, we were already north of Crinan.

But when he turned to look at me, and I saw the light like fear and wine in his eyes, I knew he wasn't telling me what he could see. He was telling me what he was going to do.

All the same, I must have got it wrong because he couldn't be contemplating what I thought he was contemplating.

But he was. And when he saw the doubt in my face he spelled it out for me, leaving no room for misunderstanding. "We're going to take the *Fairy Flag* through the Corryvreckan whirlpool."

[6]

My first reaction was that he'd get us all killed. My second was that he could get us all killed, but not as certainly as doing nothing. Corryvreckan was gambling with our lives. Doing nothing was the meek walk to the abattoir. So it was worth the gamble because we had nothing to lose. What was less clear was what we stood to gain, and how he intended to get *Flag* into Corryvreckan in the first place.

He took the easier question first. "By the time we're in there and they realise what it's like, it's going to be a question of survival. Neither of them's a sailor—if *Flag*'s going to come through they'll need us to do it, you and me. They'll be sick, they'll be scared, half the time they won't know which way is up. And if we still can't get the gun off them I'll wreck the *Flag* and make it every man for himself."

Desperate needs demand desperate measures, all right, and our need was probably quite desperate enough to warrant it. But I thought he'd overlooked something. "If it comes down to every man for himself, what happens to Duncan?"

He hadn't forgotten, he just didn't have an answer. For a moment the fire in his eyes parted and the spectre was there in the smoke, haunting him. "I don't know. I'll do everything I can to get him out and get him ashore, but I can't guarantee it. If *Flag* goes down we may none of us survive; but any way you look at it, Galbraith's going to be the hardest one to save."

That was honest, and inarguable. In any conceivable circumstances, even sailing straight back to Crinan, Duncan faced longer odds than the rest of us on making it. It was his misfortune but not Alex's fault. Moreover Duncan would not survive if Alex and I died. We had to save ourselves if we were to have any chance of saving him.

I took a long, deep, steadying breath. "All right. So how do we persuade them to sail into Corryvreckan?"

"We lie a lot," said Alex.

The one advantage we had was that neither of the ungodly was familiar with boats. That much was clear from the pantomime with the anchor-chain: anyone who knew the first thing about sailing would have known there had to be a winch, even if he had to ask where it was and how it worked. They had managed the speedboat by pretending it was a sports car on a badly drained section of the M8, and so far they were managing *Flag* by confining their attentions to the wheel and the throttles. When they needed something more sophisticated than slow down a bit and turn left, they'd be in trouble.

And if they knew so little about boats there was every chance they knew no more about navigation. A chart is a simple enough thing to read and understand, but relating its flat projection to the vast three-dimensionality of shoreline and sea takes practice. Even seamen make mistakes sometimes, which is why ships go aground. Nearly always the sand-bar is charted but the navigator thought he was approaching some other river.

We discussed—sotto voce, as all our conversations had been—which of us should open the bidding. There were arguments on both sides, but we both inclined to the feeling—with no enthusiasm on my part—that they might be more ready to believe me than Alex. He was the absolute and overt enemy; there was at least a faint whiff of neutrality still attending me. Or so we hoped.

I took a deep breath and rapped, firmly but not aggressively, on the cabin door. The wheel was just to the port side of it: whoever was steering had to be able to hear me, and with luck the other one would too. "I suppose you know you're heading straight for a whirlpool?"

For so long that I thought they weren't going to bite, nothing happened. Then the door opened, framing Mackey and the gun he held before him as a pilgrim might brandish his fragment of the One True Cross. "What?"

He wouldn't come inside to the chart-table so I took the chart up to him. "Can you read one of these things?"

"Sure," he said off-handedly, confirming our hope that he thought compass roses came in dozens, with long stems.

"Then why the hell are you taking us into Corryvreckan?" It was the note of sheer panic in my voice that sold it. Convincing fear is the trade-mark of the consummate actor, or of course the genuinely afraid. This bit I didn't have to act. "It's a death-trap. There are whirlpools in there that can swallow boats twice the size of this one. There's a tidal overfall like Niagara. The West Coast of Scotland *Pilot* reckons it's never a safe bet, in any boat, at any state of the wind or tide." I was paraphrasing here but I hadn't actually got to the lying bit yet.

I had him worried. He leaned over the port gunwale, anxiously scanning the chain of islands running away to the north. Mackey's problem was, from where we were they didn't look like islands. The clear water between them would only open up as we got closer, and we were still too far south. Yet the chart plainly showed a series of seaways from the Sound of Jura into the Firth of Lorn. Mackey's brows gathered in puckers like a curtain-heading as he tried to resolve the rising and falling land into its separate components.

"Look," I said. "Things have got a bit out of hand here. Maybe it's not all your fault. All I want now is to get my friend to hospital. If I pilot you through to the Firth, will you land us somewhere I can call for help? Take the boat, get out of the area before anyone thinks to look for you. What have you to lose?"

In fact they had everything to lose by leaving any of the three of us alive, and I knew it and knew they knew it. I wasn't hoping to persuade them otherwise, only of the wisdom of accepting my pilotage. It didn't matter that once in the Firth all bets would be off and our lives worth nothing. All our plan required was for them to think I trusted them, because if they didn't they'd wonder what I was up to and maybe guess. But if they thought they were duping me, they'd accept my offer and hand me the helm, smug in the belief that once they were safe they could revert to Plan A, which was sinking *Flag* and using the little red speedboat to get away.

Unable to make sense of the coastline he was watching, Mackey turned then and tried his luck with my face. I tried to give nothing away. It didn't matter if I looked scared and resentful, or even relieved: that was to be expected. I supposed calculating was the expression most likely to ring his alarm bells, and concentrated on the sort of open countenance much prized in historical novels but now likely to get you locked up in a pale green cell.

Finally, and without consultation although Barry was following the exchange avidly from the wheel, he made his mind up. Negligently, as if it was of no import, he said, "Aye, all right. You take us through and we'll set you off on the far side. Where is this whirlpool then?"

Now the lying began in earnest. I moved over to the gunwale beside him and pointed at an indentation in the shore half ringed with trees. "Looks like nothing from here, does it? But once you turn the corner you're into a kind of mayhem, with water coming at you from all angles and your keel trying to climb into your top bunk. It's the narrowness that does it—see?" I pointed it out on the chart. "Two practically separate seas coming together through that narrow strait. It's a ships' graveyard."

Actually once you turned that corner you were safe in Kinuachdrach Harbour, but I didn't think he'd suss that and he didn't. "So where do we go instead?"

"The Sound of Luing." I showed him on the chart, then pointed off the bow. "Look, that's it you can see opening up now. See how much wider it is?"

And so it was. As we continued north, the island of Scarba, which I'd told Mackey was Luing, began to separate itself from the northern tip of Jura, which I'd told him was Scarba, and we began to see through to the Firth of Lorn. We were far enough away that we couldn't hear the thunder and rumble of it yet, and the evening sunshine was kind. It looked positively inviting. It looked the obvious way to go.

Death-traps don't get to be death-traps by looking dangerous. The real killers are the ones that look OK until you've gone too far to turn back.

"Mind you," I said, to allay any suspicions before they had the chance to form, "this route is rough enough. They all are. There'll be some broken water, a bit of disturbance. But it's navigable, as long as you know how."

"And you do?"

"I know the Sound of Luing from Corryvreckan," I replied acerbically.

I took the helm. I made a show of placing the chart where I could see it, to emphasise the value of the proper skill and facilities. I wanted them to feel safer with me steering. The fact that I was steering them into the mouth of hell would hopefully not occur to them until it was too late to do anything about it.

I also pushed the throttles up a couple of notches. If we were going to wreck, the more daylight we had left the better. If Duncan survived the trip, the sooner we could get him ashore the better. Also, the longer this went on the more likely it was that I'd lose my nerve.

I made a big show, too, of altering course, though there was really no need—in so far as *Flag* had been on any course at all, it was a general northing and not within several points of Kinuachdrach. Still I took her round in a broad swing and settled her head on the real, genuine, one-and-only boat-eating Corryvreckan, and forced a smile. "That's better."

When we'd all settled down again and Mackey had stopped following my every move with both eyes and the muzzle of his gun, I inquired casually, "Which one of you'll take soundings for me as we come through?"

I got Mackey's eyes then, and his friend's as well. "What?"

"It's not difficult. It just means one of you leaning over the bow and calling to me how much water we have under the keel. We draw about three feet. Allowing for waves, we need a minimum of six, which'll look like four due to refraction. It's a bit tricky at first but you'll soon get the hang of it."

From the look he shot me, William considered I was the trickiest thing he had to deal with. "Is that necessary?"

I elevated both eyebrows. "It's sure as hell advisable. It would be one thing if we had a full tide over the rocks, but we'll be going through at half ebb. If we hit bottom we'll be stuck there till midnight. *Flag*'s long and she's deep: I can't judge from back here how much water there is under her bow."

"You mean you can't take this boat through that channel without someone hanging over the front shouting out how deep the water is?"

I shrugged ingenuously. "That's how I've always done it. We can try it by guess and by God, but my guess is we'll hole her. But listen, you're in charge. All I'm saying is, if I was calling the shots, no way would I go through there without a look-out in the bows." It was at least half true. The other half was that I wouldn't try it with someone in the bows either.

"All right," said Mackey, turning away. "Barry'll do it."

"Like hell Barry'll do it," retorted the big man fast. "You're the one fancies himself as Captain Bligh: if there's any hanging out over waves to be done, you'll be the one doing it."

They glared at each other for so long I began to wonder if I should propose the obvious solution. But Mackey got there on his own. "Curragh can do it."

It was gone seven o'clock when *Flag* drove her unlovely nose where angels fear to tread. The tide had been ebbing for three hours: the main overfall would be like a step, a wall of tumbling waters for *Flag* to climb. If we got that far. If the whirlpools didn't get us first.

Stifling my deep misgivings as best I could—because if the ungodly could be kept in the dark for just a few minutes longer it wouldn't matter what they guessed then—I said, "I'm going to need that lookout now."

Mackey opened the cabin door. "Curragh, get out here." Because Alex and I were now both on deck, and Duncan no danger to anyone, he didn't bother to shut the door again.

I explained to Alex for all the world as if we hadn't spent long minutes going over it in microscopic detail in the cabin. He nodded. "OK." I raised a minutely inquiring eyebrow to ask if he'd secured Duncan as I'd instructed, and with as tiny a nod he confirmed that he had.

There was nothing more to be done, except to do it. Alex went forward; I fastened both hands firmly on the wheel.

If either of them had known the first thing about boats, the ungodly would have guessed that something was wrong before *Flag* was much more than her own length into the strait. Narrow channels often develop powerful and characteristic currents, but not like this. That short hard chop of the sea, all temper and no direction, coming from nowhere and with nowhere to escape to, was telling enough. It snapped and slapped at *Flag*'s hull, pushing her this way and that, and her steering deteriorated rapidly from idiosyncratic to barely possible. The bottom of the channel must have been in a state of the utmost chaos to foster such disturbance.

While I was wrestling with the steering, scared of the speed we were doing but reluctant to sacrifice any of the manoeuvring power of those big engines when the rudder itself was so unreliable, we came on fresh evidence of the extreme and extraordinary violence of the forces at work beneath us. Whirlpools spun, deceptively glassy amid the heaving chop, like oases in a desert of warring crests. When we drew closer we could see how their centres were tugged viciously down, so that there were little spinning worm-holes into the heart of the sea. Some of them were just a few feet across, others big enough to take a boat the size of the *Fairy Flag.* I'd heard they could swallow boats whole, so that they'd never come up. I jockeyed the throttles and the inconstant wheel to keep them at a distance.

But even if they thought the choppiness was to be expected, and the whirlpools and interesting side-effect, God knows what the ungodly made of the noise. They must have been aware of it, been aware that it was growing. At first it sounded a little like peals of distant thunder. By now it was like standing under a railway arch while the Flying Scotsman snorted overhead.

It scared the hell out of me, but then I knew what it was: the sound of millions of tons of wild water battling for control of the narrow strait. Casualties were piling up in white foam on the rocks on either side. *Flag* ploughed on through the increasingly disturbed waves, heaved up now like little pyramids with the wind tearing their peaks off. The wind wasn't actually that strong, but it didn't have to be. The chaos below shoved up crests and pinnacles of water that hadn't the strength of purpose or direction to survive long. It hardly mattered. There were more where those came from.

I found Barry at my shoulder, peering anxiously over the side. The grin I gave him was nothing short of idiotic. "You think this is rough? You should see Corryvreckan."

There was another reason, beside the steering, to keep *Flag*'s speed up as high as my nerve would stand. It was so that, when I started her waltzing, the violence of the movement would be as savage and unpredictable as possible. It was perhaps a lot to hope for that it would catapult both the ungodly over the side, though you never know your luck. It might separate Mackey from his gun. It might render him incapable of using it, if he needed both hands for hanging on. It might reduce him and Barry to the death-seeking misery that is sea-sickness, heaving their guts over a rail, in which case their race was run and we could take them at our leisure.

Whatever the specific consequences, the purpose of this risky manoeuvre was to create a situation in which Alex and I, sailors both, would be more effective than two men whose experience of the sea seemed derived from pedalos on the beach at Ayr. Even when they realised what we'd done, there would be nothing they could do about it: any chance *Flag* had of coming through this depended on Alex and me being fit and free to sail her.

That was the theory. The time had come to test it.

Alex in the bows, his good left hand wrapped round the forestay, his long angular body levered out over the waves, suddenly stiffened and shouted, "Starboard!" and I spun the wheel clockwise for all I was worth.

Flag reared up like a startled horse, her port rail scraping the sky, seeming to hang over me for a moment before gravity caught her and she slid down the side of the wave, crashing at its foot and sending sheets of foam over the bows. For a dreadful half-second I waited for it to clear, with no forward vision, no knowledge of what lay around me and no certainty that Alex would still be there when it did. Then he reappeared out of the welter, drenched and streaming and with his teeth bared. He pointed with his free plastered arm and I centred the wheel.

William Mackey shoved his face, fish-belly white, between mine and the windshield. "Don't do that again!" The fear in his voice was more than audible, it was tactile.

I pretended innocence. "What? We were coming down on a rock. That's why I needed a look-out. I told you all this."

"You said this was the safe way!"

"It is. Well, the safest."

"Hard a-port," yelled Alex from the bows.

From then on everything happened quickly. *Flag* rocketed from one wave-crest to another, from one beam to the other, more often on her ear than on her feet. I wrestled the wheel with all the strength and skill at my command, fully aware I hadn't enough of either. Once Mackey shoved his gun in my back, but it was gone again before I had time to worry about it. Once Barry cannoned into me, apologising automatically but still gripping me so tightly I couldn't steer the boat.

"Let me go," I said distinctly in his ear. "Barry, let me go or you'll kill us all."

His big face slack with fear, his eyes staring almost vacantly, he somehow transferred his grip to the trailing edge of the wheelhouse and froze there, as near immobile as he could make himself.

William stayed coherent a little longer. His face hove again into my narrow field of view as I concentrated on Alex and the mayhem about our bows. His eyes were wild, with terror and anger both, rimmed with white. A froth of spit had gathered at the corner of his mouth and his hair hung sodden in his face. I guessed, without remorse, that he'd chosen the wrong moment to throw up, or possibly the wrong rail to throw up over.

"Starboard," yelled Alex, barely audible now over the crash of waves, and I did as bid.

I thought Mackey would be gone when we levelled out, but he was still there, still staring whitely at me and now pointing his gun at my eye. I shuddered. Interestingly enough, I was too scared already to accommodate any more fear, but knowing how unsteady he was with that cannon at the best of times, I knew how close I was to death. I said, "If that goes off, there's nothing you can do as quickly as this boat can flip over."

He howled at me over the storm of waters, "What have you done? Where have you brought us?"

So probably he knew, and anyway it was too late to matter and I had promised myself the pleasure of telling him. "Corryvreckan. I've brought you into hell's kitchen, and by God, if you don't give me that gun right now, I'm going to wash you down the sink."

"Damn you," he whispered. I couldn't hear him, I read it on his lips. His eyes were tormented. Not all the salt-water on his face had come over the side: some of it was tears. "Damn you to hell. Take it, and get us the hell out of here." And he slapped the gun onto the top of the console in front of me and turned away.

For long moments I couldn't take my eyes off the thing, even to lift them by the few inches necessary to see where we were going. We'd done it. Alex had conceived and together we had carried out a plan designed to push all our nerves to the edge. But when we got there Mackey's had broken first. For the first time in ninety minutes I thought we were going to see tomorrow.

I half turned, following the retreat of the man who had plotted my death. From somewhere I had not suspected I found a little gentleness. He was, after all, very young. "William, it's going to be all right. We'll get back now, get Galbraith seen to, get the rest of this mess sorted out. Whatever happens, it won't be as bad as you think and it'll get over. You won't spend the rest of your life running scared."

It was rather a lengthy speech coming from someone who should have been concentrating on her steering, and when I looked forward again Alex was back on deck and waving wildly. I waved too, and lifted the gun—carefully—for him to see. He didn't seem terribly impressed. He was making his way back up the side deck, awkwardly one-handed but not nearly as awkward as I'd have been, and shouting something I couldn't hear over the roar of the water.

The roar of the water had got an awful lot louder while I was dealing with William.

Alex reached the wheelhouse, swung one-handed round the trailing edge and landed half on his knees at my side. He was so wet it was like having a water-spaniel shake itself beside me. "Put her about," he yelled, staggering to his feet.

I looked at him. I looked ahead at the chaos of conflicting seas. I looked at the gun on the fascia. Stupidly I said, "I've got the gun."

"Put her about *now,*" he snarled and grabbed for the wheel.

And it was only then that I saw the wall, the towering overhang of water trying to force its way eastward through Corryvreckan. It couldn't have been as high as it looked, it was a mathematical impossibility, but by God it was high enough. Boats aren't designed to jump, and that's what it would have taken to get up that solid step of sea. Ploughing through it would have taxed a destroyer, and *Flag* only looked like a destroyer, she wasn't built like one.

Someone in the wheelhouse cried out in sheer, inarticulate terror. I wouldn't be surprised to learn it was me: it was the only rational response. That, and getting *Flag* turned round, which is what my two hands and Alex Curragh's one were scrabbling to do even while that cry of despair was still echoing in our ears.

We almost made it. *Flag* answered the rudder like a cow-pony for once instead of a cow, dug her props deep in the broken water and flung her head up towards the north shore. She rolled as her flank met the overfall with a clap like thunder, and for what seemed like a long time she churned on, mostly on her side, one prop still driving her while the other raced wildly in air, her head still struggling round, adamant in her refusal to admit defeat. Water poured over both sides, from the sea below and the overfall above, but she was an old campaigner and she wasn't ready to die yet. I thought that somewhere she'd find the strength and the sea-room to right herself.

I thought that right up to the moment when she turned over.

[7]

Two or three times in my life I have come close to the ending of it. Twice, which seems excessive in view of my gentle disposition and kindly nature, people have tried to murder me. But I never got as close as my last breath before, and this time that was all the margin separating me from breakfast with St. Peter. And very hard I'd have found it to explain that, while my life was certainly at hazard due to the actions and intents of others, the thing that finally saw me off was an accident, and more my fault than anyone else's.

With the wheelhouse open to the stern, the sea came in instantly as a solid body. It hit me in the back—I was still approximately at the wheel, though my legs had gone from under me and I was clutching the thing for support rather than with any expectation of being able to steer this boat that had just become a submarine—and threw me face-first against the bulkhead. Water roared in my ears and stars exploded darkly before my eyes. The sheer cold was a physical shock that made me gasp, and half the air in my lungs went that way.

What was left wasn't enough to keep panic at bay, even for the few moments it would have taken to work out which way was up. I could have swum out if I'd kept my nerve long enough to open my eyes, take stock of my surroundings and work out which way I had to go. There was time, even on half a lungful of air. What was lacking was the cold hard mental strength it needed to sacrifice those few moments in weighing up where I was and what I needed to do.

Maybe the shock was part of it, maybe I was a little stunned from my collision with the bulkhead, but mostly I think it was that my reserves of courage, of moral stamina, had hit rock-bottom and there was nothing left to draw on. After Mackey's nerve broke, the malicious spirit of Corryvreckan that we'd tried to harness to our needs had taken its revenge by upping the ante until mine broke too. So I twisted helpless in the flood, arms and legs milling slowly and mind paralysed with fear, only a few feet and one good effort from the air I was dying for lack of.

I wouldn't have made it. I'd have died there, tumbling in the alien dimensionless mayhem of an inverted wheelhouse with my lungs bursting and then flooding, my brain lanced by horror and hurt and my eyes filling up with blood, except that as I spun lost and out of control I collided with another bulky weightless body, clothes ballooning softly round it, and while I struggled insanely to fight it off, it fastened a hand in my collar and hauled me backwards out of the dark.

Light exploded around me, air gushing into my starved lungs, as we surfaced among leaping waves that tossed us all ways until we fetched up against something solid and comparatively still, and my scrabbling fingers found and clutched at a handhold. My eyes hadn't cleared enough yet to confirm it, but my brain was ticking over again and realised what it had to be: the rubbing strake along the underside of *Flag*'s hull, at the junction of vertical and horizontal chines. It was there to protect her bottom when she took the ground, but, as if he'd had some presentiment of this moment, the man who built her so long ago pierced it through at intervals. My fingers locked round it, and I think if I'd died there I still wouldn't have floated away.

As if I needed telling, a voice in my ear rasped, "Hang on—hang on there while I get your mate out." It was only then that I realised who I owed my life to: Barry, the big man from the wrong side of the Glasgow tracks, who had been more scared than any of us in the maelstrom I'd brought us to, but who had somehow swallowed his fear when the great strength of his bulky body was the only chance any of us had.

My eyes were clearing. I saw him suck in a deep breath and dive again, more effective than graceful, and disappear into the darkness at my feet, under the upturned hull. I stayed where I was, the water slapping round my shoulders, both hands fastened in the strake, wondering what he meant. The water was very cold, and I had banged my head, and it was a moment before I remembered Alex.

It was moments more before I thought of Duncan Galbraith, lashed unconscious into a bunk in the flooded cabin. The door had been open —there couldn't even have been much of an air-pocket. Poor, poor Duncan. He had to be dead, and maybe Alex dead with him, wrestling one-handed with the retaining straps we'd improvised while *Flag* lifted her keel to the sky and the black waters of the overfall crashed in on them. And it was my fault. Not because I hadn't been good enough, but because I'd got careless. Cocky. I'd thought that when I had the gun I'd won.

A few feet from me the broken water boiled suddenly and vomited two dark heads. One was Alex. His need for air was so urgent that he was whooping it in, along with some spume, as he broke the surface. Veins stood proud on his forehead and his eyes bulged. Reaching the surface had taken the last of his strength. His cheeks were white and hollow; under the half-dropped lids I saw his eyes rolling back. He wouldn't have made the boat alone.

Barry towed him over to me, took his good hand and clapped it onto the strake, heaving him halfway out of the water to make sure. He shouted at him to hold on but Alex just moved his head vaguely. Already his fingers were slackening. Barry cursed him. Then, treading water energetically, he tugged off his own belt and buckled it in a firm figure-of-eight round Alex's wrist and the pierced strake. If he passed out he'd hang there, half out of the water, until his senses returned.

The big man turned to me. "Has Willie come up yet?"

Had he? I couldn't be sure. "I haven't seen him."

"Damn. I'll go down again. About your reporter friend: I'll get him out if I can, but it's been too long." He nodded at Alex. "He was trying to get him out of the cabin. When he starts coming round he'll want to dive again. Don't let him. He's done in, and anyway if I can't find him right now there'll be no point. I'll do what I can."

I mumbled, "Thanks." I wasn't sure how appropriate it was but I needed to say something. Afterwards I was glad I had, because I never saw him again.

Flag's upturned hull, with me clinging to it and Alex Curragh lashed to it, drifted back the way we had come. Angry waves continued to beat at her, throwing spray clean over her keel, keeping her passengers wet through and fighting for breath. The deathly cold ate its way into our bones. I couldn't feel my hands, wasn't sure what prevented me from sliding off into the black depths. What strength I had ebbed into the cold water, quickly followed by my ability to think and then any strong feelings as to whether I lived or died.

After Alex regained consciousness and before we both started to lapse again, we tried to keep one another interested in survival by talking. It wasn't much of a conversation: we shouted encouragements, always unduly optimistic and often downright fatuous, over the noise of wind and wave. We assured one another that the Coastguard would be looking for us right now, and it could be only minutes before a lifeboat or helicopter came to pluck us to safety. We could last another few minutes. When the minutes had passed without sign of rescue, we chided each other for failing to allow for the distances involved. Obviously it would take a few minutes longer to reach us here. The main thing was that someone must have seen *Flag* turn over, maybe from a boat that would take a little time to reach land and raise the alarm. But they'd be here before nightfall.

Night fell.

In the end we owed our survival to no human agency so much as to the contrariness of that old sea-cow, the *Fairy Flag*, who wouldn't steer straight with two of us trying when under power and the right way up, yet revealed a gentler streak when cruising slowly backwards and upside down, buffeted by the tides of Corryvreckan. Unaided even by prayers, she picked her way through treacherous rocks and races towards the Jura shore and found a tiny scrap of stony beach, first with the stumpy mast rising from the potting shed roof.

I have no clear memory of how we got ashore. I can't say if it was me or Alex who noticed first the change in *Flag*'s motion, the grating noise from the mast, the rumble and phosphorescent flicker of nearby surf. I don't know if I dragged him through the last dangerous yards of tumbling water or if he dragged me. All I know for sure is that we ended up on the beach, crawling ashore on our hands and knees without the strength to lift our heads clear of the breaking water, still swallowing the stuff when there was no more of it under us than a toddler could safely paddle in.

And when there was even less than that we found we couldn't move at all. We'd been in the water for hours—I don't know how many but too many. We were too weak to support our own weight on dry land. As long as there was water under me I could crawl, but when my belly touched bottom I was as helpless as a stranded whale. I lay in the shallows, the foam creaming over me with every wave, and I thought I'd have to die there if it was the only alternative to climbing up the beach out of reach of the tide.

Alex got a little further, not much. I was dimly aware of him beside me, of his bare feet—God knows where his shoes had gone—by my face as he hauled himself on his elbows out of the hiss and surge of the sea. When only his legs were awash he twisted round and tried to pull me after him. But I couldn't help, even a little, and soon his meagre strength was exhausted and we slept side by side while the quiet sea withdrew and left us, half dead and draining under the summer stars.

I woke with a start and couldn't think why. It was still dark, still cold —too cold to ease the cramping chill that had invaded me from the sea. I was still wet, though some of the water and its weight had drained out of my clothes. Nothing else had changed. I listened and heard nothing but the sea. Nothing was moving but the waves.

That was it. The tide was rising again. My feet were already afloat.

It made every muscle in my body scream but I got my hands and knees under me again and made them move, mechanically if they couldn't manage an animal grace, until I was once more clear of the water. I wasn't being soaked again, not for anything.

I found Alex's shoulder and shook it. Nothing happened. I pulled his hair, gritty with salt, between my fingers, and he mumbled a sleepy complaint. "We have to move now. Get up. Get up and walk."

He did, eventually. We both did, leaning on one another like a couple of old drunks. We stumbled up the beach, beyond the wrack that marked high tide, and found a bank clad in wiry tussock-grass where the thin earth still held some of the day's heat. It wasn't much. You needed to be as desperate as us to appreciate it. But we had no dry clothes, no shelter and no means of making a fire, and that bank with its memory of sunshine and its dry grass, and the shape of it folding round our bodies while we clung together for what comfort we could find, felt to be saving our lives. Perhaps it was.

The sun rose early but for an hour there was no heat in it. I ached with cold. But I wasn't far off dry now; and where our bodies touched there was a small reservoir of warmth where a hand could be thawed out. We took it in turns to draw on this small joint account, at first instinctively, then, as our awareness of our own and each other's survival heightened, with amusement and affection. We had made it. We had passed between Scylla and Charybdis, and emerged, if not unscathed, still essentially intact. It was a communion of experience that would be between us all our days, exclusive and intimate and inexplicable.

And it was that strangely innocent intimacy, that spiritual closeness born of mutual peril, striving and success, which led to what happened next. Perhaps not only that. Eluding death so narrowly had left us with an urgent need to reaffirm life. We were hungry—for movement, for contact, for warmth. We had been badly scared and needed to repair the loss of self in our close encounter with oblivion by vigorously redefining the space we occupied. We needed to re-establish our own reality, mentally and physically and emotionally and biologically.

So I seduced him.

Afterwards, warm for the first time in twelve hours, I slept while the sun rose higher.

I dreamed. I heard again the roar of the maelstrom around me. I felt the lurch and pitch and the slow incredible toppling as the *Fairy Flag* rolled to her death. I whimpered at the image of Duncan Galbraith, strapped in his bunk all unknowing, rolling to his among the gnashing rocks of Corryvreckan. He was a good and gentle man, and deserved better.

Real violence interrupted the remembered violence of the dream. A kick in the ribs you wouldn't get from a Delhi mule shocked me awake and rolled me bodily out of the little hollow where I had found a kind of comfort. Once again tumbling out of control, with no perception of what was happening to me beyond the clear understanding that it wasn't good, I had rolled to the foot of the bank and onto hard skittering pebbles before I was able to brake my progress with spread hands and sit up and see what was going on.

I thought then that I had gone mad, on three separate grounds. I thought I could see William Mackey, and I knew he'd drowned. I thought he was pointing his gun at me, and I knew that had been lost when *Flag* turned over. Most bizarre of all, I thought he was wearing a hand-knitted Norwegian cardigan with red reindeer trooping across it, approximately half as wide again as he was.

But somebody had kicked me, and if it wasn't a dead gunman in a reindeer cardigan, who was it?

"What's the matter?" demanded William, his voice high and strident. "You look like you've seen a ghost."

[8]

Alex, whose first instinct had been to get to his feet, thought better of it and subsided onto one knee in the wiry grass. "Where have you been?" he asked quietly.

William waved his free arm, fitfully and rather vaguely, towards the strait. "Over there. Didn't you hear the helicopter?"

That was the roar I heard in my dream: not the angry waters but the rotors of Frazer McAllister's executive transport. It must have been up at first light looking for us, and Mackey, who had spent the night resting rather than exhausting himself further, had been awake enough to attract the pilot's attention.

He had been behind me, in the open end of the wheelhouse, when *Flag* turned over, and he was flung into the boiling water. Ignoring the first rule of capsising—which is that you stay with the boat, whichever way up it is and however close the shore and however strongly you can swim—he struck out for the bit of land he could see and somehow kept going until he reached it. He must have been well on his way to safety when his big friend dived again in search of him. He showed no remorse and almost no interest in his companion's fate.

From the Scarba shore where he dragged himself out of the water, he watched the dark hull of the *Fairy Flag* drift south and east until at length he lost sight of it in the twilight. But it hadn't been far from Jura then, and when the sun rose he could see it nestling among the rocks of the southern shore less than a mile away. He tried to make out if she had brought any survivors safe ashore, and just once he thought he saw movement.

"I knew then who it would be," he spat. Every word he said was aimed my way; the gun, though, was mostly levelled at Alex. His gaze flickered between us, burning with malevolent fire. I could feel his hatred licking at me. "You bitch. You tried to kill me."

Clearly the boy had no sense of irony. Laughing in his face would be unwise, so I shrugged. "I did what I had to in order to survive."

His eye glinted. "You reckon?"

Alex was looking at the gun. He was closer to it than I was. "Where did that come from?"

My heart sank. I'd assumed it was the one he had aboard *Flag*, in which case it had to be caked with salt and sand and at least as dangerous to fire as to face. If it was another gun we were in worse trouble than I had thought.

Mackey grinned at me, vividly but without much humour. "From the helicopter. I've travelled with that pilot twice a week for two years, I know all about his anti-hijack kit. I could have taken one of the sporting guns from the rack at the back, but the old devil's funny. I wouldn't want him going soft on me. Better if he doesn't know until you're dead."

I froze rigid. He meant it. After everything that had happened, all we'd been through, he still meant to kill me. A voice I didn't recognise as mine whispered, "Why?"

"Why?" he echoed, a hoot of derision in the word. He couldn't believe I really didn't know. "You have ruined me," he said then, and his eyes were indignant and unforgiving. "McAllister needed me. I'd have gone places in his organisation. You set about making a fool of me the first day we met. Damn you. You had no right."

"William," I said, and if it sounded like a plea I was past caring, "I never did anything to you that you didn't force on me."

"Oh aye? I had it worked out. My uncle wanted him." He jerked the gun at Alex but his eyes still blazed at me. "I'd have found him, but I knew fine well you'd find him first. So I followed you. You didn't even know, did you? I'd have brought him back and McAllister'd have been grateful, but what happened?"

"You beat Duncan Galbraith so badly you couldn't afford to take any of us back," growled Alex.

Mackey blinked. I think he'd forgotten that. He skipped quickly to his next grievance. "She tried to kill me! She brought the boat in here knowing it would turn over. She didn't care who she killed if she got my gun away from me. But you won't get this one." Quite slowly his frail young body, absurdly—even pathetically—clad in its reindeer cardigan and bent into a bow by the weight of his intensity, swivelled towards me, bringing the weapon with it.

Alex said sharply, "It's me McAllister wants. He won't thank you for killing her."

Mackey's eyes snapped back at him. "He doesn't have to. I'm not doing it for him. He can have you, but I'm having her." And he shot me.

If I'd thought he was ready to do it I'd have made some effort to escape. Got up or rolled aside or something. I'm sure I would: I'd nothing to lose. He not only wanted me dead, he needed me dead, as he always had since the moment of his attack on Duncan. He trusted McAllister to dispose of the other witness, but he had to deal with me himself.

I thought he'd talk about it longer. He was visibly angry, but he wasn't in the towering rage that makes taking a human life possible. I thought he'd have to work himself up to that point, that unless one of us did something to precipitate the crisis it would take him a little time to reach it. In a little time anything could happen.

But he needed no time at all. He didn't need to psych himself up, to gloat over me or humiliate or frighten me. He needed me dead, and since he'd been this close before and been cheated—by me or by events—he wanted it done quickly.

So he looked at me, sitting on my damp backside among the stones, propped up by a hand on either side, and what I saw was a triangular formation of three black eyes, all unwinking, and there was no more life or pity in Mackey's two than in the one below them that was the muzzle of his gun. At the precise moment that I realised he was going to shoot me, now, without any further discussion, he did.

He was a terrible shot. I'd guessed as much aboard *Flag*, and here was the confirmation. He couldn't have been more than six or seven yards away, and with the slope of the shore in his favour, and I didn't move a muscle and neither did Alex. Still the closest he could get to a *coup de grâce* was a nasty burning graze three inches long across the top of my left arm.

I yelled, as much with surprise as with pain—I've had worse rope-burns—and dived one way; Alex dived the other, sweeping Mackey's legs from under him, and they collapsed in a rolling, struggling heap from which issued the occasional knee or elbow, curse, threat or grunt of pain. Once the gun came out, locked in two hands, and waved wildly for a moment before disappearing again between their twisting bodies.

Alex should have had the advantage, the gun notwithstanding, being both longer and stronger. But Mackey had two good arms to fight with and Alex was both handicapped and hindered by his injury. It might have been more ladylike to leave it to them but I wasn't confident enough of the outcome. Stung by my own wound just enough to be mean, I weighed in on top of them, stamping and kneeing and gouging any piece of anatomy I didn't recognise as Alex, taking a particular toll of those bloody reindeer.

I didn't escape scot-free myself. I got knelt on, I got a fist in the midriff, and at one point a hand emerged out of the scrum, fixed a grip in my hair and yanked until I thought I'd lose it. From the way he let go when I squealed, I think it was Alex.

I didn't care. I could take a little punishment—scalp, midriff, booted ribs, bullet crease and all—if this was going to be the end of it. I was scared of the gun going off again, because in the knot of bodies there was no knowing what damage it would do and to whom, but the fear got subliminated in the sheer physical aggression of what I was doing. As long as I was strong enough to beat the crap out of those reindeer, the gun wouldn't go off.

The gun went off. At least, *a* gun went off. It sounded more like a howitzer than a hand-gun, and the shock of the blast effectively separated we strugglers on the grass. We rolled apart and for a moment none of us moved. I knew I wasn't hurt, wasn't sure about the other two.

None of us was hurt. It wasn't Mackey's gun that had gone off. At the top of the bank above us Frazer McAllister's stocky figure was planted immobile against the sky, feet apart, the long double-barrelled gun in one hand pointing up. The sun shining on his crinkly grey hair gave him a most improbable halo. He was in his shirt-sleeves—so the reindeer cardigan was his—and green wellies with some rather ancient corduroys stuffed into the tops, and he looked a little like an avenging angel and a little like an elderly Che Guevara.

I didn't know what his being here meant. I hadn't realised he was on the helicopter in person, couldn't decide what significance to ascribe to that. It hung on whether he accepted yet that Alex was not to blame for his wife's death, and now didn't seem the moment to ask him.

His voice was gravelly, the accent prominent. "Get away from that gun."

I was nowhere near it. It had fallen on the grass between Alex and Mackey, and either could have reached it with one good lunge. Alex was mostly on his back, clearly in pain from his damaged arm, and he raised his head just long enough to recognise the new arrival, then turned his face away, sick with disappointment and defeat. He had no doubt what McAllister's presence meant.

Mackey had ended up mostly on his knees. He straightened with a grin of pure malicious triumph. "Nice timing, uncle," he crowed. His nose was bleeding again and he wiped it on his sleeve.

"You found them, then." McAllister was standing quite still, his head lowered like a bull's, looking at Alex. His expression was unfathomable.

After a moment Alex grew aware of his scrutiny. Pride wouldn't let him bear it prone. As stubborn in his own way as the old tyrant himself, he struggled with hurt and weariness to pick himself up. I wasn't near enough the gun on the ground to threaten anyone, so I got up and went to him and quietly helped Alex to his feet. We stood together then and waited.

McAllister's gaze slid over to me. His voice was level, uninflected. "Dr. Marsh. How are you?"

I wasn't sure if it was a greeting or an inquiry. I wasn't even sure how I was. I'd been kicked, thumped, shot, half drowned and totally terrified. My clothes were still damp, gritty inside and out, and perforated in places. I was trying hard not to think how I must look. "I'm fine. Thank you."

"Mr. Galbraith?"

"Duncan Galbraith is dead."

"How?"

I indicated William. "He fractured his skull. I turned the boat over and drowned him."

I caught the movement out of the corner of my eye as Alex turned his head to look at me. "That wasn't your fault. If it was anyone's it was mine." Saying it altered nothing, and now it was too late to matter, but I appreciated the gesture.

Mackey said, "I was bringing them to you. They started a fight."

McAllister looked at me. "Is that true?"

"Approximately."

"How did you get here?"

"After what he did to Duncan he couldn't afford to have witnesses left over. He was taking us somewhere quiet to kill us. Corryvreckan was our only chance, so I told him this was the way through. Only I wasn't as good a sailor as I thought." I squared my shoulders at him. "But we'd have made it, if Harry had got here ahead of you. You realise he's looking for us too?"

McAllister nodded slowly. "I suppose." He let the barrels of the shotgun, which had been pointing at the sky, swing over and down and point roughly at our feet. He still held it in one hand. Something about the way he held it suggested that one hand was all he needed.

Mackey bent down and picked up the hand-gun on the grass. "Small chance," he grinned bloodily. "Uncle, you take Curragh. I'll deal with her."

"Reckon you can this time?" I demanded, burying the icy spot of horror under a show of bravado, and Alex grunted, "Only if you'll promise to stand still and not too far away."

McAllister said quietly, "Why?" I wasn't sure which of us he was asking but he was looking at William.

Mackey looked surprised. Then he answered reasonably, "Because you owe him for Aunt Alison, and I owe her." He'd assumed the question meant why do it that way rather than why do it at all.

McAllister looked at me. For the briefest moment I thought I saw a little sorrow and a little warmth through the basilisk inscrutability.

Then he looked at Alex, and I wasn't sure what I saw in his ruined face then.

My mind churning in the search for hope, it occurred to me to wonder what I would do if I was invited to buy my life with silence—about Duncan's death and about Alex's. I hoped to God I wouldn't jump at the chance.

McAllister said, "Put the gun down."

Mackey stared at him. He genuinely thought he had misheard. "What?"

"Put the gun down. You're not killing anyone."

Mackey's eyes flickered between the gun and me, between distress and a soul-deep anger. He couldn't believe he was about to be thwarted. "You cannot leave her alive," he shouted. "She's a witness against me. If you kill Curragh, she'll be a witness against you too."

"I don't intend to kill Curragh," said McAllister.

Mackey turned on him, shrieking hysterically, his body arched over the gun in his hand. "Damn you, you can't do this to me! Everything I did, I did for you. You're not throwing me to the wolves now."

The less damaged side of McAllister's lip curled. "Wee son, you never in your life did anything for anybody but yourself. If you think I'm going to kill two people to keep you out of prison, you have another think coming."

"But he killed Auntie Alison," screamed Mackey. His face was suffused with blood and rage. "He fucked her and then he killed her. You're going to let him off with that? You'll be a laughing stock!"

"Ach Willie, Willie," sighed McAllister. "That's not what happened. What actually happened between them you'll never understand if you live to be a hundred, but he didn't kill her. Did you, son?"

Alex shook his head fractionally. "I thought you did."

I found I was breathing again. Shallowly, through my mouth, but breathing.

"Then who the hell did kill her?" demanded William, exasperated beyond bearing.

McAllister looked at me. Then he looked up at the sky; there was nothing there, so it may have been to stop his eyes watering. "No-one killed Alison. It was her choice. She had an illness that wasn't going to get better, and she decided not to hang round while it got worse. She put her affairs in order and then she ended her own life. I only hope she doesn't know the trouble that's come of it."

"Trouble?" It was William. If his voice went any higher he'd need surgical intervention to recover it. "Two men are dead. I'm going to be blamed for that. You said you wanted Curragh, and I got him for you. You owe me. These people are nothing to you. I'm your nephew, and I need them dead. You owe me that!"

He might have done better not reminding McAllister of the blood-tie that could only be an embarrassment to him. The basilisk eyes went cold. "I owe you nothing, wee son. You've been trouble from the first day I saw you. Out of consideration for your mother, nothing more, I'll put my hand in my pocket once more and buy you the second-best lawyer in Scotland. I'm saving the best for myself. Thanks to you I'm likely to need him. I told you to put that gun down."

Mackey stared wild-eyed at the weapon in his hand, much as a man overboard might regard a lifeline someone was threatening to snatch away. Then he looked at McAllister's shotgun. "Why did you bring that if you don't want anyone shot?"

"Because right after you left the helicopter, Starrett realised you'd got his Beretta," McAllister retorted grimly. "He keeps that there for my protection. You'd no damn business taking it."

"Your protection? What about my protection?"

"Put the gun down."

"What about me?" screamed William Mackey.

"You're going to prison," McAllister said frankly. "But we'll plead diminished responsibility and you could be out before we've missed you. No more than five or six years, maybe."

William was in no mood for humour, not even coming from his employer. He was in no mood to listen to reason. Events of the last thirty-six hours had driven him steadily up the scale of violence, from stalking a man to smashing a man's hand to smashing his head to plotting cold-blooded murder. It was almost no distance to committing murder, and all his mental reserves were pledged to his own safety. Backing down now, taking the consequences of what he had already done, would have involved an emotional about-turn that was possible, just about, but wasn't going to happen. Jimmy Cagney wouldn't have settled for prison when one bold move could put him beyond its grasp, and William Mackey wasn't going to.

The panic was gone out of his voice. He sounded obscenely rational. "When they're dead you'll thank me." Slowly, though probably not as slowly as it felt, the muzzle of his gun started to come up.

"Put the gun down, Willie." McAllister's voice was grim. "Now. I mean it, son. If you don't drop that gun now, I'm going to blow your head off."

William thought he was bluffing. He got the pistol up level with his eye and sighted along the brief barrel, drawing a bead on the centre of my chest. My blood turned to water, my muscles to jelly. He wouldn't miss again. He held the gun in both hands to steady it, and took his time getting the aim right.

Just before he was ready to pull the trigger, McAllister blew his head off.

[9]

"It was multiple sclerosis," said Harry. "She knew what it was before her doctor did—at least she suspected. Her brother had it, was diagnosed shortly before the fire on his boat at Stromness. Alison started getting symptoms when she was pregnant, apparently. She couldn't get it confirmed, but obviously in her own mind she was sure. And she was right."

I was sitting on an examination couch back in the hospital in Glasgow, and Neil Burns was dressing my arm. He'd traded my bullet graze for an interesting osteomalacia so that he could hear the end of the story. But I'd made it too gripping: it had taken him twenty minutes to get this dressing on and he still hadn't bandaged it.

MS. I felt now I should have guessed. Orkney has one of the highest per capita rates of multiple sclerosis in the world. There were other indicators too. Pregnancy is a dangerous time for susceptible women. And patients can appear perfectly normal for a lengthy period after onset, so much so that they can have difficulty persuading even their doctor that something is seriously amiss. If she'd wanted to hide it from her husband, it would have been easy enough.

Later he'd have known, when she started to lose first the strength, then the function of her limbs. But Alison never intended him to see that. After George's experience she must have half expected this—although there appear to be both immunogenetic and infective elements in the transmission of MS, it's not a family problem in the way that, for instance, haemophilia is, but it's only human to fear the worst; and anyway the incidence of the disease in Orkney meant the fear was not wholly irrational. She knew it could happen to her, and she'd decided what to do if it did.

Ready for it as she was, she would have known what the earliest symptoms meant. She didn't have to wait for a formal diagnosis. She knew what was happening to her, and what would happen—increasing disability, reliance, loss of independence. It wasn't a life she wanted, any more than her brother had wanted it, and she took the same way out.

Finally I understood that improbable will. She had never expected to grow old, and her methodical mind had found a kind of comfort in keeping her affairs properly in order. By the time she added Alex to the list of beneficiaries, she already knew, or at least strongly suspected, that she had been touched by her island's curse, and long before that she had decided what to do if she drew a short straw. She never expected Alex to have to wait for his boat.

I couldn't find it in me to blame her. Some people cope better with incurable disease than others, but MS, like most progressive conditions, certainly has the potential to reduce existence to a considerable burden. As a doctor I have to believe that every patient is worth treating. But I'm not qualified to judge whether every life is worth having.

What I did find hard to forgive was the fact that she had left no explanation of what she intended. Perhaps she felt she owed none; perhaps she was afraid McAllister would find it in time to stop her. But if she had only left a note in her diary, so much pain and grief, and three men's deaths, could have been avoided.

With the better weather that saw Duncan and I begin our quest in *Flag*, the divers had resumed their search at the Fairy Isles and later that day they recovered Alison's body. It wasn't intact, of course, but there was more than enough for the autopsy to discover the characteristic nerve-tissue lesions and so confirm the information Harry brought back from Orkney.

Harry had taken the proof straight to Frazer McAllister. Having him call his people in would create enough time and space for Alex to be found and brought home without hazard to anyone. McAllister was convinced—he'd been more than half convinced when I visited his house the day before; perhaps if I'd been less abrasive he'd have admitted it—and issued the necessary instructions, and for twelve hours everyone was under the impression that the crisis was over.

Then news came back that his nephew and a colleague from the distillery were missing and efforts to contact them had proved fruitless. He knew or suspected that Mackey was capable of extreme and fanatical behaviour if he thought it would get him back to Glasgow. Immediately McAllister contacted Harry again.

Towards the end of the day the police located a boat yard which had hired a speedboat to two men, one rather small, one very large, for the unusually long period of three days. Most such hirings would be for an afternoon, or a full day at the outside. They had no reason to be anxious about their boat but they did recognise Mackey's description. Further enquiries established that the boat had spent the previous night in Port Askaig, and the two men had taken rooms there, only a few miles from where Duncan and I slept aboard the *Fairy Flag.*

By now, still having had no word from me, Harry was seriously worried about what was happening. He upgraded the scale and urgency of the search, using both road vehicles and boats. He asked for a helicopter but was told there'd be a delay on that. McAllister volunteered his own executive city-hopper, which got in an hour's flying over the southern half of the Sound before fading light sent it back to base. By then, of course, *Fairy Flag* the surface craft was a memory, and her upturned hull a hard target to spot among the broken waters of Corryvreckan.

At first light McAllister went up again with his pilot. They were heading out from Crinan at a thousand feet when the pilot Starrett spotted the long dark bulk among the Corryvreckan rocks. As they closed in on it, recognising it for a wrecked boat, they saw Mackey waving wildly on the Scarba shore.

Mackey, who had spent the night concocting a plausible account for the police, now saw the prospect of not having to explain to the police at all. He told McAllister there were other survivors on Jura, and while the helicopter was hopping over the strait he quietly armed himself from the pilot's emergency kit. He must have believed that McAllister would ultimately be grateful for the removal of witnesses who could implicate them both. Weighted and dropped in deep water, our bodies were unlikely to return and give the lie to an account agreed between them that the helicopter had found the boat and Mackey but no other survivors. We would be assumed to have drowned and washed away.

All the same, Mackey took the precaution of sending his uncle to search another area while he hurried to where he believed he had seen us. Presenting McAllister with a fait accompli must have seemed easier than arguing with him.

McAllister didn't know the boy was armed until he heard the shot that grazed me. Homing in on the sound, he passed close to his helicopter, and by then the pilot had searched for and missed his Biretta. There was a brace of sporting guns in a case in the back—I was never able to establish whether this was a happy oversight after the last day's shooting or if McAllister had brought them because he thought he might need them—and Starrett tossed him one and a box of cartridges. He came over the hill not sure what he would find. The rest I knew.

McAllister's helicopter flew Alex and me to Glasgow. While Neil Burns was applying his ears to my story and the slowest dressing you ever saw to my arm, elsewhere in the building his colleagues were knocking Alex's fracture back into shape. Too much had been done with it and to it for the original reduction to have survived. The ends of the broken bone had parted quite noticeably on the new X-ray, so they knocked him out and did it again.

The remains of William Mackey—an expression I use advisedly, bearing in mind he'd been killed by a shotgun at close range—followed an hour later in the police helicopter Harry had finally got hold of. McAllister stayed on the island with him until it came. When the police machine landed beside McAllister's in front of the hospital, William went down to the morgue while Harry and McAllister came along to Casualty, where we exchanged enough notes to bring all of us, and Neil Burns, up to date. When DCI Baker turned up fifteen minutes later, we went through it all again.

Four days later I picked Alex up from the hospital. The effects of exhaustion and anaesthesia, which had marked his face as intractably as scars for forty-eight hours, were fading now, leaving only a deep hollowness in his eyes. I had seen that emptiness there in the first days after the loss of the *Skara Sun*, but more recently he'd had too much to do and to worry about for the vacuum to persist. Now it was all over; already he was dwelling again on the sins and errors of the past.

He blamed himself for most of it. It was natural enough; in quiet moments I too was sure I could have done more or differently to prevent the casualty list soaring as it had. Nor could I honestly tell him he was in no measure responsible for what had happened. If he hadn't gone walkabout in the middle of the investigation, three men would be alive who were now dead. But he hadn't engineered or sought their deaths; his actions had been innocent, both legally and morally; and others were far more culpable than he. If William Mackey had lived, he not Alex would have stood trial; and Frazer McAllister wasn't out of the wood yet as far as legal repercussions were concerned. What Alex, and I, had done in good faith, and the consequences thereof, were burdens we were going to have to carry, and he might as well get used to it now.

To be fair, though, there was more on his mind today than the extent of his responsibility. The pallor of his cheek was not wholly a reflection of the guilt he felt. It was as much to do with where we were going.

While I drove I acquainted him with the ground rules. "You know you have no rights in this? McAllister calls the play. It was his idea, it's his gesture of atonement. As far as I know, and as far as you're concerned, it's a one-off thing unless and until he says otherwise."

Alex nodded, nervously. "I understand."

I glanced sidelong at him, returning my eyes to the road. "It won't be easy, you know. Not for either of you. You should expect to be upset."

He nodded again and said nothing. He thought he knew what to expect. It didn't matter that he was wrong: he'd been warned, and I'd be there for him afterwards. After that Harry would be there for me.

I parked the car in the shadow of the castle and McAllister came awkwardly, carefully, down his stone steps to greet us. He took my hand with some warmth, which was there too in his powerful, ravaged face. His greeting to Alex was more reserved, more cautious, but neither cool nor arrogant. By its nature the relationship between them was a difficult one. Only great goodwill had got us this far. After a moment, solemnly, they shook hands.

McAllister took us inside. We had to pause in the hall while he got himself up those unsuitable stone steps. He didn't take us into the sitting-room for stilted small-talk first, he took us straight upstairs to the nursery. He bent over the cot and picked up the amiable baby inside.

"Well, here we are," he said. "This is Alison's Peter. Peter, you remember Dr. Marsh? Of course you do. And this is your ma's friend Alex. Well actually, he's your da.

"What? Aye, another one. I'll explain the details when you're a little older. For the moment, just be glad you're going to inherit his looks and my money, not the other way round."

I looked covertly at Alex. The emptiness had gone from his eyes. Quite unconsciously he was leaning over the baby, as if by looking closely enough he could find Alison in it. He began to smile.

"Here, you hold him," said McAllister, proffering the infant. "Oh, you can't, can you? Look, sit you down there and hold him on your knee. Just mind he doesn't roll off—he's awful fat."

I left them alone then, and went back downstairs and made myself at home in the sitting-room. Since I was driving I couldn't help myself to the stiff slug of whisky I wanted. I settled for a stiff slug of bitter lemon instead.

A few minutes later McAllister joined me. He nodded approval at my glass—he probably thought there was vodka in it—and filled one of his own. Then he emptied it.

I said, "Are they all right?"

"Aye, sure." McAllister sat down. "Peter's chuckling his silly head off. I think the lad's crying, but that'll not do him any harm."

"What about you?"

He looked surprised. "Och, I'm all right. I'm a survivor, you mind." Then, for just a moment, he let the mask slip. "But oh God, I'm going to miss Alison."

I raised my eyes to the ceiling. "Him too."

He nodded. "Listen, I'm not making any promises. But we got him into this, Ali and me, and one way or another I'll see him through it."

I was grateful for that, glad that when I went back home to the Midlands there would still be somebody keeping an eye on Alex Curragh's welfare. Had things turned out differently I might have asked Duncan. "Thanks."

"Thank you," he said, and for all I could tell he meant it.

He refilled both our glasses. I had to own up to the bitter lemon.

He said, "There's something you should see." He went into another room, came back with an envelope. "It only turned up an hour ago. I'll take it to the police, but since you were coming I wanted you to see it first."

I took it from him and turned it in my hands. It was covered in figures and cyphers, in blue ink on one side, in black pencil on the other. It might have been Exhibit A in a trial for espionage, or a bit of office waste.

By concentrating I managed to resolve the pencilled notation as a recipe of some kind, involving salmon and something else baked until crusty—although the possibility that the guest-list was to include an award-winning author could not be discounted. Of the figures in ink I could make no sense at all.

McAllister was watching with a curious mixture of expressions. I thought I saw both grief and a solemn amusement. I thought I must have been mistaken.

I showed him the blue figures. "What does it mean?"

"Share prices. My man in London phoned through with them just as I was coming in on Sunday night. I'd been away most of the weekend or he'd have got me earlier, so by now it was pretty urgent. I took the call on the hall phone instead of in my study, and I took down the figures he gave me on a handy envelope. I did a couple of wee sums, then called him back and told him what to sell and what to buy."

I couldn't think where this was leading us. "Did you make a good deal?"

"I made a quarter of a million pounds, thank you very much."

What did he want me to say? "Congratulations. I hope you enjoyed the salmon pie as well."

"Not yet. Mrs. Lilley hasn't made it yet, and now I'm not sure she will, though it was a great success when I ate with the Camerons last week. I asked their cook if she'd mind sharing her recipe with mine, and Mrs. Lilley was in the hall too when the phone rang early on Monday morning. The envelope was still lying on the table from the previous day, but she could see from the scribbles that I'd finished with it so she took down the recipe on the other side. Then she took it into the kitchen, to copy into her recipe book.

"And then news came in about Alison, so she never got it done. She put it to one side and only got round to it again this morning."

As the confessions of a Scottish magnate, this was about as interesting as watching paint dry. I wondered if he would ever get to the point, and indeed whether there was one. "Really."

McAllister smiled slowly. "And so neither I, who had used it as a ready-reckoner, nor Mrs. Lilley, who had used the other side as a Mrs. Beeton's filofax, ever actually thought of it as an envelope. It was only after Mrs. Lilley had copied her notes off it and went to throw it away that she was struck by the blindingly obvious that had eluded us both."

It eluded me too. "Which was?"

"Which was that envelopes contain letters."

It was Alison McAllister's last letter, the one she wrote to her husband after he left for his business trip and before she left for Oban. He'd said he wouldn't be back before Monday so she had no reservations about leaving it on the hall table to await his return. The fact that his business finished a day early could have thrown all her careful plans back into the melting pot, but for the timing of that first urgent phone call and the fact that there was no other paper beside the phone.

McAllister asked me to read it and I did, and before I finished, my tears were splashing the paper. She wrote:

My dearest,

I know that what I am about to do will hurt you. That is the only regret I have.

That idiot doctor of mine still won't admit that things are wrong with me that cannot be explained by motherhood alone. But I know what the problem is, and I have done for almost a year. It's that old devil MS. I knew he'd catch up with me some day.

You remember my brother George. The circumstances of his death caused enormous shock at home, not only in the family but around the island. Strenuous efforts were made to have it recorded as an accident, or failing that as the act of a man whose mind was temporarily unhinged.

I never believed it was an accident, or that the balance of his mind was disturbed. I believed then and believe still that it was a rational response to a diagnosis that meant he'd already enjoyed the best of any life he could hope for. I wouldn't keep alive a dog that was going to grow weaker every day until it finally lost control of its most basic functions, and I could never see why my brother was expected to suffer more than a dog.

Now I find myself in the same situation and I know he was right. Not for everyone perhaps—I can admire a cheerful cripple as well as the next person—but for himself and also for me. We would both have made terrible invalids.

It's important that you understand that this is what is right for me. If I wanted to live enough to put up with that degree of disability, I might be sorry for you and Peter but I wouldn't let your interests influence my decision. I'm not doing this to save you years of coping with an invalid wife, her temper growing shorter as her muscles weaken! I'm doing it because I don't want to live in a body that restrictive.

I've gone into the science of it. I know all about remissions, how the progress of the disease can seem to be halted or even reversed for a time. I'm not doing this in a state of shock or despair. I've thought it through, and the bottom line is that, realistically, there's only one way I'm going to end up and I'm going to get out while I'm ahead.

I know you don't care for the boat so I'm going to go George's way—the Viking way. I'm sorry you won't get the insurance.

I'm afraid this next bit will hurt you too. Or perhaps you'll understand it better than I do: you always did treat my hormones with greater respect than I thought they deserved. I'm going to see Alex again. I shalln't tell him what I'm doing, but I feel the need somehow to square myself with him before turning out the light. I'm sorry I didn't handle that better, for all our sakes. I hope you'll accept Peter as my apology.

By the time you read this the thing will be done. I hope you won't be dragged away from anything important to identify the remains. It's me all right.

Is this rather long for a suicide note? There's so much I want to say to you, I feel I could fill a book—if I had the words, which I haven't. A lot of it you can probably guess: the anger, the resentment, the sense of loss for what we could have had and weren't given time for. The profound gratitude that I was able to give you our son. The fear for what comes next, tinged—you may even have guessed this—with some curiosity, even anticipation.

What I do want to state in plain words, so that you never have to wonder how much of what you guessed was what I meant to say, is this. Neither of us married for love. I didn't expect to love you, had no right to expect you to love me. But oh my dear, if it isn't love I feel for you, and have done these four years, and if it isn't love I've had from you in return, then I don't know the meaning of the word. I think it's one of the reasons I can let go now: the fact that I've had enough happiness for a lifetime in these few years with you.

Forgive me that which needs forgiving. Remember what was

worth remembering. I leave you our child, and my best hopes for both of you. Love again, if you have the chance. Be happy.

All my love,
ALISON

ABOUT THE AUTHOR

Jo Bannister is a writer who lives in Northern Ireland. A former news-paper editor, she has won several awards for journalism in the United Kingdom, including the Royal Society of Arts Bronze medal. She is the author of seven previous novels; *The Going Down of the Sun* is her fifth for the Crime Club.